A TIME TRAVELER'S
MASQUERADE

A Time Traveler's Masquerade

A McQuivey's Costume Shop Romance

PROPER ROMANCE

SIAN ANN BESSEY

SHADOW
MOUNTAIN
PUBLISHING

Library of Congress Cataloging-in-Publication Data

Names: Bessey, Siân Ann, 1963– author.
Title: A time traveler's masquerade / Sian Ann Bessey.
Description: Salt Lake City : Shadow Mountain Publishing, 2025. | Series: Proper romance | Summary: "Isla Crawford is suddenly transported from a modern costume shop to 1605, weeks before Guy Fawkes's Gunpowder Plot. Seeking refuge in a Tudor manor, she meets Simon Hartworth, who is drawn to her mysterious presence and dire warnings about Parliament's demise. Together, they must stop the traitors, even as they discover their growing attraction for each other across the centuries."—Provided by publisher.
Identifiers: LCCN 2024039083 (print) | LCCN 2024039084 (ebook) | ISBN 9781639933822 (trade paperback) | ISBN 9781649333537 (ebook)
Subjects: LCGFT: Romance fiction. | Time-travel fiction. | Novels. Classification: LCC PS3552.E79495 T56 2025 (print) | LCC PS3552.E79495 (ebook) | DDC 813/.54—dc23/eng/20240823
LC record available at https://lccn.loc.gov/2024039083
LC ebook record available at https://lccn.loc.gov/2024039084

Printed in the United States of America
Publishers Printing

10   9   8   7   6   5   4   3   2   1

For Marilee Merrell,
whose love and support of those
in the writing community make every
author feel like they're her favorite.

(But I still secretly hope it might be me.)

Remember, Remember, the Fifth of November

(A traditional English folk verse)

Remember, remember the fifth of November,
Gunpowder, treason, and plot.
I know of no reason
Why the gunpowder treason
Should ever be forgot.
Guy Fawkes, Guy Fawkes, t'was his intent
To blow up the king and parli'ment.
Three-score barrels of powder below
To prove old England's overthrow;
By God's providence, he was catch'd
With a dark lantern and burning match.
Holla boys, Holla boys, let the bells ring.
Holloa boys, holloa boys, God save the King!

CHAPTER 1

London, Present Day

Isla Crawford stared at the email on her screen and frowned. Another letter from one of Audrey Marshall's constituents complaining about the chronic lack of school funding in the country. It was the fifth email about the issue this week. At this rate, her boss would have to do more than ask Isla to write a placating response. Ms. Marshall would need to act—or at the very least, promise to act—by addressing the problem in Parliament.

"Well? Have you decided yet?"

With a start, Isla looked up from her computer. Her friend and colleague Chloe Osbourne was leaning over her desk, an expectant look in her brown eyes.

"Decided what?" Isla asked, her thoughts scattering from her current email crisis to the myriad other issues she'd been dealing with all day.

Chloe groaned. "Do you ever lift your nose from the grindstone long enough to smell the roses?"

Isla bit her lip to prevent a giggle at Chloe's idiom fusion. Isla should be used to it. Chloe blended idioms all the time, and the fact that her friend was blissfully unaware of her habit only made it funnier.

"I sometimes stop to smell the roses in Kensington Gardens," Isla said. "I think that counts."

Chloe rolled her eyes. "It's almost October. Are there even roses blooming right now?"

"Yep. Pink ones." Isla knew this because she'd seen them two days ago when she'd been on her early morning run. She didn't bother telling Chloe that she hadn't actually stopped to smell them.

"I can't believe you noticed," Chloe said.

"I notice lots of things," Isla said. "Like, you're wearing a new shirt, and the copy machine's broken."

"First," Chloe said, "I bought this shirt three months ago. That hardly qualifies as new."

As far as Isla was concerned, it did. She wasn't sure what Chloe's clothing budget was, but it had to be significantly larger than hers.

"Second," Chloe continued, "the copy machine has been broken since yesterday, and since Dave's been complaining about it all day, that hardly qualifies as a personal observation."

Recognizing that this was a battle she wasn't destined to win, Isla returned to Chloe's original question. "Okay. I'll admit, I sometimes get sucked up in my work and often spend too much time researching past parliamentary sessions, so tell me what I'm supposed to be deciding?"

"If you honestly don't know, you really do have a problem."

"Actually," Isla said, "I have lots of problems. An entire inbox full of them."

Chloe sighed. They both worked as Ms. Marshall's assistants, but whereas Chloe was in charge of coordinating events,

Isla oversaw all the politician's correspondence and press releases. "Fine. Stop thinking about those for two minutes, and tell me if you're going to be Peter Pan or Wendy for the Fall Ball."

Isla pinned a smile on her face even as her eyes darted to the date on the corner of her screen. September 29. Her heart sank. Logically, she'd known they were nearing the end of the month. She'd been typing the date on letters all week. And yet, she'd not stopped long enough to consider how quickly October was approaching. Or more specifically, October 2. That was the date of this year's Fall Ball, the annual gala held in the vast atrium at Portcullis House that most members of Parliament and their staff attended. It was a fancy affair, with live music, expensive catering . . . and elaborate costumes.

"I thought we decided I should be Wendy," Isla said. Chloe was going as Tinkerbell. Her short, blonde hair and petite stature were perfect for the part. Dave, Ms. Marshall's chief-of-staff and the only other person in their office, had initially suggested that he go as Peter Pan. Thankfully, Chloe had persuaded him that he would appear far more dashing as Captain Hook. Heavy-set Dave walking around in green tights would not have been pretty.

"Did you find a nightie?" Chloe asked.

"I have a red plaid one and a green one covered in little sheep."

"Then, you don't have a costume." Chloe folded her arms. "It doesn't matter if your hair is the same length and color as Wendy's; if you're not wearing a blue nightie, people will think you came to the ball in your pajamas."

"Just because Disney's Wendy wears a blue nightgown doesn't mean it has to be that color," Isla said. "How does J. M. Barrie describe it in the book?"

Chloe groaned. "Isla, we're not looking for historical or literary accuracy here. I know that's your thing, but as hard as it must be for you to wrap your mind around it, most people haven't read the book. As far as the general population goes, Disney's characters have it right. Tinkerbell wears green, and Wendy wears light blue."

"But—" One look at Chloe's face and Isla's argument fizzled. "I'll stop at Primark on the way home to see if I can find one that color." The discount clothing chain was her best hope of protecting her budget. "But if they don't—"

"They don't," Chloe said. "I already checked. The only blue ones they have are covered in unicorns, and the largest size is age eight."

"I have a Regency gown at home. I can wear that instead."

"You wore it last year," Chloe protested. "Besides, our office is supposed to be going with the Peter Pan theme." She leaned a little closer. "If it's just me and Dave, people will think we're dating, and that will be the end of my chances to get to know Mr. Tall, Dark, and Handsome upstairs."

There was a hint of desperation in Chloe's voice, and Isla experienced a pang of guilt. Chloe had suggested the Peter Pan theme at least a fortnight ago. And Isla had agreed to go along with it. Added to that, her friend had been gushing over Mr. Mahoney's new chief-of-staff on the floor above them ever since she'd shared the same lift with him a few weeks before. The Fall Ball was a big enough deal that it was a virtual certainty that he'd be there. It really was a perfect opportunity for Chloe to get to know him better.

"If you have any suggestions for finding a Wendy costume in the next two days, I'm listening," Isla said. "On the condition that it doesn't break my bank account."

"It won't," Chloe said. "McQuivey's Costume Shop has one. I saw it when I picked up my Tinkerbell costume. Their rental prices are cheaper than anywhere else, and you could stop by on your way home tonight. The owner told me she stays open late on Thursdays."

As much as Isla would rather go directly home after work and curl up in a chair with a good book, she did need a costume. And she was running out of time. "All right. Where's the shop?"

Chloe's eyes shone triumphantly. "It's in Pickering Place, just off St. James Street. If you take the Tube to Green Park, you'll see the alley entrance right next to Berry Bros. & Rudd."

"McQuivey's Costume Shop," Isla repeated, entering the name into her phone.

"Yeah. It's actually a really cool shop. If you have time, you should look through some of the other costumes. Maybe it'll give you some ideas for next year."

Next year. Would she still be here then? Isla dropped her phone into her handbag. Two and a half years ago when she'd graduated with her degree in political science from the University of York, she'd accepted an intern position on Audrey Marshall's election campaign team. Soon afterward, Ms. Marshall had been elected the member of Parliament for the York Central District and had asked Isla to stay on as her assistant in London. The job offer had been a dream come true. After three years of studying political history and the current issues facing Britain's government, she'd been presented with an office that overlooked the Houses of Parliament and the opportunity to work shoulder to shoulder with the politicians now leading the country.

She glanced at the email about school funding shortfalls again, and her shoulders slumped. It had not taken long for reality to dim the imagined glamour of her work in London. Despite her education, her role here was little more than secretarial. She dealt with a discouragingly large number of complaints and had no influence whatsoever on their resolution. Every day, she left the office exhausted but aching to do more than simply keep up with Ms. Marshall's correspondence or offer placating words to her constituents and the press.

"I'll take a look around the shop while I'm there," Isla said. It might be fun to browse through the costumes for a little while. The new book about Oliver Cromwell that she'd been looking forward to reading would still be waiting on her coffee table when she got back to her flat.

"Fabulous," Chloe said. "Shoot me a text to let me know how it goes. If the nightgown I saw there comes with a blue ribbon for your hair, you'll be all set. In theory, you don't even have to wear shoes."

Isla chuckled. "This may be the best idea you've ever had. If I go to the Fall Ball in pajamas and bare feet, I'll be the envy of every single female stuck wearing high heels."

"Me too." Chloe grinned. "I'll be wearing green slippers with pompoms on them." She moved back toward her own desk. "We just need to remember that when some big, tall chap dressed as a construction worker gets too close to our toes."

"Good point," Isla said. "We'd better avoid all men wearing bovver boots."

Chloe's laughter filled the small room as Dave walked in carrying a box of copy machine paper.

"Glad to see someone's enjoying themselves," he grumbled. "I had to lug this box all the way from the ground floor."

"You're our knight in shining armor, Dave," Chloe said.

Smothering a smile, Isla went back to her work. This was why she couldn't change jobs yet. She'd miss Dave's chronic crankiness almost as much as Chloe's idiom-filled cheeriness.

———·•✱·.———

The Green Park Tube station was packed with commuters heading home. Grateful to escape the chaos, Isla wove her way through the congestion toward the exit and the street beyond. Turning left, she followed Piccadilly until she reached St. James Street. There, she took a right and slowed her steps.

She loved this part of London. History seemed to seep from the very walls of the buildings that lined the street. Brick Georgian houses with their tall, elegant facades stood beside older, smaller sixteenth century shopfronts, their doorframes low and their timbered walls uneven. The modern, sleek, and shiny vehicles driving by seemed out of place on the narrow road. And yet, there was something rather wonderful about the natural melding of centuries of London life in this small section of the city.

The sign for Berry Bros. & Rudd hung suspended a few feet over the pavement. Isla approached the old wine merchant's shop curiously. She had almost reached it when she noticed an arched entrance beside it. A familiar City of Westminster sign hung on the black timbered walls beyond the archway, announcing the entrance to Pickering Place. She stepped through the archway. The alley beyond was narrower than the corridors in her office building. She followed it about twenty feet until it opened into a tiny flagstone square.

The buildings surrounding the square were at least two hundred fifty years old. They were built of gray brick, with white windows and doorframes. Black railings ran along the fronts of the houses and up the steps leading to the front doors. Shrubs in planter boxes dotted the area, and a wooden bench to one side of the square invited visitors to linger awhile.

Turning in a slow circle, Isla studied the half dozen doors. One bore a small sign. Moving closer, she made out the lettering on the brass plaque. *McQuivey's Costume Shop*. She'd found it. Climbing the three stone steps to the door, she glanced at the nearby window. Two mannequins stood beside each other. One was dressed as a Roman soldier, the other as Cleopatra. Isla pushed open the door and walked inside.

A bell rang somewhere at the back of the shop. The tap of brisk footsteps crossing the wooden floor followed, and moments later, a woman appeared between the racks of clothing. She was at least four inches shorter than Isla's five feet, six inches. Her hair was snowy white and pulled back into a tidy chignon held in place with a mother-of-pearl hair fork. She wore a purple dress with matching purple shoes, and a string of multicolored glass beads hung around her neck.

"Good evening," she said with a smile. "Welcome to McQuivey's Costume Shop."

"Thank you." Isla returned the lady's smile. "Are you Mrs. McQuivey?"

"I am, indeed." The older lady studied her owlishly through her round, wire-rimmed glasses. "And may I ask your name?"

"Isla Crawford."

"Lovely to meet you, Isla. How may I help you?"

"A friend of mine thought you might have a Wendy costume," Isla said.

"Wendy? As in Peter Pan's Wendy?"

"Yes. It's for a work costume party, and she feels rather strongly that I wear a light-blue nightgown."

"I see." Mrs. McQuivey had yet to drop her gaze. Her eyes were hazel, Isla noticed, and had an unusual sparkle. "And how do you feel about that?"

Surprised by the question, Isla shrugged. "I don't feel quite as passionately about the color of Wendy's pajamas as Chloe does, but I'm happy to wear a light-blue nightie if I can find one."

Mrs. McQuivey nodded thoughtfully. "Putting the desires of others before your own is an admirable trait."

"Oh, but I really don't mind." Isla smiled. "It's hard to complain about wearing comfortable pajamas to a work party."

"True," Mrs. McQuivey said. "Although, being uncomfortable isn't always a bad thing. After all, that's often when we're called upon to show courage and fortitude."

Isla received the distinct impression that Mrs. McQuivey was referring to something more significant than painful shoes or tight clothes, but it seemed best not to ask.

"You're probably right," she said.

"Oh, I'm sure of it. I've seen it happen time and time again." A slight frown appeared on Mrs. McQuivey's brow. "Forgive me for being presumptuous," she said, "but are you quite sure you want a Wendy costume? I would have thought you'd prefer to wear something historical."

Puzzled, Isla glanced at her own clothing. Sensible black flats, black trousers, a cream-and-sage-green floral blouse, and a gray cardigan. She wasn't wearing anything terribly dated. Her ensemble was work attire at its unremarkable finest. As far as Isla could tell, there was nothing that might give away her love of the past. "Why would you say that?"

"Oh, just a feeling I have." The older lady started toward the nearest rack of clothing. "I've discovered that occasionally, people come to the shop in search of entirely the wrong thing."

"The wrong thing?" Why would Mrs. McQuivey think she could possibly know what someone else needed?

"Completely and utterly." She tutted as though the concept were ridiculous. "Only two days ago, I had a gentleman come in wanting a policeman's uniform." With a shake of her head, she drew a hanger out from between its tightly packed neighbors and held up an elegant navy jacket, tan breeches, and crisp white shirt and cravat. "He was much better suited to be a Georgian gentleman than he was to be a London Bobby."

"Did he change his mind, then?" Isla asked.

"Of course. When you find the clothes meant for you, there's really no helping it."

Isla eyed the outfit wistfully. If Chloe had chosen a Georgian theme, Dave could have dressed up in these clothes rather than a Captain Hook costume, and Isla could have worn her Regency gown again. "I do love historical costumes," she admitted, "but I'm afraid this time it needs to be a Wendy costume. My colleagues are planning on me wearing it."

Mrs. McQuivey nodded absently, replaced the gentleman's clothing, and continued along the rack to a section filled with long gowns. She slowed, her fingers brushing against the fabric, a pensive look on her face. She reached for a hanger, went to pull it out, and then shook her head. "No," she muttered. "Not that one."

Isla waited. She wasn't sure what the older lady was looking for. She hoped it was the Wendy nightgown, but she'd not spotted anything that looked remotely like a Disney costume on that particular rack. "Would you like me to help look?" Isla asked.

"No, no." Mrs. McQuivey slid a few hangers along the rack. None of them resembled a nightie. None of them was light blue. "I shall find it, my dear."

Isla tightened her grip on the strap of her purse. Perhaps coming here hadn't been the best idea after all. "Would you like me to come back tomorrow?"

"Goodness me. That won't be necessary. I shall find just what you need in no time." She slid three more hangers down the rack, and then her fingers stilled. "There now." A satisfied expression settled on her face, and she withdrew a cream-colored gown covered in embroidered flowers. "What do you think of this?"

"It's beautiful." The elegant gown wasn't at all what she was here for, but Isla couldn't help but reach out to touch the shimmering silk. "Is it Elizabethan?"

"Well done." Mrs. McQuivey appeared impressed. "Late Elizabethan or early Jacobean, I'd say. Early 1600s, for sure. You see how the sleeves are narrow rather than the padded leg-of-mutton sleeves they wore a few decades before then?"

"Yes," Isla said. "The narrower sleeves are an improvement, but a gown like this must have been so hard to put on and so heavy to wear all day." She fingered the long-waisted stays that tapered to a point at the front. "They wore farthingales, too, didn't they?"

"Absolutely. The circular hoops were sewn into the underskirt to give their skirts the desired shape."

Isla shook her head. "I wouldn't know how to begin dressing myself. No wonder so many women relied on lady's maids to help them."

"I'm quite sure you'd sort it out quickly enough." She handed Isla the gown. "Here. Try it on and see for yourself. I'll fetch you a chemise and a farthingale."

"Oh, no, I—" Isla attempted to hand the gown back, but Mrs. McQuivey had already turned to face the rack behind them and was pulling underclothing off the hangers.

"The chemise goes first, then the farthingale, followed by the stays, the gown, and the jacket." The shopkeeper set a chemise on top of the gown in Isla's arms, and carrying the hooped farthingale, she started toward the back of the shop. "This way, my dear. And while you try that on, I'll look for the Wendy costume—if you still want it, that is."

"Yes," Isla said, a hint of desperation in her voice. It would take forever to put this costume on. She'd gone out of her way to come to the costume shop to please Chloe. She shouldn't have to please the shop's proprietor too. "The Wendy costume is really all I came for."

Mrs. McQuivey waved a hand in the general direction of the other racks. "Don't worry. It's out there somewhere. I'm quite sure I saw it recently. But you might as well try on something more *you* while you're waiting."

Isla really didn't know why the older lady thought a cumbersome late-Elizabethan gown was more *her* than a comfortable nightie, but refusing her offer seemed pointless. Particularly as Isla couldn't deny that she was unaccountably drawn to the shimmery silk gown. If it was going to take Mrs. McQuivey time to find the right costume, Isla may as well have some fun trying on this one while she waited.

"Okay." Isla spotted a couple of curtained cubicles in the corner. "Shall I use one of those changing rooms?"

"No." Mrs. McQuivey stopped opposite a dark-green door. "Use this one. There's better lighting." She smiled. "Be sure to come out once you're dressed, so I can see how you look."

Isla nodded and reached for the brass doorknob. Etched with an intricate depiction of the sun, moon, and stars, it was polished to a shine. She ran her fingers over the smooth metal, admiring the craftsman's skill before opening the door and stepping inside.

It was a small room. Perhaps it had once been a pantry or cleaning cupboard. The floor was wood and the white walls were not quite straight. A large mirror hung on one of the walls, and a row of small hooks was situated above a short bench. Hanging the various pieces of clothing in her arms on the hooks, Isla set her purse on the bench and kicked off her shoes. No matter what Mrs. McQuivey said, it was going to take serious concentration to put this costume on correctly.

Several minutes later, Isla smoothed her hands down the floral silk skirt and surveyed herself in the mirror. A small smile danced on her lips. The gown fit perfectly. Although the stays were restrictive, she could not help but notice how well they accentuated her small waist. And below the stays, the wide hoops of the farthingale held out the gown in a perfect dome.

Isla swayed from side to side. Like a silent bell, the gown's hem swooshed across the floor, gently brushing her bare feet. The neckline was lower than she was used to, but a wide Medici lace collar ran around the back of her neck, drawing the eye upward. Her light-brown hair fell in gentle waves to skim the shoulders of the beaded jacket that was almost exactly the same color blue as her eyes. She smiled again. She felt like a princess.

"Are you managing, my dear?" Mrs. McQuivey's voice reached her from the other side of the door.

"Yes, thank you." Somehow, she'd navigated the inordinate number of ties and pins. "I think I've put everything on right." Knowing that Mrs. McQuivey would not be satisfied unless she saw Isla in the costume for herself, Isla turned from the mirror and opened the door. "What do you think?"

She stepped out of the changing room and onto a gravel path. She gasped, staggering sideways. This time, her feet met grass. A breeze caught her skirt, and the fabric flapped against her bare ankles. She looked up. The costume shop was gone. In its place, a vast lawn stretched out before her. A gravel driveway circled the grass, lined with large trees and bushes. On the other side of the lawn, a gray-stone manor house filled the view, complete with small-paned windows, more chimneys than she could count, and half a dozen stone steps leading to a wide wooden door.

Isla swallowed hard and closed her eyes. She'd never had a hallucination before, but this had to be one. A rumble filled the air. It sounded like thunder. The skies had been clear when she'd entered the shop. She stumbled back a pace, wincing as her feet encountered the small rocks again. She'd always been told that you didn't feel pain in dreams. Was the same true for hallucinations?

"Mrs. McQuivey?" Isla attempted to clear her constricted throat. "Mrs. McQuivey?"

There was no reply. Spinning around, Isla reached for the changing room doorknob. It was gone. In its place, an old-fashioned latch hung on a black door. The door was unusually short and appeared to be the only entrance into a stone hut of some sort. Isla depressed the handle and wrenched the door open. Wood, chopped in tidy stacks, filled the space within. Panic welled. It looked like a woodshed. But how could that be? Moments ago, it had been a changing room.

"Mrs. McQuivey! Where are you?"

Another gust of wind rattled the nearby branches, and gray clouds scudded across the sky, blocking the lowering sun. A crack of lightning was followed almost immediately by a second roll of thunder. The storm was close. Even as Isla framed the thought, she felt the first droplets of rain. Within seconds, the isolated drops became a deluge. The gravel hissed as the rain hit the ground at full force.

Turning her back on the woodshed, she lifted her sodden skirts and dashed for the closest trees. Water ran down her face, dripping off her hair and clothing. Her feet slipped on the wet grass, and she stumbled, falling to her hands and knees. A sob escaped her. This couldn't be happening. Wrestling yards of heavy, drenched fabric, she pulled herself upright and stumbled on. Another crack of lightning lit the sky, and a new awareness filled her. She couldn't take cover beneath the trees. Not until after the storm passed. Her gaze shifted to the distant manor house. Who lived there? Would they know how to help her?

Another clap of thunder. And then a hawk's piercing cry. She shivered, fear tightening her chest. How could she be in a costume shop one minute and outside in a completely unfamiliar location the next? It made no sense. And where was Mrs. McQuivey? Or Pickering Place? She fought back another sob. With no sign of the older lady or a landmark she recognized, Isla had no choice. She was soaked to the skin and couldn't feel her feet anymore. Her only hope of avoiding hypothermia was to seek shelter at the house.

CHAPTER 2

Copfield Hall, Surrey
September 1605

Cursing his bad luck, Simon Hartworth lowered his head against the driving rain and urged his mount across the courtyard behind Copfield Hall. The wide brim of his cavalier hat offered his face a modicum of protection, but no manner of headwear or cloak could compete with this storm. He slid from his saddle and tugged on the wet reins. If he'd left London ten minutes earlier, he would have arrived ahead of the storm. As it was, he would be giving some poor stableboy a devil of a job and trailing a small river of water into his sister's entrance hall.

Pulling open the stable door, he led his horse inside. Physical relief from the pelting rain was instant, but the rattle of water hitting the clay tile roof overhead continued. One of the nearby horses snorted nervously. Simon's mount tossed his head and pulled away.

"Steady, boy." Simon ran a wet hand over the horse's equally wet neck. "Your lot will improve soon enough."

"Evenin', Lord Bancroft." A thin lad of about twelve years of age approached and inclined his head respectfully.

"And to you, Ezra. Although, I daresay it would be better for us both if the rain had held off." He handed the stableboy his reins. "I fear Blaze will need some extra attention. It has been a long journey, and the last few furlongs were particularly unpleasant."

"Don' you worry none, m' lord." Ezra eyed the black thoroughbred appreciatively. "A good rubdown'll do wonders t' settle 'im."

"I am sure it will. And perhaps a little extra feed would not go amiss either."

Ezra grinned. Simon visited Copfield Hall often enough that this was a familiar conversation. "Yes, m' lord."

"Very good. I shall leave him in your capable hands."

The pummeling of rain on tile had yet to abate. Simon gazed upward and frowned.

Ezra must have caught his look. "Would ya be wantin' to wait out th' storm in th' stables, m' lord? I can fetch ya a blanket."

Simon had a fairly good idea of what a stable blanket would smell like, and it was quite possible his sister, Martha, would not let him set foot in the house if he added that level of malodor to his already sopping state. "It's good of you to offer," he said, "but I believe I shall take my chances on making a run for it."

Ezra's grin returned. "Best o' luck t' ya, m' lord."

"I may need it." Simon lifted the lever on the door. Cinching the front of his cloak closed with one hand, he exited the stables and started down the gravel path at a steady jog. The light was dimming, and the cloud cover made it difficult to assess the exact time. Given that Martha was expecting him, she'd probably planned to have him join them for an evening meal. After his unpleasant ride, he'd be glad of some warm food. He only hoped he'd not kept the household waiting long.

The path took him around the large manor to the front of the house. Impeccably tended flowerbeds lined the edge of the lawn. Farther away, trees, shrubs, and narrow paths cut through the vast green expanse, showcasing a small portion of Simon's brother-in-law's extensive property. Normally, Simon would have paused to take in the view from this vantage point. This evening, however, he wanted nothing more than to be indoors, sitting beside a fire, wearing dry clothing.

Angling his head away from the driving rain, he took the stone stairs up to the front door two at a time, landing on the top step less than an arm's length from someone else. The person issued a startled cry. He staggered sideways, barely catching himself on the lip of the top step. "I beg your pardon. I did not see you."

"Oh! But you *can* s-see m-me?"

At the sound of a female voice, Simon's head shot up. He'd been so consumed with escaping the rain, he'd all but barreled into a young lady. Attempting to shake off his chagrin, he focused on her rather odd question. After his uncivilized approach, she deserved a reply. "Of course, I see you now. I foolishly kept my head down because I did not expect anyone else to be here."

"Wh-where exactly is 'here'?"

"Why, on the doorstep." He studied her more carefully. If her sopping silk attire and stuttering speech were any indication, she was a young lady of some means who was in extremis. He met her blue eyes. Was it fear that shone in them?

"Wh-whose doorstep?" She was shivering with cold, and there was no hiding her desperation. "Please. Can you t-tell me wh-where I am?"

"Copfield Hall," he said. A quick glance over his shoulder assured him that he'd not missed seeing a carriage in the drive.

He'd just come from the stables, and there'd been no sign of any recently arrived horses beyond his own. Had she truly arrived here on foot? And with no hat or cloak? Where were those who should have been attending her? Even if her carriage had broken down on the road, she should not be here alone.

"Wh-where exactly is C-Copfield Hall?"

"Surrey," he said. "It is the home of Lord and Lady Maidstone."

Her hands were clasped tightly before her, but whether that was due to anxiety or extreme cold, he could not tell.

"Are you . . . Are you Lord Maidstone?"

"I am not." Heaven help him. Had all remnants of common courtesy been washed away by this rain? First, he'd almost leveled the young lady on Maidstone's completely unforgiving stone stairs, and then he'd been so confounded by her unexpected appearance, he'd neglected to introduce himself. "I am Lord Bancroft. My sister is married to Lord Maidstone."

"Oh." Her chin trembled.

"Do you know my sister?"

She shook her head. "I d-don't . . ." A shudder coursed through her entire body.

Simon did not wait for more. He pounded on the door. She could add "interrupting a young lady midsentence" to his list of current faux pas if she wished. As far as he was concerned, the time for conversation was past. He was cold, but with no cloak, she must be frigid.

The Maidstones' servant had obviously been standing nearby because he opened the door straightway.

"Send for my sister, would you, Hobbes," Simon said, thankful that he knew the man well enough to bypass pleasantries. Too late, he realized that although he'd offered the mysterious young woman on the doorstep his name, he had yet to learn hers. He reached for her elbow to guide her inside. "This young lady needs immediate assistance."

If Hobbes was surprised by his request or by the young lady's appearance, he was sufficiently well-trained not to show it. He bowed politely. "Yes, my lord." And then, with barely a glance at the bedraggled stranger, he started toward the parlor.

"Come," Simon said, guiding the young lady farther into the entrance hall. "Martha will know how to best help you."

—— · ✳ · ——

Isla gazed around the vast room. The wood floor was polished to a shine, as were the wood panels on the walls. Small, leaded windows allowed in the last remaining light of early evening, but most of the room's illumination came from two large candelabras standing on tables on either side of a staircase. Three oil paintings hung on one wall depicting ships at sea. On the opposite wall, a family crest hung over the archway that led into a darkened passageway. It was the direction the man who'd played the part of a butler had gone.

Was he an actor? None of this made any sense. If she wasn't hallucinating—and the pain she was feeling in her feet suggested she wasn't—then she had no idea how she'd arrived at this place. Or who these people were.

"Wh-why are you all d-dressed up like this?" It didn't seem to matter how tightly she wrapped her arms around herself; she couldn't control her chattering teeth.

The man beside her—Lord Bancroft, supposedly—glanced down at his ensemble. The soggy ostrich feather in his flamboyant hat drooped, but even that didn't fully detract from his heroic musketeer appearance. "Given the storm we encountered," he said, "I'm grateful for my cloak. Did you not think to don one before venturing out in such inclement weather?"

She had to give him points for staying in character, but suggesting that he was more sensibly dressed than she was wasn't going to win her over. "N-no. There wasn't a c-cloak with the costume." She raised the hem of her wet skirts a fraction. "Or shoes, for that m-matter."

The shock on his face appeared genuine. "How far did you travel without shoes?"

"From the ch-changing room."

"The changing room?" His shock turned to confusion.

"Yes." She shivered. She was out of the rain and wind, but this room was not nearly warm enough. Someone needed to crank up the heat. "Th-the one that l-looks like a woodshed or s-something."

"Simon!" A woman who appeared similar in age to Isla hurried toward them from the passageway. Her dark, curly hair was piled on top of her head in an elaborate updo. The farthingale beneath her red gown must have been even wider than Isla's because her dress swayed back and forth like a pendulum as she crossed the floor. "I am so glad you are arrived safely."

Attempting to muffle her chattering teeth with her lip, Isla studied the two people curiously. Their dark hair was similar, as were their brown eyes. Despite their significant difference in height and Lord Bancroft's neatly trimmed beard, they certainly looked enough alike to be siblings.

"As am I." Lord Bancroft removed his hat and greeted her with a brief kiss on the cheek. "But as you can see," he continued, "I am not the only one seeking shelter from the storm tonight."

The woman turned her attention to Isla. "Good evening," she said politely. "I am Lady Maidstone."

"Isla C-Crawford," Isla said.

"You are most welcome, Miss Crawford." She hesitated for a fraction of a second, and when Isla didn't correct the title, she smiled. "I am anxious to hear more about you and learn what brings you to Copfield Hall. But first, we must get you out of those wet clothes."

"Th-that would b-be marvelous," Isla said. "My b-blouse and trousers are in the ch-changing room."

Lady Maidstone offered Lord Bancroft a puzzled look.

"Miss Crawford came from the direction of the woodshed," he said.

"Yes. B-but it wasn't a w-woodshed when I went in. It was a ch-changing room." Even as Isla spoke the words, she could hear how ridiculous they sounded. But seeing as all these people were dressed in period costume, they had to be in on the charade. "I'm feeling p-pretty miserable r-right now, so m-maybe we could end this prank?"

"I am very sorry, Miss Crawford," Lady Maidstone said. "I can appreciate your discomfort completely. The prank, however, I am struggling to comprehend."

"This!" Isla waved one arm to encompass the room and everyone in it. "It's l-like we all l-landed in the Elizabethan era."

Lord Bancroft cleared his throat. "Given the political volatility in our nation at present, it might be well to remember that Queen Elizabeth died over two years ago."

Isla stared at him. "Elizabethan doesn't refer to Queen Elizabeth II, you know."

"There is no Queen Elizabeth II," he said.

"Right. Because she d-died in 2022." Isla's irritation was mounting. She was going to give Chloe an earful when she saw her next. It was one thing to talk Isla into going to a costume shop she'd never heard of before; it was a whole other thing to take advantage of her visit to play a practical—and completely unfunny—joke on her. It was about time they ended this farce so Isla could go home. "Queen Elizabeth II was on the throne f-for ages," she said, "and maybe one day, people will r-remember her reign like they d-do with the f-first Queen Elizabeth." She raised her soaking skirts a few inches off the floor. "But I guarantee, th-they won't be dressed like this."

Lady Maidstone exchanged a look with her brother. It seemed like it was one part warning, one part concern. Good. Maybe he'd stop playacting now.

"I think we'd best resume our conversation after you've both changed out of your wet clothes," she said. "Simon, your trunk arrived yesterday and is in the green room, as usual. I imagine you'll find Anson there also. Miss Crawford, you and I are of a similar height. I believe I can find you a gown to wear from my wardrobe. You are of a more slender build, but my maid, Maggie, is masterful at pinning. I have no doubt she will be able to fit something to you without any difficulty."

"But my own c-clothes are in—"

"The changing room," Lady Maidstone finished for her. "So you said. But seeing as the storm has yet to subside, I think it would be wise if you borrowed something of mine for the time being."

"What of shoes, Martha?" Lord Bancroft asked.

Isla raised her hem just enough to expose her purple feet. "A pair of socks would be g-great, especially if you don't have any sh-shoes in a six."

"In a six?" Lady Maidstone frowned. "What is that?"

"My shoe size," Isla said. "I usually w-wear a six, but I might be okay in a f-five and a half."

"How remarkable." The lines on Lady Maidstone's forehead weren't completely gone, but she seemed intrigued. "My cobbler traces my foot to make a pattern when I need a new pair of shoes. I do not believe he has ever told me how my foot size compares to that of other ladies. He has certainly never given me a number." She gestured toward the stairs. "Come this way. We shall see if my shoes are also a six."

Isla wasn't too excited about following Lady Maidstone to yet another unknown location, but the promise of dry clothes was too good to pass up.

"Thank you for your h-help, Lord Bancroft," she said.

With a startled look, he inclined his head. "My pleasure, Miss Crawford."

She managed a weak smile and then turned to follow Lady Maidstone across the hall. When they reached the bottom step, she glanced back at him. He was watching her, his expression troubled. Lady Maidstone must have noticed, too, because she paused, her hand already on the banister rail.

"Locate your manservant and trunk, Simon," she said. "I have Miss Crawford's situation well in hand, and you need to change your clothing almost as badly as she does. You are dripping water on my floor." She started up the stairs. "Miss Crawford and I shall meet you and Hugh in the parlor within the half hour."

CHAPTER 3

Have you ever heard the name before, Maidstone?" Simon stared out of the drawing room window in the general direction of the woodshed. The darkness and rain made it impossible to see the distant structure, but he knew where it stood.

"Miss Isla Crawford? Can't say that I have." Simon's brother-in-law sat in one of the armchairs closest to the fire, a thoughtful look in his eyes. "Didn't someone in Northumberland's family marry a Crawford?"

"If she's from the north, it might explain her unusual speech." He shook his head, trying to capture something that yet eluded him. "It's not so much her cadence as her choice of words. She sounds English, and yet she does not."

"Scottish?" Maidstone guessed. "Or it could be that she hails from some out-of-the-way place in Wales."

"If that were the case, I don't suppose Martha and I would have understood her at all."

Maidstone chuckled. "I cannot argue with that." He set the glass in his hand on the small table beside the chair and rose to his feet. "Stop worrying, old fellow. It should not be hard to discover how the young lady came to be here all alone. I daresay Martha will know her entire life story by the time they come downstairs."

Simon appreciated Maidstone's optimism, but the gentleman had not seen the deep-seated fear and desperation in Miss Crawford's eyes. Such raw emotion was the product of a significant ordeal. Something far greater than being caught in the rain.

Footsteps and voices sounded in the passageway. Maidstone tossed Simon a meaningful look. "It appears you shall not have to wait much longer to have your questions answered."

Moments later, Martha led Miss Crawford into the room. Martha acknowledged Simon with a smile before moving to stand beside her husband. "Miss Crawford," she said, "I should like to have you meet my husband, Lord Maidstone. Hugh, this is Miss Crawford. She is most recently from London but was raised in York."

Maidstone bowed. Miss Crawford offered a hesitant smile. Simon simply stared.

Martha had touted her lady's maid's skill in Simon's presence before, but Maggie had truly outdone herself this evening. Gone was the sopping wet, disoriented stranger who had washed up on the Maidstones' doorstep. In her place was an elegant young woman whose damp hair was pinned to her head in a flattering mass of gentle curls and whose rose-colored gown complemented her complexion perfectly. Her blue eyes—even brighter now than they'd appeared in the shadowy entrance hall—were framed with thick, dark lashes. And although she retained an air of hesitancy, the only word Simon could summon to describe her now was *breathtaking*.

"Welcome to Copfield Hall, Miss Crawford," Maidstone said.

"Thank you, Lord Maidstone." Almost as if it were an afterthought, Miss Crawford inclined her head slightly. "I'm very grateful for Lady Maidstone's kindness." She brushed her hand down her skirt. "It's wonderful to be dry again."

"Ah, yes. I heard you were caught in the storm." Maidstone turned to Simon, drawing him into the conversation. "Were you en route from London, as Lord Bancroft here was?"

"I was in London," she said. "Pickering Place, to be exact." She clasped her hands, her gaze darting from Maidstone to Simon. "To be honest, I don't know exactly how I got from there to here."

"Miss Crawford is alone," Martha said. They'd clearly had this conversation upstairs. "She has no escort, no carriage, no mount, and no luggage."

Disbelief rippled through Simon, and he saw a similar emotion touch Maidstone's eyes. Martha had obviously had more time to assimilate this rather shocking state of affairs, because she tucked her arm through her husband's and continued calmly. "I have told her that she is welcome to stay at Copfield Hall until she has acquired a way to safely return home."

"There is no safety to be had in returning to London at present," Simon said.

Miss Crawford swiveled to face him. "Why? Has something happened there?"

"If you have truly just come from the city, I would have thought it impossible to be ignorant of current conditions."

"Has there been a riot? A bombing?" Panic tinged her voice. "Please, tell me."

"The plague," he said. Was he truly the only one in the room who was mystified by half of what Miss Crawford said? "Surely you know that the alarming number of deaths from the disease has caused the theatres to close their doors and the king to delay the opening of Parliament."

"The plague?" She swallowed. "You mean COVID?"

"Pardon my ignorance," Maidstone said, "but what exactly is COVID?"

Miss Crawford reached for the back of the chair closest to her and gripped it tightly. "A disease," she said tightly. "But maybe not the one you're talking about?"

"I don't believe so." Simon eyed her warily. "The one I am referring to is also known as the Bubonic Plague or Black Death."

"Yes." Her voice dropped to a whisper. "I thought that might be it."

"It is the reason almost all members of the House of Lords have vacated their London homes."

"Including you," she guessed.

"Yes. My country residence is a considerable distance from London, in Derbyshire. The Maidstones are good enough to allow me to stay here when I am required to return to the city within a relatively short period of time."

"Although we regret the terrible suffering occurring in London, Simon's extended visits to our home have delighted our sons," Martha said, seemingly attempting to redirect the conversation to something lighter.

Her approach proved successful, for Miss Crawford's eyes widened. "You have children?"

"We do." Martha smiled. "And if I had taken you down the east wing of the house, you would doubtless have heard them in the nursery. They will be so jubilant when they learn of Simon's arrival, I fear their voices will not be contained to that part of the house."

Simon grinned. Much as he appreciated Martha and her husband's company, in his opinion, Copfield Hall's biggest draw was his rambunctious nephews. The boys had a way of making the most difficult of circumstances seem less trying and the most challenging problems more manageable. "Are you telling me that I must wait until tomorrow to see them?" he asked.

"Absolutely." Martha eyed him sternly. "As Hobbes has already informed me that supper is ready, I believe we should relocate to the dining room and enjoy the meal uninterrupted."

Simon accepted her directive with an exaggerated sigh. "Very well. But your cook had better have outdone herself if there is to be any hope of assuaging my disappointment."

"I believe she has," Maidstone said. "I have it on good authority that there will be braised eel for supper tonight."

"Ah." Simon guessed Martha had specifically requested the dish because she knew he liked it so well. "I daresay braised eel may be worth the sacrifice."

Maidstone chuckled and led Martha to the door. Left with only one polite option, Simon offered Miss Crawford his arm. She gave him a mystified look, but when he raised an eyebrow, she tentatively set her hand on his sleeve.

"I shall not eat you," he said. "You have my word."

"I'm glad to hear it," she replied, lifting her chin slightly. "It may ruin your appetite for the braised eel."

Surprised but unaccountably pleased by her response, Simon fought back a smile. Miss Crawford may say exceptionally odd things, but it appeared that she was not without a sense of humor.

———— ·•✶•· ————

Isla stared at the long, brown object on the pewter plate before her and suppressed a shudder. Braised eel. She might have tried it if she hadn't known what it was. But thanks to Lord Maidstone, she did know. And she was genuinely worried that if she put a piece in her mouth, she might gag.

Across the table from her, Lord Bancroft was already half-way through the portion on his plate. Isla shuddered again. Live eels gave her the creeps; cooked eels weren't much better. The first course had been roast beef, lamb, and turnips. She hadn't expected or needed a meal of eel and leeks after that. Would she be considered horribly rude if she left it untouched? Lady Maidstone had been incredibly kind, and the last thing Isla wanted to do was insult her, but eating eel . . . She honestly didn't think she could do it.

After stabbing a small piece of leek with the short, sharp knife she had found beside her plate, Isla slid the vegetable into her mouth and chewed slowly. If she knew Lord Bancroft better, she'd offer him her eel, but since she'd only just met the man, it would probably be weird to suggest it. Not that every conversation they'd had so far hadn't been weird. Her chest tightened. Pretty much everything about her situation and sur-roundings right now was surreal.

She was sitting at a large, rectangular, wooden table in a wood-paneled room in a Tudor manor. A fire in the large fire-place augmented the light from the candles lining the center of the table. The dishes were filled with simple foods, yet they tasted unfamiliar. Ale filled the goblets, and the others in the room—all dressed in elegant Jacobean clothing—appeared com-pletely at ease. It truly seemed as though she were the only one who felt out of place.

"Bring me up-to-date on news from London, Bancroft," Lord Maidstone said. "Do whispers of death threats directed toward the king continue?"

Lord Bancroft grimaced. "In almost every social gathering. And I see no reason for them to stop. Not until the monarch is willing to offer the Catholics some concessions."

Death threats? Catholics? What on earth were they talking about? Isla set down her knife. It clattered against the rim of the plate. Instantly, silence fell over the table, and everyone's gaze landed on her.

"I'm sorry," she said. "I didn't mean to interrupt."

Lady Maidstone cleared her throat. "At the risk of causing offense, Miss Crawford, would you be willing to tell us your religious leanings?"

"My . . . my religious leanings?"

"Yes." Lady Maidstone didn't look away. "Do you align yourself with the Protestant faith or Catholic?"

During an evening filled with odd questions, this one might win the prize.

"When I go to church, I attend Church of England services," Isla said.

The tension left Lady Maidstone's shoulders. "That makes life easier, does it not?"

"I . . . I suppose so. Why did you ask?"

"There always seem to be negative repercussions when one is seen fraternizing with Catholics." Her expression dropped. "It is awful. And I hate that we have to even consider it, but for the sake of the boys . . ."

"You have nothing to apologize for, Martha." Lord Maidstone set a comforting hand over his wife's. "Today's political upheaval is not of your making. Neither is the rift it has caused between those of differing religions."

Isla's thoughts spun. This discussion and the distress it had engendered felt incredibly real. And heavy. Heavier than pretense should ever be. She allowed her gaze to traverse the room again. There were no electric plugs or cords, no items made of plastic or rubber. Nothing remotely modern. Was it possible that this historically perfect building was no set, these people weren't acting, and she'd actually traveled back in time? No. It couldn't be.

More than ever before, she wanted to escape the room and this bizarre conversation. But her newfound doubts lingered. What if this wasn't fake? Ever since she'd stepped out of the changing room, she'd been in such a state of shock and disbelief that she'd not allowed herself time to think. To *really* think. What if the inconceivable had actually occurred? What if she really had been dropped into the past? She needed to shake off her shock and focus. And she'd better start drawing on whatever she could remember from all her college history classes too.

In a final act of defiance against the preposterous situation, she raised her eyes to meet Lord Bancroft's. "What's today's date?" she asked.

"It is the twenty-ninth of September," he said.

"And the year?"

He gave her an odd look. "Sixteen oh five."

Sixteen oh five! Isla attempted to keep her breathing even and racked her brains for anything she could attach to the time period. Queen Elizabeth had just died. King James was on the throne. But there were factions who didn't believe he belonged there. And if she remembered right, those factions were almost exclusively Catholics who longed for a monarch who would restore the rights they'd enjoyed under the reign of Queen Mary.

"Would you say that King James is more concerned with uniting England and Scotland under one monarch than in uniting people of differing faiths in those same countries?" she asked, offering a silent prayer that she'd remembered right.

"Undoubtedly." Lord Bancroft was still staring at her. "Although few outside those serving in Parliament recognize it."

For a monarch who would be instrumental in producing the King James version of the Bible, his lack of sensitivity to varying religious beliefs made no sense. But Isla's schooling had taught her that history was riddled with such contradictions.

"It must have been a disappointment to the Catholics that Mary Queen of Scots' own son would treat them so badly," she said.

Something flickered in Lord Bancroft's eyes, but before Isla could identify the emotion, he turned to Lord Maidstone. Isla followed his gaze. The sandy-haired man was looking unusually grave.

"If your bent is truly toward the Church of England, Miss Crawford," he said, "I would suggest that you curb your public criticism of the king's treatment of Catholics. There are assuredly others who share your feelings, but there are equally assuredly spies circulating at every social function, keeping track of anyone who speaks ill of the king. Once those names reach Cecil, those people are considered potential traitors to the crown."

Cecil. Isla was obviously supposed to know the name. It sounded vaguely familiar. It also sounded as though he wielded a great deal of power. "How do you know who the spies are?"

"Guesswork," Lord Bancroft said. "Those who appear a little too interested in conversations not meant for them. Those who encourage Catholics who practice their religion in secret to speak openly of their religious observance. Those who appear at inns where the proprietors are known to turn a blind eye to clandestine gatherings."

"Unfortunately, they are rarely obvious." Lord Maidstone's expression remained grim. "I have lost some good friends to Cecil's witch hunts."

"What happened to them?" The moment the words were out of her mouth, Isla regretted them. Lady Maidstone bowed her head as though inexplicably burdened. "I'm sorry. You don't have to answer that."

"If you truly do not know, it is best that I enlighten you," Lord Maidstone said. "They were taken to the Tower. Most are already dead."

"Because they were practicing Catholics?" It was almost too terrible to comprehend.

"Yes. And they were seen as a threat." Lord Maidstone straightened his shoulders. "Now, perhaps you better comprehend why Martha asked about your leanings. No one in this room harbors ill feelings toward those of the Catholic faith—quite the opposite, in fact—but I believe I speak for Lord Bancroft when I say that neither of us will ever be sufficiently swayed by religious fervor to condone an assassination attempt on the king."

"I understand." And she did. It had taken her a few minutes, but the penny had finally dropped. Unfortunately, the new awareness brought more fear than comfort. "Thank you for your warning; I'll be more careful from now on."

Slipping her trembling hands beneath the table, she fought for composure. She should have registered the importance of the date the moment Lord Bancroft had enlightened her. Sixteen oh five was no ordinary year in British history. It was the year Guy Fawkes and his fellow conspirators had attempted to blow up Parliament and the king.

CHAPTER 4

The priest brought his prayer to a close. In unison, the ten men in the Duck and Drake Inn's upstairs room raised their heads. All but one kept his eyes on the religious leader as he offered an acknowledging nod to Robert Catsby. Catsby was the person responsible for calling this meeting. He insisted upon beginning all their clandestine gatherings with a mass. It was a worthy practice, and Guy Fawkes could not fault the man for doing it. Even if it meant that one more person was aware of the connection between the conspirators in the room.

For his part, Guy chose to ignore the priest and study his associates. Every gentleman within these four walls claimed full devotion to the Catholic cause, and despite the Anglican leanings of their current monarch and his henchmen, a heady sense of power, determination, and influence pervaded the small, dimly lit room. With swords unsheathed, these men had sworn an oath of fellowship and secrecy. Guy thrilled at the memory of the night he had joined them. It had marked the beginning of real change. There would be no more waiting for King James to fulfill vague promises. Diplomacy had long since proved to be a futile endeavor. The time for action had come, and it would commence with ending the monarch's reign.

Unaware of the true reason for the gathering, the priest offered a final blessing on those in the room before slipping out through the door. For a few seconds, no one spoke. The whisper of footsteps in the outside passage faded. In the distance, another door closed. And then Catsby rose to his feet.

"You are undoubtedly aware of the king's recent edict, demanding that the opening of Parliament be delayed until November 5." His lip curled contemptuously. "King James's assertion that the plague has become overly rampant in London is a characteristically weak excuse. He simply wishes to take more time to flatter Scottish noblemen on yet another royal hunt."

Jack Wright scowled. "No matter the reason, he has thrown our plans into commotion."

Across the room, Kit Wright shook his head. "Where's your faith, brother? A delay is merely a delay. It is not the termination of our efforts."

"Well said, Kit." Thomas Percy played the part of Gentleman Pensioner to perfection. His attitude was as haughty as was his voice. "Our plans shall move forward; only the date of the end of the Church of England's stranglehold on this country will change."

Catsby looked askance, and Guy smirked. Notwithstanding Catsby's undisputed leadership, Percy was well positioned to put the older Wright brother in his place. Percy's pedigree set him apart from most of the men in the room. His connections were impeccable. They'd gained him access to a house across the street from the House of Lords, which had been a godsend when they'd been searching for a way to enter the revered building. Those same credentials also gave Percy admittance to the royal residence.

Guy leaned back in his seat, watching the interaction between the gentlemen with interest. It would not be long before

Jack Wright backed down and resumed his rightful place. If Catsby was the group's leader, Percy was his deputy. And Guy? Well, everyone here knew his position. To the outside world, he was John Johnson, manservant to Thomas Percy. To those in this room—and a handful of others currently working with the Spanish on the Continent—he was a fearless combatant and foremost authority on the use of gunpowder. No matter the lowly station he had assumed since returning from Spain, he was indispensable to the success of Catsby's plan, and everyone in this group knew it.

As though Catsby's thoughts had mirrored his own, the tall, broad-shouldered man turned to Guy. "What say you, Fawkes? Can the gunpowder withstand the wait?"

Thirty-six barrels of gunpowder sat in an undercroft beneath the chamber where the House of Lords gathered. They'd been painstakingly transported there under the cover of darkness from Robert Keyes's house in Lambeth.

"The damp coming from the Thames is the greatest threat," Guy said. It was a factor he'd rarely had to consider in Spain's dry climate.

"How great a threat?" Catsby pressed.

Guy shrugged. "Until I have inspected the barrels, I cannot say for certain."

"Can you access them within the next twenty-four hours without drawing attention?"

Guy did not deign to answer the question directly. Over the last few weeks, he'd been in and out of the undercroft more times than he could count. Always at night. Always with an associate keeping guard across the street. "Assign a watchman to go with me tomorrow evening, and you shall have your answer by the next morning," he said.

Catsby gave a satisfied smile. "Wintour, go with Fawkes."

Thomas Wintour exchanged a brief nod with Guy. "I shall be on the corner of Margaret Street and King Street at half past midnight tomorrow."

"Very well," Guy said. It would be easy enough to exchange a few words with Wintour before venturing into the Parliament building. At that time of night, the street should be empty—the king's mandate had worked in their favor in that regard, at least. Few members of the upper class remained in London; even fewer were venturing outside their homes.

"When you have ascertained the status of the barrels, send word to me at the Bell Inn in Daventry," Catsby said before turning to the remaining men. "On the assumption that Fawkes discovers nothing amiss, we shall set our plans in motion on November 4. I advise each of you to leave the plague-ridden city until that date. Contracting the disease will do nothing for our cause. Do not spend time alone together. No hint of collusion or subversion must reach Cecil. He will not rest until he uncovers the source of the faintest of whispers."

Every man nodded. They would scatter, but it would not be hard to locate them when the time was right. Rookwood and Grant would return to their respective horse farms. Sir Digby would undoubtedly join a hunt in the Midlands. Robert Wintour would likely wait for his brother, Thomas, to return from standing guard before joining his family. There would be no questions asked if the Wright brothers traveled together, nor if Bates remained with Catsby. Bates was Catsby's right-hand man and would be expected to go wherever his master went.

"I believe I am overdue for a visit to your country home, Catsby," Percy said.

Catsby eyed him narrowly. "In case you have forgotten, you possess a well-furnished manor of your own, Percy. Make use of it. My wine cellar is depleted far too quickly when you come to stay."

Percy grinned, not the least perturbed. "Your loss, Catsby. I have a feeling the month of October shall see you pacing your spacious rooms just as a caged animal would."

As expected, Catsby ignored the goading. No one in the room had witnessed Catsby ruffled. He was a man of deliberation followed by brisk action. During the months that had passed since they'd first met, Guy had come to appreciate Catsby's calm, measured approach. It was a quality that boded well for a leader and his followers.

"That is all, gentlemen," Catsby said. It was time to disperse— slowly, one at a time, so that no one in the lower room of the inn was aware that a meeting had occurred on the upper floor. "Fawkes. I wish you well."

Guy rose, grateful to be the first to leave. It was safer that way. He eyed Percy speculatively. If the gentleman followed Catsby's orders and relocated to his own house in the country, he would be surrounded by retainers and would have no need of his so-called servant, John Johnson. Perhaps this dismissal might last a little longer than Guy had anticipated.

He started for the door, his thoughts shifting from the inn near London to a small house outside York. He'd not seen his former home or his mother in over ten years. If he were forced to flee the country after the events of November 5, it was unlikely that he would see either one for years to come. He reached for the door and opened it a fraction. The passage beyond was quiet. With ears pricked for the sound of an unexpected footfall, he opened the door wider and stepped out. He had an important task to perform. Once that was behind him, he would consider making a journey up north.

———— · ✴ · ————

Isla rolled onto her right side. The mattress beneath her rustled, the noise penetrating her troubled sleep. She'd bought a new memory-foam-topped mattress not more than six months ago. It never rustled. Afraid to open her eyes, she held completely still, listening for the grind of a London bus's engine or the honk of a taxi's horn outside her bedroom window. Instead, she heard a rooster crow. She tensed. There were no roosters in Knightsbridge. There was probably a city ordinance prohibiting them.

Reluctantly but unable to put off the inevitable any longer, she opened her eyes. A narrow chink of light spilled through the small gap between the shutters at the window. It was just enough to illuminate the dark beams running across the ceiling and the large fireplace filled with the ashes of yesterday's fire.

The heavy fabric hanging from the top of the four-poster bed in which she lay blocked her view of the rest of the bedroom, but there could be no doubt about where she was. Last night, she'd done her utmost to persuade herself that if she fell asleep in the seventeenth-century bedchamber, she'd wake up in her modern London flat. It hadn't happened.

She snapped her eyes closed again. "Stay calm. Stay calm." Her words were barely audible, but they circled the room in a taunting whisper.

Somehow, she'd fumbled her way through an entire Elizabethan meal. At least, she'd thought it was Elizabethan, but she'd been wrong about that too. She clenched the blanket. Sixteen oh five. The beginning of the Jacobean era, with all its political turmoil and domestic hardships. When the significance of the date had finally hit her, shock had left her virtually speechless.

In retrospect, Isla realized that her continued silence at the table may have come across as rudeness, sullenness, or shyness, but she would accept any of those labels over having a complete meltdown or saying something that would send her to the Tower of London. She took an unsteady breath. What *was* the right thing to say? If she had truly traveled back in time, did she tell the people living here about the dangers the government was about to face? Or would giving them that kind of information somehow rewrite history? Over the last few months, she may have wished for more influence at work, but this was taking responsibility for the workings of Parliament to another level.

She pulled back the bedcovers. The room felt chilly and damp, but she slid out of the bed anyway. When her bare feet touched the wooden floor, she shivered. There was a small pile of logs lying beside the fireplace, but with no matches in sight, she had no idea how to start a fire. Helplessness mingled with panic. Starting a fire without matches was only the beginning. She didn't know the first thing about how to survive in a seventeenth-century world.

Attempting to tamp down her fears, she focused on what she could do. Her best chance of warming up was to put on a few more layers. The gown Lady Maidstone had loaned her lay across a nearby chair. Her costume shop clothing hung on a clothes rack in front of the empty fireplace. Tiptoeing across the floor so as to limit how much her feet actually touched the cold surface, she reached for the cream-colored floral gown. It was dry.

Isla wasn't sure whether the speed at which she donned the clothes was due to practice, or if she was just desperate to warm up. Either way, she dressed quickly and hurried over to the window. Opening one of the shutters a fraction, she peeked outside. This bedroom faced the front of the house. Morning mist hung over the trees, shrouding the world beyond. Puddles caused by the rain the night before appeared like pockmarks on the gravel driveway, and the grass glistened with moisture. Beyond the nearest cluster of trees, she could just make out the tiled roof of the woodshed.

She gripped the window frame. Was it a woodshed? Or was it some kind of time portal? The thought that she might actually be experiencing life in 1605 was mind-blowing. And completely terrifying. She had to check the shed one more time. Before anyone else was awake. If she had actually traveled into the past, there had to be a way for her to go back.

With a whispered apology to Lady Maidstone, Isla slipped her feet into her hostess's size-six shoes and crossed the room. She opened the door carefully. It creaked, but the hall beyond was silent. Just enough light was coming through the chinks in the shutters to guide her down the stairs and to the front door. There was no sign of a servant, so Isla turned the enormous key in the lock. The bolt drew back with a loud thud. She stood very still. Voices reached her from the back of the house. Something clanged. A pan in the kitchen maybe? Not waiting to find out, she opened the door and stole outside.

Closing the door behind her, she ran down the steps and cut across the gravel driveway to the grass. The damp ground muffled the sound of her running feet, but it was slippery. She slowed her steps slightly. She'd fallen in this area once before and still had grass stains on her gown to prove it. Moving more carefully, she wove around a small grove of trees, and suddenly, the woodshed was right before her. From the safety of the trees, she glanced up and down the driveway. There was still no sign of anyone, so she stepped onto the path and cautiously approached the shed door.

The black wood and wrought-iron latch were discouragingly familiar. She walked around the right side of the shed. An empty wheelbarrow was parked against the wall. She continued past it to the back of the small building. It pressed up against a thick hedge, and even though she could just make out the muted greens of a field beyond, there was not enough space for anyone or anything to pass between the wall and the dense foliage.

Doubling back, she walked around the front of the shed to study the other side. Three large logs lay on the ground, and if the dusting of wood chips on the grass was any indication, this was the spot where much of the wood for the house was chopped. There was no sign of any tools. Presumably, the Maidstones' servants knew better than to leave axes or saws outside in an area where unexpected rain was common.

Like it or not, it seemed that there was no other entrance or exit to the woodshed. The black door was the only one she could have come through the night before. She stared at the unimposing entrance to the woodshed with mounting trepidation, then she reached for the latch. It lifted. She pushed open the door and stepped inside. The wood was stacked just as it had been before. Tidy rows piled almost as high as the uneven roof. No painted walls, no mirror or hooks, no polished wood floor.

Isla fought back tears as her hope crumbled. Lord Bancroft was right; this building was nothing more than a woodshed. She would never understand how she'd come here. And if there was a way for her to return to modern-day London, she didn't know where to begin looking for it. She pressed her hand against the roughly hewn doorframe, her thoughts and fears tumbling over each other. What was she to do? Without ID, money, a home, or family—at least, none who would know her, even if she knew where to find them—she was basically destitute.

And what of the life she'd left behind? How long would it be before her parents, siblings, friends, and coworkers realized she was gone? Her heart ached at the thought that her mother and father would never know what had happened to her—or how much she loved them.

"Miss Crawford?"

At the unexpected voice, Isla gasped and swung around. "Lord Bancroft!"

"Are you quite all right?"

All right? No. Not remotely. "I . . . uh . . ." She fought for control of her emotions.

He must have sensed her helplessness, because his eyebrows lowered. "If I can be of assistance, I am willing."

"Thank you. You've already been marvelous. I just don't know if you'll . . ." She shook her head. The man was hardly more than a slight acquaintance. If she told him the truth, he'd think her a certifiable nutcase. But what other choice did she have? She didn't know nearly enough about the early 1600s to survive another twenty-four hours without help. Besides, she had nowhere to go and no one else to turn to besides him and the Maidstones.

"I have a considerable number of well-connected friends and associates," Lord Bancroft said. "Lord Maidstone has even more. No matter what has happened in your past, between the two of us, we are well positioned to give you aid."

Isla wrapped her arms around herself. "I'm not sure that anyone here can help me."

"I should like to try."

Hope made a valiant attempt at surfacing through her deepening despair. "Why? We hardly know each other."

Shrugging off his cloak, he stepped forward and set it around her shoulders. It was heavy and warm and smelled of horses and leather. He drew it around her. "First, any young lady wandering rural Britain in late September without a cloak is, of necessity, in need of aid. Second, my father taught me that being born into privilege simply means that one is in a better position to offer assistance to others."

Isla stared at him. "Your father is a remarkable man."

"He was. He died when I was eighteen years of age. That was ten years ago, but I miss him fiercely even now."

"I'm sorry. Is your mother still alive?"

He shook his head, regret in his eyes. "She followed him to the grave two years later. Martha and I are the only ones left now."

"I have an older brother and sister," she said. "Both married and living their own lives. My parents still live in York." She paused, the ramifications of her new situation settling on her with even greater weight than Lord Bancroft's cloak. Would she ever see any of her family members again? Battling an unexpected surge of emotion, she cleared her throat. "They . . . uh . . . They . . ."

"If you wish to return to York, that can be arranged," he said.

"Thank you, but they won't be there."

He frowned. "Forgive me. With the prevalence of the plague in London, I assumed they would be in residence in York. Are they visiting friends or relatives elsewhere?"

"No." Isla took a deep breath. There was no easy way to explain this. "They won't live there for over four hundred years."

"I beg your pardon?"

"I honestly don't know if there's anything you can do to help me, but if you're willing to suspend disbelief for a few minutes, I'll tell you exactly where I came from."

Lord Bancroft's frown deepened. "'Suspend disbelief' is not an expression I am familiar with."

"Sorry." Isla rallied her thoughts. Perhaps her unusual expressions were something she could use to her advantage. "I'm afraid my speech is probably full of unfamiliar words and expressions."

He acknowledged her comment with an inclination of his head and a slight smile. "I have been trying to ascertain the origin of your unusual vocabulary. Have you spent time in Wales?"

Isla shook her head. Under normal circumstances, she would have laughed. At the moment, however, she was too stressed to even smile. If Lord Bancroft didn't believe her, she would be in even more trouble than she was now. "I'm simply asking you to listen to what I tell you with an open mind," she said.

"Of course."

That was easier said than done. As was uttering the words she needed to say.

"I'm from the future." The sentence tumbled out, and Isla hurried to continue. "I know it sounds crazy, and I have no idea how it happened, but it's true. I promise."

"You are from the future," Lord Bancroft repeated. His voice showed no hint of emotion, but she caught the twitch in his jaw.

"Yes. One minute, I was in a changing room in a costume shop in Westminster in 2025, and the next minute, I was caught in a storm on the Maidstones' front lawn in 1605." She gestured toward the woodshed. "I know it sounds mad. I walked out into a completely different world. Well, not a different world, exactly, but a completely different time."

Lord Bancroft's jaw remained tense. "And you expect me to believe this?"

Tears pricked Isla's eyes. "No. I don't. It's too far-fetched. But it's all I've got because believable or not, it's the truth." She clasped her hands together tightly and willed the tears to stay at bay. "I don't know what to do. The only people I know are you and Lord and Lady Maidstone. All I have are the clothes I'm wearing."

"I beg to differ," he said. "The shoes and cloak do not belong to you."

"You're right." She slid the cloak off her shoulders and offered it to him.

"Put it back on," he said gruffly. "It's far too cold out here to be without one."

"But it's yours, and now you're without one." She didn't understand him. One minute, he was calling her on the carpet, and the next minute, he was being chivalrous.

"My jacket is warmer than your gown," he said. "And no matter how ludicrous your tale, I am not so inconsiderate that I would walk away from you with the cloak."

Isla's heart sank. "Are you going to walk away, then?"

"If I had a modicum of sense, I would be halfway to the front door by now."

"Yes." She looked down at the cloak in her hands, and a tear escaped. "You would."

There was a moment of silence, and then with a frustrated grunt, he took the fabric from her and draped it across her shoulders again. "There is a bench on the other side of the grove of trees," he said. "I shall give you five minutes of this so-called suspended disbelief, and then I shall decide what is to be done."

With you. The additional words went unsaid but hung in the damp air between them. Isla drew the cloak more closely around herself. He had offered her more than she'd dared hope for. For now, it was enough.

CHAPTER 5

M iss Isla Crawford was of an unsound mind. It was the only logical reason for her outlandish claims. A world filled with carriages that ran without horses, hot and cold water accessed from within the house, and contraptions that allowed people to fly. Such things were beyond anything Simon had ever imagined. Beyond anything the foremost authorities in any scientific field had likely ever imagined. It was completely preposterous. And yet Miss Crawford spoke of the contrivances with such earnestness and detailed description, he found himself envisioning these miraculous devices and advancements.

"And you say this horseless carriage can travel faster than my mount at full gallop?" he asked. At some point, she would surely be caught in her own fabrications.

She eyed him more thoughtfully than he had anticipated. "How fast can your horse go?"

"How would you have me measure it?"

"Do you use miles?" she asked.

"I am familiar with the distance," he said. "The measurement was set forth in Queen Elizabeth's reign."

"Okay, how many miles do you think your horse could travel in an hour?"

Okay? Her speech was peppered with oddities. They were impossible to ignore. Had she purposely made up words to persuade him to believe her story? "If he were given his head, Blaze could travel the best part of forty miles in that time." Blaze was the fastest mount Simon had ever owned, and he could not help but allow a touch of pride in his response. He did not add that the horse would be completely exhausted by the time it reached its destination.

Unfortunately, Miss Crawford did not appear overly impressed.

"My car can go double that without any difficulty," she said. "But there are other cars made especially for racing that can go five times that speed."

Faster than a gale-force wind? Miss Crawford's grasp of speed and distance was obviously as erred as her concept of time. "That is impossible."

"But I've seen it! When I was younger, my brother made me watch the Indy 500 and the Monaco Grand Prix with him on the telly. Those cars were going close to two hundred miles per hour."

Indy 500. Grand Prix. Telly. What on earth did those words mean? Simon had never considered himself a dunce. Indeed, in his youth, he'd excelled in his classes. But at least half of what Miss Crawford had just said was lost on him.

His bafflement must have shown on his face because the vibrancy she'd exhibited when she'd spoken of *cars* evaporated, to be replaced by an air of disappointment.

"I understand," she said. "When you haven't seen or experienced something for yourself, it's hard to imagine that it exists. Up until yesterday, I would never have believed time travel was possible." Her shoulders drooped. "And yet, here I am."

She looked away, and Simon received the uncomfortable impression that she might be crying. Blast it all. He'd offered her five minutes of his time, and they'd been sitting on this damp bench for close to thirty. But he was no nearer knowing what to do now than he had been when she'd first told him she'd arrived from the future. The young lady was quite obviously delusional, and the safest thing to do would be to send her on her way with a cloak, a pair of shoes, and some basic provisions. Yet he could not shake the impression that the logical solution was not the correct one.

He needed more time to think this through. More time to observe her. And more time to listen—to her and to his feelings.

"May I have your permission to share what you have told me with Lord and Lady Maidstone?" he asked.

She nodded and wiped her fingers across her cheeks before turning to face him. "I think they need to know, don't you?"

"I do." At the sight of her tear-stained face, Simon experienced a pang of self-reproach. No matter its ludicrousness, it was clear that she believed her own story, and Simon could not help but admire her courage. Had most young ladies of his acquaintance conceived of a situation so desperate or frightening, they would have been too distraught to leave their beds this morning.

"I should probably be the one to tell Lord and Lady Maidstone." Her fingers were clasped around the edges of his cloak, her white knuckles the only outward sign of her anxiety. "Although, if you'd like to be there, too, I'm fine with that."

"Then, I shall join you," he said. Not only would he benefit from the retelling, but it might also be best if someone else were in the room when Miss Crawford attempted to convince his brother-in-law of her fantastic account. Simon had no idea how Maidstone would react. "Unfortunately, if you wish to speak with Lord and Lady Maidstone together, the meeting may need to be postponed a little while. My sister is rarely awake this early."

"Oh." She appeared momentarily nonplussed. "I'm afraid I have no idea what time it is."

"I would guess we are approaching nine o'clock," he said.

She blinked. "I am usually at work by now. What time does your sister get up?"

"She should be available within an hour or so," he said, but his attention was drawn to her earlier comment. "What manner of work are you referring to?"

"I'm an assistant to a member of Parliament."

Simon eyed her with concern. "Forgive me, but you are a young lady."

"Yes." A smile tugged at her lips, and with shock, he realized how badly he wished to see her happy. "Then again, my boss is also a lady."

"Your boss? What is that?"

"The person I work for," she said. "The member of Parliament for the York Central District in 2025 is Ms. Audrey Marshall."

Simon attempted to gather his wits. He could scarcely comprehend a scenario that included ladies in the chambers of Parliament. It was as unthinkable as a gentleman taking to the air in flight. He ran his fingers through his hair. This conversation had become fully out of hand.

"She was voted into power by the people of Yorkshire," Miss Crawford said, and then, as if sensing his disbelief, she continued. "By the turn of the nineteenth century, women in England will begin entering the workforce, taking on jobs in the mines and on farms. That movement continues to grow as new industries spring up across the country. In the early twentieth century, women are granted a vote in elections, and in the England I know, there are very few things that a woman cannot aspire to do or achieve."

"Including running the country," Simon said.

Miss Crawford's smile blossomed. "We've already had a couple of female Prime Ministers. From the mid-1700s on, that's the highest elected position in the country."

Simon's mind was reeling, and he could not tell where to place the blame. Miss Crawford's outrageous claims about life in the future were staggering, but the fact that it was becoming more and more difficult to believe that she could fabricate such things was far more disturbing. If she was truly who she claimed to be, the ramifications of her arrival here were immeasurable. Then again, his visceral response to the warmth of her full smile may well be the most immeasurably concerning thing of all.

He needed to leave this bench and experience some normalcy, but he couldn't very well leave Miss Crawford here alone. Until he and the Maidstones determined the seriousness of her instability, she should not be left alone anywhere in the house or on the grounds. Being among other people would be a good thing. Preferably people who would accept the unusual young lady's presence without questioning her background and who would not care one jot if Simon was struggling to string his thoughts into a coherent whole.

He rose to his feet. "Come," he said. "We have conversed long enough for now. I have completed my morning ride, and you have ascertained that the Maidstones' woodshed is nothing more than a woodshed. It is time that we returned to the house. After so fraught a discussion, I believe we would both benefit from a visit to the nursery."

"Now?" She stood. "Didn't you say Lady Maidstone won't be up yet?"

"I did. Which is precisely why it is the perfect time." The thought of being with his nephews lifted his spirits. "If Martha is in her chambers still, the boys will be free to be their naturally boisterous selves."

"The boys or you?" Miss Crawford asked.

Grateful that their conversation had turned to a more lighthearted subject, he grinned. "I believe it would be safer if I opted not to answer that question."

"I see." She eyed him speculatively. "I am beginning to understand why Lady Maidstone was so reluctant to have you visit the nursery last night."

With a soft chuckle, he offered her his arm. "Being with Will and Sam will be a pleasant diversion from your troubles. You shall see."

— · ✳ · —

The servant, Hobbes, was at the door when Isla and Lord Bancroft entered the house. Lord Bancroft offered the man his hat, and rather reluctantly, Isla handed over Lord Bancroft's cloak. There was no fireplace in the entrance hall, and the temperature in the drafty room didn't feel any warmer than it had outside.

"If Lord or Lady Maidstone inquire after me or Miss Crawford, please tell them we have gone to the nursery and will join them for breakfast shortly," Lord Bancroft said.

Hobbes inclined his head politely. "Very good, my lord."

Somewhat surprised that Lord Bancroft was willing to postpone eating in exchange for time with his nephews, Isla walked with him across the hall and up the stairs. On the landing, they turned right, away from the room Isla had used the night before. They hadn't gone far when the sound of young voices reached them from the end of the hall. Lord Bancroft continued until he reached a closed door on the left.

Pausing, he set his hand on the doorknob. "Prepare yourself," he warned. "They may be a little rambunctious."

Isla smiled. "I have three nephews. It's been a while since I've seen them, but I know all about rambunctious boys."

He nodded, and although Isla received the distinct impression that he wasn't fully convinced, he opened the door and ushered her in ahead of him.

A fire burned brightly in the fireplace, and the room was blissfully warm. A rug covered a good portion of the wooden floor, and a large, multipaned window let in the morning sunlight. In one corner of the room, two young boys who looked so alike, they had to be twins occupied the small stools positioned at a low wooden table. A middle-aged woman stood nearby, her gray gown covered in a white apron. Isla guessed that she was the nursemaid. The boys were eating their breakfast, but the moment they caught sight of Lord Bancroft, all thought of food seemingly fled. Scrambling to their feet, they hurled themselves at the gentleman with cries of delight.

"Uncle Simon!" they called in unison.

The young boy wearing tan breeches and a red jacket narrowly beat his brother in the green jacket across the room, and seconds later, Lord Bancroft had a child attached to each leg.

"What is this?" Lord Bancroft said, feigning shock as he tousled both boys' fair hair. "The last time I visited, two four-year-olds dressed in gowns lived here, and now there are two young men."

"We had a birthday, Uncle Simon!" the boy in green cried. "And Mother said we must wear breeches."

"Just as Father and you do," the child in red said.

"Good heavens," Lord Bancroft said. "Does that mean you are too grown up to play with me?"

"No!" They both laughed, and then the one in green reached for Lord Bancroft's hand.

"We have new animals. Come and see!"

"Just a moment." There must have been something in Lord Bancroft's voice that caused the boys to pause, because the tugging on his arm suddenly stopped. "I would not have thought that you would both so quickly forget your manners?"

The boys exchanged a chagrined look, and then slowly, reluctantly, they turned to face Isla.

"Miss Crawford," Lord Bancroft said, "may I introduce Master Samuel Winslow and Master William Winslow. Sam and Will, this is your mother's houseguest, Miss Isla Crawford."

The boys bent at the waist in a bow. Isla bobbed a curtsy, thankful that no one seemed to notice or care how poorly she'd executed it. The children straightened and glanced at Lord Bancroft. He raised an expectant eyebrow.

"Good morning, Miss Crawford," they chanted in unison.

"Good morning, boys," Isla said. "It's very nice to meet you."

Lord Bancroft then gestured to the woman still standing beside the table. "Miss Crawford, this is Miss Tomlinson, the boys' nursemaid."

"Good morning," Isla repeated.

"And to you, Miss Crawford," the older woman said.

"We shall not interrupt you for long, Miss Tomlinson," Lord Bancroft said.

"Not to worry, my lord. The boys generally play for a bit after their breakfast."

As though waiting for that very cue, the boy in red—Isla still wasn't sure which was which—resumed his tugging on

Lord Bancroft's arm. "Now?" he asked. "Can you see the animals now?"

"Very well," the gentleman said. "And perhaps Miss Crawford would also like to see them."

"Would you?" the boy in green asked, appearing surprised.

"Absolutely," Isla said, pleased when her enthusiastic response garnered a grin. "Show me your favorite one first."

With whoops of delight, the twins ran to the corner of the room where an assortment of rudimentarily carved wooden animals were set up end to end in a straggling line.

Isla leaned a little closer to Lord Bancroft. "Which one is Sam, and which one is Will?" she whispered.

"My guess is that Will is the one in green," he muttered. "But until I see the back of his neck, I cannot tell for certain. Will has a small birthmark there that sets him apart."

Given that both boys had shoulder-length hair, spotting the birthmark was going to be tricky, but Isla crossed the room beside Lord Bancroft, willing to follow his lead.

"Look!" The boy in green raised a wooden animal to show her. "My new one is a fox, and Sam's is a bear."

Lord Bancroft had been right. Mentally assigning the green jacket to Will, Isla reached for the toy. The wood had been smoothed to a shine, and although the creature was without eyes or a mouth, its long snout, thin legs, and thick tail made it easy to identify.

"Wow! That's brill!" Isla said.

Will's brows came together. "What's 'brill'?"

"Brilliant," Isla answered.

When the confusion in Will's eyes didn't clear, Isla tried again. "It's marvelous!"

This time Will smiled. "It's just like a real one!"

"Yes." Isla smiled even as she made a mental note to think more carefully before she spoke. Lord Bancroft obviously wasn't the only one struggling to interpret her modern words and slang.

"My favorite is the hare," Lord Bancroft said, picking up a small wooden piece with long ears. "They run faster than the wind."

"Foxes eat hares," Will cried, pouncing on Lord Bancroft.

"So do bears," Sam yelled, and within moments, the three of them were entangled in a wrestling match on the floor that involved a great deal of giggling on the part of the twins and mock groans of pain from Lord Bancroft.

"Save the hare!" Lord Bancroft shouted. "He's done nothing wrong!"

Will rolled over, clambering for the small toy in Lord Bancroft's hand. "But bear says he tastes delicious."

"Bear thinks everything is delicious," Lord Bancroft countered, swinging his arm above his head. "He should try frog."

Isla laughed. It was the first time she'd laughed since she'd stepped out of the changing room, and it felt wonderful.

"Frog, I tell you." Lord Bancroft was virtually hidden beneath the boys' flailing arms and legs. "Bear and fox would like frog so much better."

Sam's leg swung out, and Isla shifted a little to the left to avoid the melee. Her foot knocked over a couple of the wooden animals still on the floor, and when she reached for the closest one, she discovered that it was a frog.

"Frogs do taste delicious," she said, raising the toy in one hand. "But bear and fox will only discover that if they catch him."

Gathering her skirts in the other hand, she darted across the room. Behind her, the boys scrambled to their feet, and suddenly, they were chasing after her.

"We love frogs!" Will cried, with Sam hot on his tail.

Isla laughed and circled back around to Lord Bancroft. "Here," she called, tossing him the wooden frog as he came to his feet. "I can run, but in this gown, wrestling is beyond me."

"Uncle Simon has the frog!" Sam yelled, and as one, the boys tore past Isla to attack Lord Bancroft again.

"Good heavens! Whatever is happening in here?" At the sound of their mother's voice, Will's and Sam's feet came to a stuttering halt, and their attention diverted to the door.

"Mother! Uncle Simon is here!" Will said breathlessly.

"And Miss Crawford," Sam added.

"Yes, of that, I am fully aware," Lady Maidstone said. "And I would think half the population of Little Twinning also knows it by now. I've never heard such a fracas."

"I apologize, Martha," Lord Bancroft said, looking not the least bit sorry. "It was my doing."

Lady Maidstone gave him a long-suffering look. "Honestly, Simon. If Miss Tomlinson weren't such a saint, you would cause her to leave her position. She's the one who is left to deal with Will and Sam after you've turned them into human tornadoes."

Lord Bancroft had the decency to offer the nursemaid a more sincere look of apology. "Forgive me, Miss Tomlinson. Next time, I shall take them outside and allow you some time away from the human tornadoes."

"Taking them outside does not sound any more calm and decorous," Lady Maidstone said.

"Of course not." He winked at her. "Where would be the fun in that? I would simply be providing Miss Tomlinson with a well-deserved respite."

Lady Maidstone set her hand on her forehead and groaned. "One day, you shall grow up, Simon. The boys may rue the day, but I shall cheer."

Lord Bancroft smiled and dropped to one knee beside the twins. Placing an arm around each of them, he spoke to them in a low voice. "Boys, I need you to treat Miss Tomlinson especially well today. Mind her every word, and do exactly as she says the very first time she asks. Is that understood?"

The boys nodded solemnly. "Yes, Uncle Simon."

"Well done." He tousled their hair again and rose to his feet. "I knew I could count on you."

"Will you come back to the nursery soon?" Sam asked.

"That all depends upon how well you listen to Miss Tomlinson today."

"We will be very good." Sam nudged Will.

"Yes, very good." Will gave Isla a shy look. "Can Miss Crawford come back too?"

Isla sensed Lady Maidstone's surprise, but she kept her attention on Will's earnest expression. "If I'm still here the next time your mother allows a visit, I would love to come again."

"You run fast," Will said as though that fully explained the personal invitation.

Lord Bancroft's cough sounded suspiciously like smothered laughter.

"Thank you, Will," Isla said.

The little boy beamed. "Next time, I will show you my top. It goes around and around."

"I'd love that."

"I have a top as well," Sam said.

"Maybe we could try spinning them at the same time," Isla said.

"A race!" Will cried.

This time, Lord Bancroft did nothing to hide his laughter. "No more unruly competitions, or your mother will never allow me or Miss Crawford into the nursery again."

"Yes, indeed," Lady Maidstone said, the look of fondness that she gave the twins belying her serious tone. "Next time, we shall have your uncle meet you outside in the yard. You can show him how well you ride Marigold."

The boys cheered, and Lady Maidstone smiled. Isla glanced at Lord Bancroft. Humor danced in his eyes as he watched Sam's and Will's enthusiastic response, and Isla received the distinct impression that he knew exactly what they were feeling. He'd probably had a similar joyful zest for life as a child.

"Unlike the two of you, your mother, Miss Crawford, and I have yet to eat this morning, so we shall leave you now," he said, reaching for the door. "But if I learn that you behaved well for Miss Tomlinson the remainder of the day, I shall see you in the yard tomorrow morning."

Lady Maidstone bent down and gave each boy a kiss on the top of their heads before sending them back across the room to their waiting nursemaid. "Is it wrong that I wish they could stay young a little longer?" she asked. "Breeching them seemed to age them by at least five years."

Lord Bancroft ushered her and Isla out of the room. "They are wonderful little gentlemen," he said. "And I speculate that you shall find something to enjoy at every age that lies ahead."

"Even thirteen?" she asked.

He grinned. "Just because I persecuted you at that age does not mean Will and Sam will do the same."

"I shall hold fast to that hope," Lady Maidstone said, looking utterly unconvinced. And then she turned her attention to Isla. "I have yet to ask how you are faring this morning, Miss Crawford."

Lost. Terrified. Overwhelmed. Half an hour ago, those would have been Isla's foremost emotions. Now, thanks to a little time with two five-year-old boys and their playful uncle, she was able to answer more calmly. "I slept well. Thank you for allowing me to stay."

Lady Maidstone looked pleased, but it was Lord Bancroft who spoke first. His expression had turned from playful to grave. "Miss Crawford has some rather startling information to share. Perhaps after we've eaten, we could reconvene in the parlor and have Maidstone join us to discuss her situation."

"Of course." Curiosity lit Lady Maidstone's eyes, but she led them down the stairs without pressing for anything more. "I shall inform Hugh that we require his presence at the top of the hour."

Isla inched closer to Lord Bancroft. "Thank you," she said softly.

He gave her a puzzled look. "For what, exactly?"

For listening to her bizarre tale. For not abandoning her outside. For requesting time with Lord and Lady Maidstone on her behalf. Now that she thought about it, she owed Lord Bancroft a great deal of thanks today. But the moment he'd mentioned a meeting, her chest had tightened, and she'd realized again what a gift her time in the nursery had been. "For taking me to meet the twins," she said. "You were right. Spending time with them was exactly what I needed."

"You were certainly up to the task when faced with Will's and Sam's high spirits," he said. "It must be that you truly do have young nephews."

"I do. Ages six, four, and two." She paused. "Everything I told you about myself this morning is the truth."

They'd reached the bottom of the stairs. Lady Maidstone had gone ahead, but Lord Bancroft paused and gave Isla a searching look. "Including where you came from?" he asked.

"Yes," she said, meeting his dark eyes and willing him to believe her. "Including that."

CHAPTER 6

Ten minutes before Martha's appointed meeting time in the parlor, Simon knocked on the door of his brother-in-law's study. Not wanting to leave Miss Crawford to her own devices, he had waited until Martha had her fully engaged in a discussion about the selection of wool twill at her London haberdasher's shop before excusing himself. He was sufficiently familiar with Martha's penchant for fabric to know that she would maintain the conversation—and, therefore, keep Miss Crawford beside her—until they met with Maidstone.

"Enter." Maidstone's voice reached him through the closed door.

Simon walked in and closed the door behind himself.

Maidstone looked up from the book he was studying. "Bancroft." He stood and glanced at the timepiece on the mantel. "Forgive me. I had thought Martha wished me to meet with you at the top of the hour."

"She did. She does," Simon said. "And I apologize for interrupting you before then, but I thought it might be prudent to have a private word before we meet with the ladies."

"By all means." He gestured toward a nearby chair and reclaimed his own. "What is on your mind?"

"Miss Crawford," Simon said, dropping onto the seat. "To be brief, she claims that she has come here from the future."

Maidstone's brows rose. "The future?"

"Indeed. She aims to tell you and Martha how she arrived when we gather in the parlor, but I thought you might be glad of a few extra minutes to consider how you wish to proceed after she makes her statement."

Maidstone frowned. "The young lady did not give the impression of being a lunatic last evening. Confused and a little odd, most definitely. But I blamed that on her being caught out in the elements for who knows how long."

"Agreed." Simon paused. His intention had been to simply give Maidstone time to ponder upon an unexpected and difficult situation. But perhaps he owed him more than that. "I was with the young lady earlier this morning. After I heard her claim, I thought it best that she not be left unattended."

"Most wise," Maidstone said. "I am grateful to you."

"She is now with Martha, and I assume they will go to the parlor together. As far as I can ascertain, she shows no sign of being a threat to anyone. In fact, I would go so far as to say the opposite is true. She was fully engaged with the boys and appeared genuinely happy with them."

Maidstone's frown deepened. "She was with my sons?"

"For no more than half an hour." Had he done wrong by taking Miss Crawford there? Simon was suddenly stricken with the thought that he may not have made the same choice had Sam and Will been his own children. "With Miss Tomlinson ever present, I did not think it a great risk."

"Hmm." Maidstone seemed unconvinced.

"In truth, one of the reasons I took her to the nursery was to gauge the boys' response to her. It is my belief that children are far more discerning than most adults realize. If Sam and Will want little to do with someone, the chances are good that they have a valid reason, regardless of how well hidden the adult's character flaw may be." Simon had witnessed the twins' interactions with some of the Maidstones' neighbors. Their disinclination to be around some of them was remarkably telling.

"How did the boys respond to Miss Crawford?" Maidstone asked.

"Very well. In fact, Will asked that she return to play with them another time."

"Until we know more about her state of mind, she is not to have access to my sons without another trusted adult present," Maidstone warned.

"I will personally relay that message to Miss Tomlinson," Simon said, guilt that he'd taken Miss Crawford to the nursery without checking with Maidstone or Martha warring with his earlier estimation that it had been the right thing to do.

Maidstone's nod was curt. "Sam's and Will's opinions aside, what is your estimation of the young lady?"

"She appears fully lucid. Until she starts speaking of her future world." Simon shook his head, more troubled by his inner conflict than he cared to admit. "Her story is wholly unbelievable. Her manner of delivery, however, is most convincing."

The clock on the mantel whirred, preparing to chime.

Maidstone rose again. "I appreciate the forewarning, Bancroft. If you conceive of some way of proving Miss Crawford's assertion, do not hesitate to speak up in the parlor. I believe we would all benefit from some clarity on Miss Crawford's place of origin. The young lady, in particular."

Proof? Simon's thoughts swirled as he came to his feet. What could they possibly ask Miss Crawford that would give them something substantive upon which they could base their decisions?

Unfortunately, Simon was no closer to answering that question twenty minutes later when he stood to the right of the fireplace in the parlor, his eyes on his sister and brother-in-law, who were seated beside each other. Across from them, Miss Crawford had just concluded her account of her arrival here, and an uncomfortable silence now blanketed the room.

Maidstone cleared his throat, obviously unsure how to proceed. Simon understood. He felt similarly—although the cause of his discomfort had changed. The first time he'd heard Miss Crawford's tale, he'd felt trapped by his desire to maintain gentlemanly behavior in the face of seemingly blatant lies. This time, however, his unease came from the disturbing realization that regardless of how completely preposterous Miss Crawford's claims may be, his inclination to believe them was greater than it had been.

Maidstone came to his feet and paced to the fireplace before swiveling to face her. "I must say, Miss Crawford, this is all rather a lot to absorb."

"I understand, my lord." Miss Crawford's hands were clasped so tightly that her knuckles were white. "If I hadn't experienced it firsthand, I wouldn't believe it either."

"The twenty-first century, you say?" Martha's voice was little more than a squeak.

"Yes. It was 2025, to be precise."

Martha eyed Miss Crawford's clothing and then ran her hands across her own purple gown. "Tell me, have the farthingales widened or narrowed?"

Miss Crawford blinked, likely as stunned by Martha's question as Simon was. His sister had a young lady sitting in her house, claiming to have arrived from the future, and her first question was on the diameter of women's hooped underwear?

Simon offered Maidstone a stupefied look, but Miss Crawford was already replying.

"There are no farthingales at all," she said. "Women wear much simpler dresses, and they usually end at the knee."

Martha gasped. "Ladies show their legs and ankles?"

Despite the tension in the room, the corners of Miss Crawford's lips turned upward. "They do. And men wear trousers that go to their ankles, rather than breeches that stop at the knee."

"Good heavens." Martha's hand went to her chest as though this revelation were somehow more shocking than the fact that Miss Crawford had entered a world so far removed from her own.

"Ladies often wear trousers too," Miss Crawford continued. "I went to the costume shop looking for a pale-blue nightgown, but I was wearing trousers when I walked in."

Martha, it seemed, was momentarily speechless.

It was probably a good thing because her silence offered Simon an opportunity to interrupt. "Forgive me," he said. "I do not think choice of wardrobe in the seventeenth century, the twenty-first century, or one's imagination is the most important issue to discuss at present."

"No, indeed," Maidstone said. "Although, I confess, I am not sure quite where to begin."

"Is there anything you might tell us that would more fully persuade us to believe that you are from the future, Miss Crawford?" Simon asked.

"I . . . I've told you about some of the advancements already."

"You have, but I have no way of knowing if those are fabricated," he said.

She caught her lower lip between her teeth. "You want something that you would know, but I would not unless I were from the future."

Put in that light, his request sounded unreasonable. But despite Maidstone's request, Simon had yet to come up with another avenue that might offer them clarification. "If possible," he said.

"It's been a few years since I studied this time period, and I don't know what was common knowledge." Miss Crawford's brows came together as though she were thinking deeply. She looked at him hesitantly. "When Queen Elizabeth died, her face was caked with Venetian ceruse. She used it to cover the scars on her face caused by smallpox, but doctors think the lead in it may have contributed to her death."

"Good heavens!" Martha looked from Simon to Maidstone. "Did you know this?"

"The queen's face was always painted white," Maidstone said. "It would be a reasonable assumption that she used Venetian ceruse."

"Did it cause her death?" Martha asked.

"I do not believe any doctor could claim that," Simon said. "For years before her death, the queen refused to allow anyone to examine her."

Miss Crawford's face fell. "Perhaps modern doctors conjectured that diagnosis."

Or she could have imagined it herself.

For a moment, no one spoke. Maidstone cleared his throat again. "I realize—"

Miss Crawford gasped. "In 1604, King James met with Anglican and Puritan scholars at Hampton Court to discuss the need for a new and definitive version of the Bible." Her voice rang with a peculiar mixture of desperation and surety. "It will take over seven years to compile, but ultimately the King James version of the Bible will become a standard text around the world."

Simon glanced at Maidstone. Was he aware of this meeting? Maidstone met his eyes and gave an almost imperceptible nod. He knew of it. Simon did not. Which begged the question, How had Miss Crawford come to hear of it?

"Who told you of that meeting, Miss Crawford?" Maidstone asked.

Her shoulders sagged. "No one. I read about it in a history book."

"Did it happen, Hugh?" Martha asked.

"It did. Although very few gentlemen outside the king's privy chamber and the invited religious leaders knew of it."

Martha's eyes widened. "Does that prove that Miss Crawford is telling the truth?"

Proof was a very strong word, and if Maidstone's expression was any indication, he was reluctant to use it.

"Someone in attendance at that small gathering may have shared information that was not meant to be made public," he said. "I was told of the meeting in confidence by the Lord Chamberlain."

Miss Crawford lifted her chin slightly. "No one told me anything, my lord."

"You read it in a book," Simon said dryly.

"Yes. In *The Oxford History of Britain*, to be precise."

Maidstone eyed her guardedly. "If you were in my position, Miss Crawford, which of those two scenarios would you believe?"

Miss Crawford held his gaze for two heartbeats before turning to Martha. "You have been extremely good to me. I understand if you wish me to leave. If you'd be willing to point me in the right direction, I could start walking toward London, and perhaps I might . . ." She swallowed.

Simon stood completely still. Might what? Be accosted? Did she truly believe she could safely walk all the way to London unattended? In borrowed shoes and without a cloak, no less?

"I might be able to find work somewhere along the way," she finished.

Obviously choosing to gloss over Miss Crawford's ridiculous suggestion, Maidstone ran his hand thoughtfully across his short beard. "What skills do you possess, Miss Crawford?"

She hesitated. "I'm actually a pretty good press secretary, but I don't think being computer savvy and having experience with Excel, Adobe, and the press corps will do me much good here."

Simon exchanged another look with Maidstone. He'd understood a minute fraction of the words Miss Crawford had just spoken, and he guessed his brother-in-law was in a similar position. If nothing else, Miss Crawford's incomprehensible speech gave some credibility to her origin.

"You are not going anywhere until we have determined exactly why you have come," Martha said with surprising firmness.

"But I have no idea why I'm here," Miss Crawford said.

"Then, we shall simply have to work together to sort it out."

"Martha, I appreciate the sentiment." Maidstone offered Miss Crawford an apologetic look before continuing. "But I must remind you that we have yet to come to a firm decision on Miss Crawford's tale."

"Well, I believe she is speaking the truth," Martha said. "Quite apart from the knowledge she shared about the king, no young lady of unsound mind could speak so clearly about clothing, fabrics, and fashions. I would further submit that if everyone in Little Twinning is willing to believe that Mary Peasly can locate underground water using two sticks, then the three of us should be willing to believe that Miss Crawford can visit from another time. She has offered us more evidence than Mary ever has."

Maidstone shifted uneasily. "Even if her account is true, if Miss Crawford is in ignorance of the reason for her coming, it is highly unlikely that any of us will uncover it."

"Nonsense." Marth was at her take-charge best. "Two heads are better than one—and together, we are four heads."

Miss Crawford smiled tremulously. "That is exactly the kind of thing my friend Chloe would say."

"I daresay I would like her very much."

"Yes." Miss Crawford's smile grew, and Simon was struck once again by how that single act brightened her entire countenance. "I think you'd get along famously."

Martha looked from Miss Crawford to Maidstone and then to Simon. "I know you gentlemen believe me foolish to focus so much on clothing, but your lack of attention to that detail has caused you to miss what I believe is an important clue."

"I am very willing to stand corrected," Maidstone said.

"Tell us again exactly what Mrs. McQuivey said as she was going through the clothing racks with you, Miss Crawford," Martha said.

"She acted as though she were searching for the costume I'd gone in for, but she suggested that I'd probably like something historical better."

"And afterward?" Martha prompted.

"She looked at a few gowns and passed by them."

"Did she say anything in particular when she did that?"

Miss Crawford hesitated as though trying to remember. "It seems like she said, 'No, not that one,' a couple of times."

"Exactly," Martha said, sitting back in her chair with a satisfied expression.

"Exactly what?" Simon asked.

Martha ignored him. "What about when she pulled out the gown you're wearing now?"

"She asked me if I liked it, and when I told her I did, she insisted that I try it on."

"Because it was the right one," Martha said.

"The right one," Miss Crawford echoed, a flash of something that looked remarkably akin to awareness entering her blue eyes.

His frustration mounting, Simon ran his fingers through his hair. "Martha, either I am more dense than I had previously believed, or you have already adopted Miss Crawford's unusual manner of expression. I cannot speak for Maidstone, but personally, I am struggling to follow your logic."

Martha gave a resigned sigh. "I do not know who this Mrs. McQuivey is, but she quite obviously has a greater understanding of the changing room with the green door's peculiar power than she shared with Miss Crawford. I would be willing to wager that she has implemented its magical abilities before. Given what Miss Crawford has told us about her experience, I would also suggest that Mrs. McQuivey has a special ability to discern when someone is needed elsewhere. The exact location and time period may not come to her directly—as Miss Crawford has just illustrated—but it does eventually come. And when that happens, she sends the person off to do what they are called upon to do, wearing the appropriate clothing."

When Martha paused, the ensuing silence was an echo of the earlier one, but this time, all eyes in the room were upon his sister.

"You . . . you think I was meant to come here?" Miss Crawford asked.

"It stands to reason, does it not?" Martha said.

As far as Simon was concerned, absolutely nothing that involved Miss Crawford and her appearance at Copfield Hall could be classified as reasonable.

"Your insight has some merit, Martha," Maidstone said. "But if what you believe is true, it would have been helpful if Mrs. McQuivey had given Miss Crawford some information about what was ahead."

"Yes, it would." Miss Crawford shook her head helplessly. "Mrs. McQuivey made some comment about courage and fortitude rising when we are most uncomfortable. Maybe that was her way of warning me that I was about to be in over my head."

With a concerned expression, Martha reached over and set a hand on Miss Crawford's. "Are you horribly uncomfortable here?"

"Yes. No." She attempted a smile. "I'm sorry. You've all been marvelous. Kinder than I deserve. It's just that I have no idea how to live in your world."

"We can help you," Martha said firmly. "Until you have ascertained what you were sent here to do, you must stay at Copfield Hall. Hugh, Simon, and I can be your tutors."

Simon stiffened. He had no jurisdiction over whom Martha invited to stay at her home or how she wished to employ her time, but he did take exception to being volunteered for a task he did not agree to. Teaching Miss Crawford the niceties of seventeenth-century polite society fell firmly into that category. "I may not be here long enough to participate in Miss Crawford's schooling, Martha," he said.

"Then, we shall simply be glad of the time we do have you," Martha said.

Miss Crawford's cheeks had pinked. "There's no need for you to do anything." She stood. "Really. I've imposed on you all long enough already."

Martha glared at him and then rose to stand beside Miss Crawford. She tucked her arm beneath Miss Crawford's. "At the risk of sounding selfish, I am not yet ready to share you with anyone else. There's too much I wish to learn from you." She paused. "You see, this arrangement will work splendidly. You may ask me questions, and I shall do the same to you."

"Is there anything in particular that you are struggling with, Miss Crawford?" Maidstone asked.

Simon set his jaw. Blast it all. Even Maidstone was siding with Martha. Had the man truly accepted Martha's convoluted reasoning? Did the fellow not see what a quagmire he was stepping into? Even if the unthinkable had happened and Miss Crawford had come from the future for a particular reason, who knew how long it would be before she determined what she must do or where she must go? And in the meantime, how was her unexpected presence and background to be explained to their acquaintances? In a society fraught with distrust, spies, and treachery, the mysterious Miss Crawford could trigger all manner of unwanted attention.

"Yes, is there?" Martha's smile was warm. "What should we begin with?"

Simon stifled a sigh. It seemed that his sister and her husband were willing to take that risk. Miss Crawford had quickly won over Maidstone and Martha, not to mention Will and Sam, but Simon refused to be so easily swayed. He had opened his heart to a young lady once before only to have her cast him aside when he was no longer needed. The experience had taught him that it was safer to maintain barriers, no matter how intriguing or needy a young lady appeared to be. Especially when, according to her claims, she could quite literally disappear at any moment.

"I feel so stupid," Miss Crawford said. She appeared close to tears. "You're so kind. But honestly, I know almost nothing about how to function in your world. I don't know how to light a fire, write with a quill, address nobility, ride a horse—"

"I beg your pardon." Simon took a stunned step away from the fireplace. He knew full well that he should not have interrupted the lady, but the words had escaped him before he could call them back. "Did you say that you cannot ride a horse?"

"Well, I rode a pony once. On the beach. But I was only eight years old, and the old man who owned the ponies had them on a rope." She looked at him hesitantly. "Does that count?"

"No, it most certainly does not."

"Well," Martha said as though that settled everything. "I would suggest that you spend a good portion of this day with me and Maggie. Between the two of us, we can teach you a great deal about Jacobean households. Hugh can be available for any questions we cannot answer. Then first thing tomorrow, you could join Simon when he visits Will and Sam outside the stables." She shot Simon a challenging look. "If he is of a mind to assist you, Simon would be the best person to introduce you to riding."

Martha had pinned him into a corner. He should have been irritated, but somewhat surprisingly, that was not the emotion that rose to the fore. "Very well." He offered his sister a capitulating nod and allowed the unexpected surge of anticipation to swell. "I shall ask Ezra to have Belle saddled when he readies the ponies for the boys."

"Is . . . is Belle a big horse?" Miss Crawford asked.

Simon detected a flicker of fear in her eyes.

"Not at all," Martha reassured her. "Belle was my horse for many years. She's always been a gentle mount—and is all the more so now that she's aging. We should have sold her when I acquired my new mare, Violet, but we were too attached. And she will be a good training horse when the boys transition from a pony to a full-sized mount."

"Which should be any day now," Maidstone said.

Martha frowned at what was likely yet another reminder that her sons were growing up. "True, but tomorrow, Belle shall be your ride."

"Thank you." Miss Crawford glanced at Simon. He caught the uncertainty in her eyes a moment before she turned back to Martha. "Answering a few questions seems very little payment for all your kindness. I wish I could do something more."

"You may yet do so," Maidstone said. "I would advise you to keep pondering what your reason for being here may be. I daresay once you discover it, we shall be grateful that you are come."

Her smile was small, but the air of despair that had hung over her appeared to lift a fraction. "I hope you're right," she said.

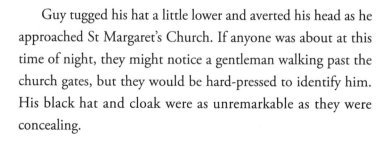

Guy tugged his hat a little lower and averted his head as he approached St Margaret's Church. If anyone was about at this time of night, they might notice a gentleman walking past the church gates, but they would be hard-pressed to identify him. His black hat and cloak were as unremarkable as they were concealing.

When he reached the corner of the church grounds, he spared a quick look to his right. A shadow silhouetted against the low wall shifted. He narrowed his eyes. A white glove appeared from beneath a dark cloak. Thomas Wintour's signal. Guy made no acknowledging sound or sign. There was no need. Wintour knew he'd seen him.

Given the choice, Guy would have preferred to work alone. Placing his trust in others did not come easily. But now that the gunpowder had all been transported to the undercroft at the Palace of Westminster, there was too much at stake to risk being seen entering the ground floor storage room. Wintour knew that as well as any of the conspirators. It was unlikely that anyone would be in the vicinity at midnight, but the king's henchman, Cecil, was known to do the unexpected, and his spies had been trained to do the same. It was pure foolishness to not employ a lookout when Wintour was perfectly capable of doing the job.

Guy paused to listen. A gust of wind rattled the dry leaves on a nearby tree. The lap of the Thames River hitting the boat moorings reached him from the other side of the building before him. An alley cat screeched, and a distant shout followed. It was the closest the city of London could come to complete calm.

Slipping his hand beneath his cloak, he drew the large key from the purse at his belt and moved swiftly across Old Palace Yard. Within moments, a building's roofline loomed above him, blocking the moonlight and darkening his path. He slowed his steps. A fall would not serve him well.

Instinct told him he was nearing the stairs. Straining to see through the darkness, he picked out the slight change in hue on the ground ahead. He stopped and stretched out his leg. Instantly, his toe touched the edge of a step. With a triumphant smile, he moved forward. Three stairs down. Four more paces forward. He'd been wise to make a mental note of those details the first time he'd come. He reached out his hand and felt the wooden door. Moments later, he had the key in the keyhole. The bolt slid back with a thud. Guy counted to three. No unexpected sound or movement. Opening the door, he slipped inside and closed it behind him.

The air was dank and musty. He wrinkled his nose with distaste and bent to feel for the lantern and flint he'd left beside the door. His fingers brushed against the lantern standing beside a small pail of sand. He seized it, locating the flint moments later. As soon as the wick within caught light, Guy raised it above his head. A scurry of tiny paws sounded at his right. He swung the lantern in that direction and caught the glow of rats' eyes coming from the wood stacked along the wall. He clenched his jaw. He had no desire to share this space with the vermin, but if they wished to make this their home for another month, so be it. When the time came for Guy to light the fuse attached to the barrels of gunpowder, they would be the first to go.

He started toward the wood, making note of how well the logs and faggots camouflaged the barrels hiding beneath. Casks of wine and cider—enough to supply a household for over a year—lay stacked in front of the wood. Percy had thought it prudent to store decoy barrels in the room just in case it was visited by someone outside their band. Guy could not fault his logic. Casks of wine and cider were appropriate items for the cellar below the Lords' Chamber. He smirked. They would also contribute well to the upcoming conflagration.

He moved slowly around the room, assessing the level of moisture on the stone walls. He hated the damp. Spain had spoiled him. Long, hot days were brutal when one's battalion was relocating across the parched hills on foot, but he preferred it to the bone-chilling wetness associated with being near the Thames. He'd had enough of that damp discomfort when he and the other conspirators had spent months digging a tunnel from Percy's lodgings to the palace. Guy grimaced at the memory. Water from the Thames had continually seeped into the tunnel, and after over a year of digging through the night, they had hit the seemingly impenetrable barrier of the palace's foundational walls.

With their original plan stymied, this undercroft—with its dank air and rats—had been an unforeseen gift. Guy had discovered Mrs. Ellen Bright clearing out the room that had been used by her late husband for his coal merchant business. Anxious to be free of the lease, she had been more than happy to have someone else assume it, especially a gentleman so accommodating as Lord Percy's manservant, John Johnson. Guy picked up the crowbar leaning against one of the casks of wine. There was a satisfying irony in the exchange of commodities that had occurred in this space. Coal that could fuel a household had been replaced by gunpowder that would fuel a revolution.

Setting the lantern several feet from the nearest barrel, Guy removed half a dozen logs and used the crowbar to pry off the barrel's lid. Removing his glove, he ran his fingers through the dark powder in the barrel. Dry. The tension in his shoulders eased. This barrel was up against the wall. If the gunpowder within had been unaffected by the moisture on the stones, the chances were good, the remaining barrels were safe from contamination as well.

Guy replaced the lid and repositioned the logs. Sliding the crowbar behind the barrel, he picked up the lantern and swung it in a slow arc. The cache was enormous, and his chest swelled with pride at all that the conspirators had gathered under cover of darkness. With key in hand, he moved back to the door. It was time to leave. He would send word to Catsby that all was well with the gunpowder, and then Guy would head north and lie low until the appointed time. Percy had left London already. There was no cause for Guy to remain in the plague-infested city any longer.

Setting the lantern down beside the flint, he took a handful of the sand in the bucket and tossed it onto the floor at the undercroft's entrance. Then he extinguished the flame and slowly opened the door. No warning signal from Wintour. No footsteps passing by. The conspirators' plan was secure, and the unwitting Mrs. Bright had no idea what she had facilitated. On November 5, the downfall of the English government and the annihilation of the king were all but certain. Of course, if Mrs. Bright's personal lodgings were anywhere nearby, the widow would never know what she had done until the next life. Thirty-six barrels of gunpowder were going to level far more than the House of Lords alone.

CHAPTER 7

One of the Maidstones' servants accompanied Isla along the gravel path that led toward the stables behind the manor. The sun was attempting to make an appearance between the clouds, which seemed an appropriate reflection of Isla's state of mind. The fear and helplessness that had filled her heart yesterday morning was not gone, but a flicker of hope was attempting to dispel her lingering distress.

She'd spent most of the previous day with Lady Maidstone and Maggie. They'd been unfailingly patient with her. It had taken Isla eight attempts to light some kindling with the spark from a flint, three attempts to lace a bodice tightly enough, and two attempts plus much exertion to plump up the straw-and-feather ticks on the bed. Lady Maidstone had sat with her for hours, peppering her with questions about twenty-first-century life while Isla had tried to write with a quill. Her first efforts had been embarrassingly bad, and when she'd told Lady Maidstone that it looked as though a drunken spider had fallen into the inkwell only to stagger across the paper, her hostess had been hard-pressed to fight back her laughter.

In one hour, Isla's efforts had improved enough to resemble the work of a sober ink-covered spider walking in a relatively straight line, but she had a horrible suspicion that Sam's and

Will's penmanship would outclass hers. There had been more than once during the painstaking exercise when Isla had wished that Lady Maidstone could appreciate how extraordinarily fast Isla typed, but explaining computer keyboards after she had already tried describing televisions, radios, and telephones had seemed more trouble than it had been worth.

By the end of the day, mental and emotional exhaustion had overcome her small successes, and she'd asked if she might be excused from joining the family for their evening meal in favor of going to bed early. Lady Maidstone had been good enough to send some warm milk and bread to Isla's room. Isla had enjoyed it far more than the bite of braised eel she'd eaten the day before, although she'd been surprised by how much she'd missed seeing the gentleman who had enjoyed that food so much.

She didn't know how Lord Bancroft had spent his day after she'd left the parlor or even if he was any closer to believing her story now than he had been at first. She only knew that the knowledge that she would spend time with him and the twins this morning had made facing today's challenges a little less daunting.

"Look at me, Uncle Simon!" The young boy's voice rang with excitement, and Isla increased her pace.

"Nicely done, Will." Lord Bancroft came into view. He was standing near the stables, watching his nephews circle the wide yard on two dappled gray ponies. Each of the ponies was being led on a rope by a stablehand. "Be sure to sit up nice and tall."

The boy wearing a pale-blue jacket and breeches straightened his small shoulders, and Isla made the appropriate mental note: Will was wearing light blue. Sam was dressed in navy. She turned her attention to Lord Bancroft. This morning, his jacket and breeches were a dark green, plush fabric, his boots were black leather, and his white shirt collar was wide and trimmed with a narrow band of lace. He chuckled at Sam's attempts to urge his small pony to move faster, and she caught herself smiling in response.

She was obviously adjusting to her new environment better than she'd thought. If any of the men she'd gone out with at uni or since she'd moved to London had shown up at her door dressed the way Lord Bancroft was now, she would have politely but immediately turned him away. At this precise moment, however, she found herself battling a completely opposite reaction. Dressed in his elaborate clothing, with his well-trimmed beard, thick dark hair, and dark eyes, Lord Bancroft was distractingly handsome.

"Miss Crawford!" Sam spotted her and released his grip on the reins long enough to wave.

Will immediately turned in his saddle. "We're riding, Miss Crawford!" he called.

"So I see," Isla said. "And it looks like you're both slaying it!"

Lord Bancroft gave her a troubled look. "'Slaying it'? As in, killing the ponies?"

"Oh, good grief." Isla covered her face with a hand. "I promised myself I'd do better with my slang." She peered at him between her fingers. "Do you think they heard me?"

"Undoubtedly," he said dryly. "As did the stablehands."

Isla groaned and turned back to the circling ponies. "You're doing marvelously, boys," she called. "I need you to show me how it's done."

"You must sit up nice and tall," Will said, echoing Lord Bancroft's instructions as he drew closer. "See? Just like this." He raised his chin, and Isla fought back a smile.

"I shall try to remember," she said.

"That's good." Will offered her a winning smile before beginning his circuit again.

The servant who had accompanied Isla to the yard bowed to Lord Bancroft, and upon the gentleman's nod of dismissal, the servant bowed again—this time to Isla—and started back toward the house.

"How are you this morning, Miss Crawford?" Lord Bancroft asked, his question drawing her attention away from the departing servant.

"I'm well, thank you." Wishing she'd asked Lady Maidstone whether she was expected to curtsy every time she greeted her hostess, Lord Maidstone, or Lord Bancroft, she ended up bobbing up and down awkwardly.

"How did your initiation into seventeenth-century life go yesterday?" he asked. "I had thought to ask about your day at the evening meal, but Martha told me you chose to retire early."

Isla eyed him warily. "Did she also tell you I wore out my fingers trying to write with a quill?"

His lips twitched, but he manfully kept a full smile from appearing. "She may have mentioned that it was a challenging task for you."

Isla raised her right hand so he could see the black ink stains on her fingers. "It was an exercise in mortification."

This time, he released his laughter.

"I feel completely daft," Isla said, "even if it does further demonstrate that I'm telling the truth."

He sobered immediately. "I would surmise that you are dealing with the unknown far better than most in your situation."

"Does that mean you do believe my story? Or is it just your version of a pep talk before I make an even bigger idiot of myself on a horse?"

"I continue to fight an internal battle with regard to your story, but the 'suspending disbelief' you spoke of is a little easier than it was. As to the other, I have no idea what a pep talk is, but I am quite sure you will not make an idiot of yourself on Belle."

As relieved as she was to hear that his skepticism was lessening, a knot of nervousness formed in her stomach. Will and Sam were making riding look far too easy. And enjoyable.

"Miss Crawford?"

She heard the concern in Lord Bancroft's voice and turned to meet his uneasy gaze with the honesty she knew he deserved. "I'd be lying if I told you I wasn't afraid. I neglected to tell you earlier that my eight-year-old self got her foot tangled in the pony's stirrup on Formby Beach and promptly fell onto the sand. I can count on one hand the number of times that I've been near a horse since then."

His look softened. "I will not allow anything bad to happen to you."

"How can you be so sure? Horses are animals. They have wills of their own. And I've heard that they can sense fear in a rider."

"All those things are true, but Belle is mild-mannered and very well trained. She will treat you gently."

"Do you have a helmet I can wear?"

His brow furrowed. "You will be riding around the yard and possibly across an empty meadow—not going to war."

"Right." Given that Sam and Will were riding without helmets, it should not have come as a surprise that she would be too. It was no wonder that the life expectancy in this century was so low.

"Are you ready?" he asked.

She wanted to say yes. Half an hour ago, she'd thought she was. But now that the stablehands were leading Sam's and Will's ponies toward the nearby building, her nervousness was increasing.

"How will this work exactly?" she asked.

"As soon as the ponies are restabled, the stablehands will bring out Belle. Miss Tomlinson will take the boys back to the house, and we shall focus on the basics of mounting and walking the horse. When you feel sufficiently comfortable in the saddle, I shall have my horse readied, and we can take a short ride together."

When, not *if*. Isla swallowed. Lord Bancroft had considerably more confidence in her ability to pick up the necessary riding skills than she did. "I'll do my best."

He smiled. "Of that I have no doubt." He paused. "Tell me, these cars that you claim you drive, was it a hard skill to learn?"

"I suppose so." Isla thought back to her first driving lesson with her father. "Timing depressing the clutch with releasing the break or pressing the accelerator was tricky. And I shifted into the wrong gear more than once, which stalled the car."

"You see," he said, "if our roles were reversed, even after you had broken down the most basic instructions into language I understood, I would surely struggle to make the vehicle move."

"Are you trying to make me feel better about not knowing what to do on a horse?"

He did not answer. Instead, he offered her his arm. "May I make a prediction, Miss Crawford? I would hazard a guess that once you have a feel for the horse's gait, you will fall in love with riding."

She set her hand on his sleeve. She wasn't trembling quite as much as she had been moments before. "Can I make a prediction too?" she asked. "If you were to ever get into a car—especially a nippy little sports car—you'd figure out how to operate it in record time, and you'd drive it very fast."

He laughed. "I rather like your prediction."

"Yeah," she said, smiling at the thought. "Me too."

———·•✳•·———

"Impossible," Miss Crawford said, eyeing Belle as though he'd just told her that mounting the horse would take her back to the twenty-first century.

"I assure you it is not," Simon said. "There are countless numbers of young ladies who successfully ride sidesaddle every day."

"I'm sure there are," Miss Crawford said. "It's not the side-saddle I have an issue with. It's getting on it with these enormous hoops under my skirt."

Simon shifted uncomfortably. He had never considered how ladies managed their farthingales when using a sidesaddle, but he had no desire to discuss the complexities of a lady's underwear in front of a stablehand. "Ezra will hold Belle steady," he said, "and if you will allow me, I can help you into the saddle."

Her gaze shifted from the patiently waiting horse and stablehand to her wide skirts. "Will you give me two minutes?" she asked.

"Give you two minutes?"

"Yes." She lifted the hem of her offending skirts and ran past the door to the stables. "And don't let anyone come behind the building until I come back," she called.

Simon ran his hand across the back of his neck. Blast it all, trying to understand this woman was like trying to make sense of a butterfly's flight path. Just when he thought he understood what she was about, she took off in a completely different direction. Should he dismiss Ezra and continue this ill-fated riding lesson alone? At this rate, he and Miss Crawford would spend the entire morning discussing the difficulty of sitting upon a sidesaddle rather than actually riding a horse.

"Are you needed in the stables, Ezra?" he asked.

"It's all right, m' lord," the lad said. "Duncan's takin' care o' the ponies. 'E knows t' bring Blaze out when 'e's got 'em settled."

"Very well." They would wait Miss Crawford's allotted two minutes, and then he would go after her.

He heard her running footsteps moments before she appeared around the back of the stables.

"I'm sorry for keeping you waiting," she said, her blue skirts billowing loosely around her legs as she slowed to a walk. "I'm ready now."

He stared at her. "What did you do?"

"Took off the farthingale." She said it as though she'd simply taken a pin out of her hair. "I left it under the bush behind the stables. I'll pick it up again before I go back to the house." She set her focus on the sidesaddle. "If you tell me what to do, I think I can manage to sit on the horse now."

Counting his lucky stars that Miss Crawford had not also hiked her skirts to her knees, and that Ezra was the only other witness to her unconventional approach to a riding habit, Simon pointed to the pommel atop the sidesaddle. "Your right leg will hook around the pommel to anchor you to the saddle. Although both legs will be to one side of the horse, you will be able to face forward." This saddle was an improvement over the traditional sidesaddle with a wooden platform for the ladies' feet that had been commonplace before Queen Elizabeth's reign, but as far as Simon was concerned, there remained significant room for improvement.

"Right leg around the pommel," Miss Crawford repeated. "Got it."

"Are you ready, Ezra?" Simon asked.

"Yes, m' lord."

"Hold her steady." Simon placed his hands around Miss Crawford's tiny waist. A frisson of awareness pulsed through him, setting his senses humming. He cleared his throat, hoping the action would also clear his mind. "On the count of three, Miss Crawford."

She gave a small nod. He counted and then lifted her onto the saddle. She slipped sideways, reaching for his shoulder to steady herself. Belle shifted slightly, and Miss Crawford gasped.

"I have you," he said, taking her hand. "Relax."

"I'm perched on an animal ten times my size," she said, her eyes wide. "Relaxing is a bit hard."

"Think of Sam and Will waving at you from their ponies," he said.

She took a deep breath, and her viselike grip on his hand eased.

"Well done." He guided her fingers to the reins. "Take these. Ezra will remain at Belle's head, and I shall remain at your side. We're going to walk slowly around the yard, just as the boys did."

"Emphasis on *slowly*, right?" she asked.

He nodded solemnly. "Snail's pace."

————·•✳•·————

Isla had to admit that she'd seen more improvement after one hour on a horse this morning than she had after the same amount of time with a quill yesterday. Just a moment ago, a second stablehand had brought Lord Bancroft's horse out to join them. Even with her limited experience, Isla recognized a majestic animal when she saw one. Blaze was stunning, and if his pricked-up ears and alert eyes were any indication, he was ready for more than a sedate walk around the yard.

Despite Belle's placid demeanor, Ezra kept a reassuring hand on Belle's bridle while Lord Bancroft mounted his horse. Isla waited, grateful that she'd relaxed enough in the saddle to actually enjoy the experience. She wasn't ready to canter off alone, but her knuckles were no longer white, and she could appreciate the thrill of being outdoors astride a powerful animal.

Lord Bancroft guided his horse closer. "What do you think, Miss Crawford? Are you ready to venture out of the yard?"

"I think I am."

He smiled. "I am glad to hear it."

Isla willed away the flush of warmth his obvious pleasure at her response brought on. She had not left the house or its immediate surroundings since her arrival, but now that she felt more comfortable astride her mount, her eagerness to see more than the woodshed and yard was hardly surprising. Her strong desire to share a new experience with Lord Bancroft, however, was a little more disconcerting. And it was something she'd rather not admit to. "What did you have in mind?" she asked.

He pointed toward a wooden gate in the nearby hedge. "If Ezra opens the gate for us, we can take the horses into the meadow. There's a footpath that leads to the crest of the hill and a lookout of sorts. It's not far, but it will give you a feel for riding on something other than the hard-packed dirt and gravel of the yard."

"That sounds perfect."

"Shall I open th' gate, then, m' lord?" Ezra asked.

"If you'd be so kind," Lord Bancroft said, angling his horse so that he was within reach of Isla. "I believe Miss Crawford can manage."

Ezra relinquished his hold on Belle's bridle and hurried across the yard. Belle tossed her head as though glad to be free of that added restriction. Isla tightened her grasp on the reins. She might have doubts about her ability to manage the horse unaided, but Lord Bancroft didn't. It was time to dig a little deeper for some confidence.

"How will Belle know when to move?" she asked.

"If I allow Blaze to take the lead, Belle will follow." He offered Isla a reassuring look. "These two are well used to each other. Martha and I have ridden them together many times."

"Okay."

"Okay?"

"No fair!" Isla said. "I can't think about using old English words when my whole focus is on staying in this saddle."

He grinned. "Reasonable enough. I shall come up with my own interpretation. You used this word the last time we were talking about Blaze, so I imagine *okay* means 'I wish I had ridden many more times also.'"

"Or it could just mean 'very well,'" Isla suggested.

He shook his head. "That is far too prosaic. I prefer my interpretation."

"Okay," Isla said, and then when she realized what she'd done, she began to laugh. "In my current state, I can't win this battle of words."

"That is just as well," Lord Bancroft said, humor dancing in his eyes. "It will enable us to concentrate on the ride instead."

They rode through the gate side by side. Lord Bancroft kept Blaze at a steady walk and—just as he'd told Isla she would—Belle kept pace. Ezra closed the gate behind them, and Isla adjusted her position in the saddle to take advantage of the view.

Sheep, some standing alone and others in small clusters, dotted the field. Their bleating filled the air, and although a few stopped their grazing to stare curiously as the two riders cut through the pasture, most continued with their meal undeterred. Above their heads, a few puffy clouds hung suspended in the blue sky, and after all the rain of the last few days, it was good to feel the warmth of the late autumn sun.

"The leaves are starting to change colors," she said, her attention on a small grove up ahead. "They're beautiful."

"They are," Lord Bancroft agreed. "I always enjoy coming to Copfield Hall, but I confess, the countryside around here puts on its very best show at this time of year."

"What about the area where your family home is located?" she asked.

"Bancroft House is in the Peak District," he said. "It has its own beauty, but the countryside is more wild and rugged than Surrey's. Rather like the weather."

"York's temperatures are often chillier than London's too," Isla said.

He looked at her curiously. "Do you miss the north?"

"Sometimes. I miss my family—although they've never felt quite so inaccessible as they do now."

"So I imagine."

They rode on. Grateful that Lord Bancroft didn't feel the need to fill the time with pointless chatter, Isla allowed the gentle sounds of nature to calm her overarching anxiety. The steady hoof falls pounding the ground, the bleating of the sheep and occasional song of a bird, the creak of leather, and the bark of a distant dog. It struck her then. There was no rumble of an engine—no vehicle on a road, no piece of farm machinery in a field, and no airplane in the sky.

"The quiet is lovely," she said.

"I agree." They had reached a small stand of trees, and he reined Blaze to a halt. Belle immediately paused beside the larger horse. Isla watched as Lord Bancroft dismounted and walked around his horse to stand opposite her. "Come," he said, reaching up. "There is something I would like to show you."

Releasing her hold on the reins, Isla swiveled slightly and leaned forward to set her hands on Lord Bancroft's shoulders. He reached for her waist. His shoulder muscles tightened beneath her fingers, and then she was airborne. Moments later, her feet were on the ground. She staggered sideways.

"Careful," he warned, not relinquishing his hold on her. "It may take a moment to adjust to being upright."

"It's like my legs have forgotten how to work," she said.

He met her alarmed expression and chuckled. "It will not take long for them to remember." Sliding her hands off his shoulders, she gripped his biceps and took a wobbly step. His hold on her waist remained firm. "Take your time."

She averted her eyes from his. Taking her time was all well and good, but if she didn't put some space between her and Lord Bancroft soon, her heart would fail her before her legs. She took a second shaky step back. "I think I'm okay." She shook her head in frustration. "I mean, I think I can manage now."

Slowly, he lifted his hands. She took another step. This one was more stable.

He smiled and offered her his arm. "Well done. The ground is a little uneven here, but I think you will find the short walk worth the effort."

When faced with the choice of maintaining some distance or falling flat on her face in front of the gentleman, Isla chose to save herself from the possibility of further humiliation. She set her hand on his arm and attempted to ignore the way her heart instantly responded.

He led her around the trees. On the other side, the ground fell away in a gentle slope, opening into a stunning vista. The rolling hills were crisscrossed by stone walls and hedgerows. Isolated cottages and farmhouses punctuated the fields and wooded areas. Cattle, horses, and sheep grazed in the green meadows, while other fields burst with golden sheaves of grain. In the hollow immediately below them, a cluster of buildings was strung along a winding dirt road, and on one end, a tall spire marked a church.

"Oh!" Isla was momentarily speechless. "It's beautiful."

"I think the same every time I view it." He gestured toward a nearby fallen tree. "If you are not afraid of a little dirt clinging to your clothing, you can sit and take it all in."

Isla lifted her hand from his arm and crossed the short distance to the log. Grateful that her legs seemed to have recovered, she sat on one end of the fallen tree and gazed out at the view. Her seat shifted slightly, and she looked over to see Lord Bancroft claim a spot a little farther down the log.

"Tell me what I'm looking at," she said.

"Surrey," he said. "In all its glory." But then he pointed to the spire below them. "That's St. Augustine's Church and the village of Little Twinning. Beyond the wooded area to your right, you can just make out the chimneys of Greenbriar Manor, home of Lord and Lady Whitely, the Maidstones' nearest neighbors of note."

"As in, they have titles?" Isla asked.

"As in, they have titles, land, money, and influence," he said.

"Ah, I see. Very important neighbors indeed."

He gave her a quizzical look. "Am I to understand that such things are not so significant in your world?"

"Not really," she said. "The titles still exist, but they're more honorary than anything. In fact, most people with titles are desperate to come up with ways to pay for the upkeep of their enormous homes." She paused. "Over the centuries, it's become easier to move within and across Society's ranks. There are more opportunities for men and women to follow vocations that really interest them rather than simply following in their fathers' footsteps."

"Such as you choosing to work in the government," he said.

"Yes." She smiled. "My father's a school teacher, and my mother's a nurse. They probably thought I was completely bonkers—I mean, mad—for wanting to work in politics, but they never stopped me."

"That sounds rather marvelous."

She tilted her head, studying him curiously. "What would you choose to do if your options were unlimited?"

"Since I will never have that luxury, I've not given the matter any consideration."

"But if you could," she pressed.

He appeared thoughtful. "If I were not a member of the House of Lords, I believe I would search for another avenue that would allow me to affect a positive change in the country."

"That was my primary reason for entering politics."

"I would have guessed as much." He hesitated. "Affecting a positive change aside, I think perhaps I would have enjoyed breeding race horses."

"Or—if the century of your birth were no object—driving race cars," she said.

The flicker of humor that she was coming to recognize in his eyes had returned. "You believe I would like that, do you?"

"Yes," she said. "You'd probably enjoy riding a bullet train too."

Shaking his head slightly, he looked away, his focus reverting to the scene before them. She watched a seagull sail by; she was content to wait for him to speak again.

"Are you any closer to grasping why the lady at the costume shop may have sent you here?" he finally asked.

It was not what she'd expected him to say, but the question deserved an honest answer. "I think about it constantly. I've considered and rejected more possibilities than I can count, but I don't think I'm any closer to a reason now than I was when your sister suggested it." She shrugged helplessly. "I don't have any special skills that would help your family members or even the people of Little Twinning. In fact, I'd say I am rather lacking in such things."

"You made great strides in your equestrian abilities today."

She frowned. "Do you think I'm here to learn new things?"

"Perhaps. Although, regardless of your assertions to the contrary, I am quite sure you have a great many strengths." He paused. "What do you consider to be your greatest abilities?"

It was a spectacularly awkward question to answer outside a job interview, but Isla understood Lord Bancroft's motivation. She clasped her hands together and tried to respond objectively. "I think I'm a good secretary—I have above-average office and people skills. I'm organized, and if it's a subject I feel passionate about, I can remember more details than most."

"What do you feel passionate about?" he asked.

"Politics, human rights issues, history." She stopped, feeling suddenly self-conscious. "I'm sorry. The fact that my history is your actual life makes this feel very odd."

"Try not to think about that. Instead, consider what you might know that could be of assistance to us."

"I've only ever lived in the cities of York and London. I can't think of anything I could do or say that would be of worth to people in Jacobean rural England."

"If you had arrived in London, would there be something?"

Isla's thoughts immediately leaped to the gunpowder plot. Her grip on her fingers tightened. The date of Guy Fawkes's attempt to blow up the House of Lords was unnervingly close.

"Miss Crawford?"

She had hesitated a fraction too long, and Lord Bancroft was watching her a little too closely.

"Is there something?"

"Yes."

He released a tense breath. "You realize that as members of the House of Lords, Maidstone and I are in the country only because the opening of Parliament has been delayed due to the plague resurgence. All those who have the ability to leave the city have done so. If you were meant to influence current events in London, it stands to reason that you may also have had your arrival there postponed."

"But the event . . . the crisis that lies ahead . . . it will be averted."

"You are sure of that?"

She nodded. Her presence in London during the weeks preceding November 5, 1605, could not possibly have any impact on the outcome of the gunpowder plot. The players in that conspiracy were all in place years before the event.

Lord Bancroft had yet to look away. "And yet the very thought of it has the power to rob you of words and cause you to clench your fists."

"It will go down as one of the most infamous events in British history," Isla said softly.

His eyes widened. "When will it occur?"

She forced her fingers apart. "Soon."

Rising to his feet, Lord Bancroft extended his arm to her. Hesitantly, she gave him her hand. He took it and drew her upright. "If you are willing, I think we should continue this conversation at the house in the presence of Maidstone and Martha. The timing of your arrival may have nothing whatsoever to do with the event you know is coming, but given that you have yet to come up with a sound alternative, I think it would behoove us to at least consider it."

"You believe me?"

"It is becoming harder not to, and I am unwilling to allow my own reservations or stubbornness to cause you to dismiss something that may be of great import."

He was right. As much as Isla didn't want any involvement in Guy Fawkes's treasonous activity, she'd be a fool to ignore it. "If Lord and Lady Maidstone are available when we get back to the house, I'll share as much of it as I can remember."

A light squeeze of her hand accompanied his encouraging smile. "Perhaps your exceptional attention to detail is exactly what is needed after all."

CHAPTER 8

Simon waited for Maidstone to take a seat beside Martha before claiming a chair near the fireplace for himself. "Thank you for interrupting your morning activities to meet with Miss Crawford and me," he said.

"Is everything all right?" Martha's concerned gaze moved from Simon to Miss Crawford and back.

"Yes," Simon said. "At least, that is our hope."

He did not need to look at Miss Crawford to sense her discomfort. But was she fully aware of how much the atmosphere in the parlor had changed in twenty-four hours? Gone was the aura of polite skepticism that had been clearly visible on every face. Everyone's focus had subtly shifted from what to do *about* Miss Crawford to what to do *for* her.

"I assume you have gathered us because you have an update on Miss Crawford's situation," Maidstone said.

"In a manner of speaking," Simon said. "Although it is not so much an update as a possible clue to her reason for being here."

"Oh, do tell!" Martha said enthusiastically.

At his sister's instant and eager response, Simon experienced a pang of unease. Had he jumped to a conclusion without truly thinking it through? "I would have you bear in mind that we are still simply exploring possibilities at present."

"Yes, yes," Martha said. "But a possibility—no matter how tenuous—is more than we had yesterday."

He could not argue with that. He glanced at Miss Crawford. She was perched on the edge of her seat, her back taut and her hands clasped together on her knee, but she met his look without flinching. She was ready.

"It occurred to me this morning that just because Miss Crawford arrived at Copfield Hall, we should not assume that her area of influence is to be limited to this family or this area of the country."

Maidstone stroked his beard thoughtfully. "You are operating under the premise that if the plague had not caused the evacuation of so many from London, she may have found herself there instead."

"Exactly." Having Maidstone's train of thought parallel his own did much to boost Simon's confidence. "That said, I asked Miss Crawford if she knew of anything of significant import that was to occur there soon."

"And?" Martha leaned forward. "I assume there is."

"Apparently." Given Miss Crawford's stricken expression at the lookout, Simon had a sinking feeling that Martha's eagerness would soon turn to something more akin to fear. "I have not asked for details. I thought it better that we hear what she has to tell us as one."

"Very good of you," Maidstone said. He reached for Martha's hand in a rare show of tenderness. "We are ready to hear what you have to say, Miss Crawford."

Miss Crawford acknowledged Maidstone's invitation with a slight nod. "Thank you, my lord." She paused, concern filling her eyes. "To talk about events that are in your future but my past feels very strange. I don't want to say anything that might change the course of your lives—or of history in general."

"As commendable as that is, I would rather hear the whole of it rather than a watered-down version that leaves me guessing," Maidstone said. "You may be assured that we will act with similar caution."

She looked at Simon.

"I agree," he said. "Tell us what you know."

"There is a plot underway to kill the king and destroy the government," she said.

Maidstone shrugged. "Unfortunately, there are usually several of them floating about."

"Not like this one," Miss Crawford said.

Maidstone's eyebrows shot up at her emphatic tone, but Simon was coming to know the young lady. She would not speak so forcefully without good reason.

"How is this one different?" he asked.

"It has been planned for years," she said. "The players are well connected and affluent and are fueled by a deep-seated hatred of those who have treated Catholics harshly. Everything they need is already in place, and they are waiting only for the opening day of Parliament to execute their plot."

"What do they have planned?" Maidstone asked.

"They intend to blow up the Palace of Westminster when the king, his retinue, and all members of the House of Lords are in the building," she said.

A log shifted in the fire, the sound unnaturally loud in the deathly silent parlor. Martha raised her free hand to her mouth to muffle a cry, and Maidstone found his voice.

"An act such as that would throw the country into a state of total anarchy."

"I think that is their hope," Miss Crawford said.

"But . . ." Martha's face was completely void of color. "Would that not kill everyone in the building?"

"Everyone in the building and within at least a quarter-mile radius of the area," Miss Crawford said. "They've stashed thirty-six barrels of gunpowder beneath the chamber."

Thirty-six barrels of gunpowder! How was that even possible? As the frightfulness of this treacherous plot took root, Simon could not remain seated. He leaped to his feet, then paced to the window and back. "When you first told me you knew of an infamous event that would soon take place, you also said that it would end well."

"Yes." Miss Crawford's hands were tightly clasped again. "The authorities will learn of it and capture the men responsible before the gunpowder is lit."

"How?" Simon asked.

Maidstone raised his hand. "I beg your pardon for interrupting this line of questioning, but before we go into the details of how this shocking incident shall be averted—and may God be praised if it is—I believe it would be in our best interest to know who is responsible for this treachery."

"Fair enough." Simon paused at the fireplace. "Can you give us names, Miss Crawford?"

She grimaced slightly. "This would be way easier if I had internet access."

"I beg your pardon?"

"Nothing." She rubbed her forehead as though trying to encourage memories to resurface. "I wrote a research paper on this event when I was at university, but it's been four or five years since I studied the material. There were about a dozen men in the conspiracy. I can probably come up with names for most of them, but the lesser-known ones will be harder to remember."

Martha rose from her chair and walked to her small writing desk in the corner. "I will write them down. That way, if you remember more later, we can add to the list."

"Thank you, Martha," Simon said.

Miss Crawford waited until Martha's quill was raised above a fresh sheet of paper. "The most well-known is Guy Fawkes," she said. "He is the one who was placed in charge of gathering and lighting the gunpowder."

"Guy Fawkes?" Maidstone gave Simon a puzzled look. "Is he familiar to you?"

"Not at all," Simon admitted.

"That's not terribly surprising," Miss Crawford said. "He grew up in Northern England—York, actually—but he left the country about a decade ago to fight for the Catholics in Spain. While there, he took upon himself the name Guido Fawkes, and that's where he learned so much about the use of gunpowder. He returned to England at the urging of Robert Catsby and has been posing as Thomas Percy's manservant, John Johnson, since then."

"Do you mean to tell me that Catsby and Percy are in on this?" Maidstone asked.

Miss Crawford nodded. "Catsby is the ringleader of the conspiracy. Percy has provided invaluable access to the royal palace and to a residence that is close enough to the Parliament buildings to allow the conspirators to try tunneling their way beneath the House of Lords."

Maidstone uttered a quiet curse. Simon echoed the sentiment. Miss Crawford had not been exaggerating when she had told them this band of men was well connected. Catsby's family was known to be recusant Catholics but were affluent landowners. And Percy—although reputed to be a bigamist, an embezzler, and an all-too-ready swordsman—was the great-grandson of the Earl of Northumberland.

"Who else?" Simon asked.

"There were two Wintour brothers," she said.

"David Wintour?" Maidstone asked.

She shook her head. "I don't think so. I seem to remember their names were the same as Catsby's and Percy's, so Thomas and Robert." She frowned. "There were another set of brothers. Men who Guy Fawkes knew in school." She closed her eyes, and Simon wondered if she was visualizing notes she'd taken in class. "Wright!" she said, opening her eyes. "That was their last name. John and Kit Wright."

"I believe Kit Wright is Percy's brother-in-law," Maidstone said grimly.

"Several of them are related," Miss Crawford said. "Keeping track of how they were connected helped me remember their names. Another one was Francis Tresham. He's Catsby's cousin."

"I would not trust Tresham if my life depended upon it," Simon said. "And I know of no other gentlemen who would."

"Catsby's servant, Thomas Bates, was involved too," she said. "And a couple of horse breeders."

Horse breeders? Simon's thoughts whirled. He knew most of the reputable horse breeders in England—at least by name and reputation. "Where were they from?"

"The Midlands, I think," she said.

"Smythe, Townsend, Grant, Rookwood?" Simon rattled off the names of the best-known horse breeders from that part of the country.

"Rookwood," Miss Crawford said, seizing on the unusual name immediately. "And I think the other was Grant. Their responsibility was to supply the conspirators with getaway horses to escape London during the chaos that would ensue after the explosion. And one of them was to organize some kind of hunt at which Lady Elizabeth was to be kept until they brought Duke Charles to join her."

"Blast it all, they've thought of everything," Maidstone said, running his fingers through his hair.

"Not everything," Simon said. "They must have made at least one error, or else they would not have been found out."

"True." Maidstone released a tense breath. "Perhaps the time has come to learn what will cause their downfall."

Simon looked over at his sister. "How many names do you have, Martha?"

"Eleven," she said.

Frustration lit Miss Crawford's eyes. "There were more. Two or three, I think. Some of them joined the group just before November, and so they played a lesser role in my history books."

"You've done well to remember eleven of them," Simon said.

She offered him a grateful smile. "If the other names come to me, I'll let you know."

"Join us again, Martha," Maidstone said. "And we shall have Miss Crawford tell us what lies ahead for these scoundrels."

Martha left her writing table and took her place beside Maidstone. Simon opted to stay on his feet.

"Whenever you are ready, Miss Crawford," he said.

"I believe most of the conspirators have temporarily left London," she began. "I don't remember where they all went or even when they will reunite, but they'll regroup within a week or two of November 5. As Lord Maidstone said, they've thought through every element of their plot, including having a ship at harbor, ready to transport Guy Fawkes away from England after he escapes the city."

Maidstone grunted his displeasure even as Simon marveled at the traitors' forethought. "How are they to be prevented from seeing their plot through to its nefarious end?" Simon asked.

"A member of the House of Lords will have a dinner party at the end of the month," she said. "During that party, a letter will be delivered to a servant, warning his master to stay away from the chambers on the opening day of Parliament. At first, the gentleman isn't sure whether to take the message seriously, but he decides to take it to Robert Cecil, who brings it to the attention of the king when the king returns to London. The king orders a search of Parliament House."

"And they find the gunpowder," Martha guessed.

"Not immediately," Miss Crawford said. "But men go back on the evening of November 4. That's when they discover Guy Fawkes in the undercroft and arrest him."

"Why on earth would they wait until the final hour?" Maidstone said. "A few minutes too late and all would be lost."

"Cecil would want to catch the perpetrators red-handed," Simon said grimly. "To send a message to all other would-be traitors."

"I think that's right," Miss Crawford said. "Cecil must be very good at his job, because within a week, every member of the conspiracy is accounted for—most are dead."

"Cecil is extremely powerful," Simon said, "and utterly ruthless when crossed."

A flicker of awareness lit Miss Crawford's eyes. "He's the one you said has spies everywhere."

"He is. And I would hazard a guess that the letter you refer to will not be the first Cecil has heard of this conspiracy."

"Perhaps not," Maidstone said, "but it is obviously the catalyst for action that saves countless lives and the government as we know it." He came to his feet. "Who is the gentleman who receives the warning note?"

Lines crossed Miss Crawford's forehead. "I've been trying to remember. He's titled. Lord Mount or Mont-something, I think."

"Lord Montague?" Martha suggested.

"No."

"Lord Montgomery?"

In obvious frustration, Miss Crawford shook her head. "I don't think that's it either."

"It will come to you," Simon said, genuinely believing it was true. Already, he was astounded by her ability to recall so many details from a history lesson given years before. "What of the person who sent the letter? Did one of the conspirators succumb to a prick of conscience?"

"I don't know."

Maidstone leaned forward. "You do not know, or you do not remember?"

"I don't know. Nobody does." She shrugged. "It's one of the great mysteries surrounding the gunpowder plot. Many historians believe it was sent by one of the conspirators. The most popularly held belief is that it was Tresham because his sister was married to the gentleman." She paused. "That's it! That's how we can figure out who received the warning. He's Francis Tresham's brother-in-law."

"Lord Monteagle," Martha said. "His wife, Elizabeth, is Mr. Tresham's sister."

Simon stared at his sister. "How ever did you know that?"

Martha shrugged. "Ladies have to talk about something whilst the gentlemen are discussing politics. Familial relationships are a common enough topic."

Along with *desired* familial relationships, no doubt. Simon was well aware that ladies regularly bandied his name about in parlors, wishing to make a match for their daughters or granddaughters. Setting that discomforting thought aside, he focused on what Miss Crawford had been about to say. "So, centuries later, no one knows who sent the letter?"

"No. Lord Monteagle didn't recognize the handwriting. I assume Cecil didn't either."

"No one ever claimed responsibility?" Maidstone asked.

"Not as far as historians know."

"Miss Crawford." Martha's voice was unusually hushed. "What if you are the one who wrote it?"

CHAPTER 9

Isla's mouth went dry. Lady Maidstone had to be joking. When Lord Bancroft had first suggested that her reason for being at Copfield Hall at this particular time might have something to do with the gunpowder plot, she'd wondered if perhaps she was meant to warn him and Lord Maidstone to stay away from London. Or maybe alert them to the dangers of being associated with the men involved in the conspiracy.

"I really don't think I should get entangled in this," she said. "As far as I'm concerned, history has already been written."

"True," Lord Maidstone said. "But what if Martha is correct? Is it possible that you have always been an integral yet anonymous part of that history?"

Isla's thoughts spun. How was she supposed to make sense of the past, present, and future when they collided like this? "But what if I'm not? What if, by getting involved, I mess things up? If Guy Fawkes is successful because I do the wrong thing . . ." She swallowed, the magnitude of that disaster washing over her in an overwhelming wave.

Lord Bancroft moved from his place at the fireplace to take the chair beside her, his dark eyes reflecting the turmoil she was experiencing. "As challenging as this is to grasp, we must do our best to think it through."

He was right. She needed to remain calm and think clearly. "You said that most historians believe Tresham sent the note. Why has that not been generally accepted?" he asked.

"Most think it was Tresham since he was a relatively new addition to the group of conspirators and his sister would be directly affected if Lord Monteagle were in the chambers when the explosion occurred. But Tresham vehemently denied it, and no one was ever able to place him in the vicinity of Lord Monteagle's house on the evening of the dinner party."

"If the conspirators have kept their plans secret for years, it does seem unlikely that one of them would terminate that allegiance immediately before the culmination of all their efforts," Lord Maidstone said.

"Unless the mounting pressure caused one of them to crack," Lord Bancroft said.

"Is there any reason why we could not wait to see if a note is delivered during that dinner party?" Martha asked. "If it is, then we know history has remained on course without Miss Crawford's intervention. If it is not, then we assume she has always been the originator of the warning note. Miss Crawford could have a letter ready and can see that it is delivered to Lord Monteagle by that evening's end."

Lord Bancroft gave his sister a startled look. "When did you become so wise?"

"I believe she always has been, Bancroft," Lord Maidstone said, an unmistakable air of pride in his voice. "You simply did not notice."

"In fairness, it may have been difficult to see beyond my older-sibling overbearing tendencies," Lady Maidstone added.

Lord Bancroft gave her a wry smile. "Ah, yes. The overbearing tendency is something I am well acquainted with."

"Well, be that as it may," Lord Maidstone said, "I believe Martha has hit upon a sound solution."

Isla could think of half a dozen solid reasons why it was a terrible solution—most of them involving her inability to fulfill the assignment without drawing all sorts of unwanted attention. She started with one of the most basic. "You do realize that I can barely write a single legible word with a quill. A whole letter is completely beyond me."

"If Lord Monteagle's dinner party is not until the end of the month, you have almost four weeks to practice," Lady Maidstone said, seemingly unperturbed. "I have no doubt you shall have wonderful penmanship by then."

Isla had no such confidence. "But how would we know if another letter is delivered?"

"It would be all but impossible unless we are guests at Monteagle's dinner," Lord Bancroft said.

"That is easily accomplished," Lord Maidstone said. "Monteagle owes me a rather large favor for giving him the name of a captain willing to transport cargo for him from India."

"You think he would be willing to extend an invitation for four?" Lord Bancroft asked.

"Without question." Lord Maidstone leaned back in his chair as though everything was settled. "I have only to suggest it to him."

Isla fought back her mounting panic. "I don't think I can navigate all the unknowns of a seventeenth-century dinner party without people noticing my mistakes. The last thing I'd want to do is draw extra attention, but between not knowing the right etiquette or vocabulary, I'd be a walking disaster."

"She has a point, Maidstone," Lord Bancroft said, and Isla wasn't sure whether to be grateful for his support or offended that he thought her such a liability.

"One of us would have to be at her side the entire evening," Lord Maidstone said. "A subtle prompt every once in a while is all that would be required."

Lord Maidstone's faith in her should have brought her comfort. Unfortunately, it didn't. Lord Bancroft obviously wasn't convinced, and he'd spent far more time with her. He was a firsthand witness to her many blunders.

"It may not be quite that easy," Lord Bancroft said. "It will raise eyebrows if you or I remain at Miss Crawford's side all night, and Martha will undoubtedly be pulled away by someone at some point."

"You are right," Lady Maidstone agreed. "But there is a simple solution to that difficulty."

"What is that?" Lord Bancroft asked.

"Miss Crawford goes to London as your betrothed."

Isla's stomach lurched, and she reached for the arm rests, digging her fingers into the polished wood even as Lord Bancroft glared at his sister.

"I certainly hope you are jesting," he said.

"Not at all. Neither am I being overbearing. I am thinking through our options in a calculated—and might I even say *wise*—manner."

"No," he said, his eyes narrowing. "In this instance, you may not use the word *wise*."

"Steady, Bancroft," Lord Maidstone interjected. "I believe we should all hold back judgment until Martha has had a chance to say her piece."

"Thank you, Hugh." Martha met Lord Bancroft's glare without wavering. "Simon, you know full well that if you attend this dinner party without an attachment, Lady Monteagle will ensure that several other unattached young ladies are also in attendance. She will have you circulate the room and talk to every one of them. You will also doubtless be seated between two of her favorites at the dinner table. She will not seat two ladies together, which means Miss Crawford will be separated from me. Hugh's rank will have him sitting near the head of the table, and Miss Crawford's lack of rank will place her nowhere near him.

"In addition to that, if you wish to see Miss Crawford more than once or twice during the fortnight that we shall be required to be in the city, Society tongue-waggers will require that you have a compelling reason for making those calls. If not, they will surely create one of their own."

"You can't be serious." Isla looked from Lady Maidstone to Lord Bancroft. "The only way I can sit beside Lord Bancroft at dinner or be seen with him outside that party is if we are engaged to each other?"

"Or married," Lady Maidstone said. "But in this instance, that would be taking the charade a little too far."

Lord Bancroft's jaw tightened. "I am glad you think so."

"But that's crazy!" Isla said.

Lady Maidstone inclined her head. "Call it what you will; it is the way of things in this century."

"And what happens to this supposed betrothal after November 5?" There was an edge to Lord Bancroft's voice that Isla hadn't heard before.

"If Miss Crawford disappears as quickly as she came, we could claim that she succumbed to the plague," Lady Maidstone said.

"And if she does not?"

Isla's grip on the arms of the chair tightened. If she never returned to the twenty-first century, what would become of her?

"You can have a change of heart and call off the betrothal."

With a groan, Lord Bancroft ran his fingers through his hair. "Do not gloss over the implications of that disastrous act, Martha."

"Why would it be disastrous?" Isla asked.

"Neither of us would be viewed in a favorable light following a broken betrothal, but whereas you might be granted some clemency due to a lady's prerogative to change her mind, I would be hard-pressed to escape the stigma of committing a breach of contract."

"So, Miss Crawford must be the one to sever the arrangement," Lady Maidstone said.

This conversation was beginning to take on the fuzzy and ludicrous properties of a dream—or rather, a nightmare.

"Is all this really necessary?" Isla asked.

"If you wish to have ready access to my brother's assistance with whatever lies ahead in London," Lady Maidstone said, "it is all but imperative."

"I believe Martha has the right of it, Bancroft," Lord Maidstone said. "I realize that it is easy for us to say that, not having to live with the consequences of this pretense ourselves, but if we do not do everything in our power to ensure that Monteagle receives the warning letter, our entire nation is at risk."

Lord Bancroft released a slow breath. And then he turned to Isla, his troubled eyes meeting hers. "Are you willing to enter into this mock betrothal with me, Miss Crawford?"

"Do you think we can manage it?" she asked.

His smile was thin, but it was something. "I do. As Martha said, you have time to learn a great deal before we arrive in London. Indeed, by then, you may not need my aid at all, but if you desire it, I am willing to provide it."

The seriousness of what lay ahead was mind-numbing, but if she did not have to face everything and everyone alone—if

Lord Bancroft were at her side throughout it all—perhaps she could do what was required of her.

"Then, yes," she said. "I'll play my part. And for the record, I'm absolutely sure I'm going to need your help."

"We shall see to your wardrobe right away," Lady Maidstone said. "You will have to learn the correct forms of greeting and table etiquette, an elegant curtsy and acceptable subjects of conversation. Oh, and you must practice your penmanship every day."

"Oh dear," Isla said. "This is going to be like trying to drink out of a fire hydrant."

Lord Bancroft gave her a perplexed look. "What is a fire hydrant?"

Isla moaned. She was in so much trouble. "Who are we kidding? I'm going to have to remain mute from the moment I arrive in London."

"That would certainly add a new level of difficulty to the challenge," Lord Bancroft said. "But it might work."

"Absolutely not," his sister said. "We shall simply add current word usage to your daily studies."

Isla must have appeared as overwhelmed as she felt, because Lord Bancroft's expression changed from quizzical to concerned.

"I daresay that would be helpful," he said, "but Miss Crawford has something else she must do first. Could you spare her for an hour or so before she begins her training?"

Isla had absolutely no idea what Lord Bancroft was talking about, but if it bought her a little time to regroup, she was all for it.

"Certainly," Lady Maidstone said, looking almost as surprised by Lord Bancroft's announcement as Isla felt. "I shall use the time to go through my wardrobe with Maggie. I am sure we can find some gowns there that would look quite splendid on Miss Crawford." She nodded as though it were decided. "Whenever you are ready, Miss Crawford, you may come to my chamber to make your choices."

"Thank you," Isla said. "You've been incredibly kind."

"On the contrary," Lady Maidstone said. "If we are correct, your willingness to act will save the lives of countless people, including my husband and brother. You are the one who should be thanked."

An uncomfortable weight settled on Isla's shoulders. Regardless of her long list of inadequacies, there was no room for mistakes with the task ahead.

"Come," Lord Bancroft said, rising to his feet.

Startled, Isla stood. "Where are we—"

The slight shake of his head cut off her question. "I shall deliver Miss Crawford to your chambers shortly, Martha," he said.

Curiosity shone in the lady's eyes, but she nodded. "Very well."

"I daresay you'd best locate Maggie and warn her of what you have planned, my dear," Lord Maidstone said, vacating his chair. "Meanwhile, I shall set about drafting a missive to Monteagle, encouraging him to invite all four of us to dinner."

"Thank you for taking that on, Maidstone," Lord Bancroft said.

Lord Maidstone inclined his head. "Given that my assignment is undoubtedly the easiest of this entire scheme, I shall endeavor to ensure that our places at Monteagle's table are guaranteed."

Guaranteed. The word carried with it an exactness that was about as far from Isla's capabilities right now as it could be. Battling her mounting apprehension, she barely felt the light brush of fingers at her elbow. She darted a glance at Lord Bancroft. He nodded, and with a firm but gentle touch, he steered her toward the door.

She followed his lead, remaining silent until the parlor and the Maidstones were behind them, and they were approaching the staircase.

"Where are we going?" she asked.

"The nursery."

She stumbled to a halt. Had she totally lost her mind? She had no memory of scheduling a nursery visit. "Are Sam and Will expecting us?"

"No." His smile was fleeting. "I have not known you long, Miss Crawford, but I recognized the look on your face in the parlor. It was the same one you exhibited when we spoke in the grove of trees yesterday morning. On that occasion, I was the one in need of time in the nursery to clear my head. I thought in this instance, perhaps you might benefit from it." A flicker of uncertainty entered his eyes. "After all that was just handed you, a spinning-top competition might be just the thing to turn trepidation into laughter. Better than a lesson on seventeenth-century protocols, at least."

To Isla's horror, tears pricked her eyes. She had friends who'd known her for years who would not have been so sensitive to her feelings. She blinked a few times and fought for control of her emotions. "That's very kind of you, my lord, but I don't want to reward your thoughtfulness by making you feel bad."

He frowned. "Would you rather not go to the nursery?"

"Oh no, I want to go very much. It's just that if we have a spinning-top competition, you will probably lose every game."

The lines on his forehead disappeared, and a smile emerged. "So you think. As a gentleman, I should probably warn you that Will is the undisputed champion of spinning tops, but I am a close second."

"Ah, but you haven't played against me yet," Isla said, starting up the stairs. "And Sam might surprise you too. Especially if I give him some pointers."

Lord Bancroft's soft chuckle followed her up the staircase, and for the first time since she'd dismounted Belle, Isla found herself looking forward to what was to come next.

—— · ✳ · ——

"Mine is still going!" Sam jumped up and down with excitement as Will's peg top tumbled to a stop beside Simon's foot.

"Well done, Sam," Miss Crawford said, clapping her hands and smiling widely. "I knew you could do it!"

Simon forced his gaze away from her radiant face to focus on his excited nephews. The boys were already setting up for a rematch, and as Miss Crawford prepared to start them off, Simon experienced a wave of gratitude that his instincts had not failed him. She had needed this time in the nursery. Her troubles had not disappeared, but Will and Sam had helped her forget her worries long enough to experience childlike joy.

Simon had not allowed himself to think through the many and troubling ramifications of his counterfeit betrothal or Catsby's dastardly plot. That would come later—when he was alone. Given what lay ahead, even without thinking it all through yet, he had a feeling both he and Miss Crawford would be making regular pilgrimages to the nursery over the next few weeks.

"I won again, Uncle Simon!" Sam was jubilant, and to his credit, Will was allowing his brother a moment of glory.

"I am proud of you," Simon said. "And of you, Will. You have both become champion top spinners, and I think it is time I contrive a new game to play with you so that I may stand a chance of winning."

The twins laughed delightedly but were obviously not ready to abandon their activity just yet. Setting their tops to spin again, their attention quickly reverted to the wooden toys.

Miss Crawford moved to join Simon beside the small table. "Thank you for bringing me here."

"Martha is one of the most generous people I know," he said, "but sometimes her enthusiasm can be overwhelming. You will undoubtedly spend a great deal of time with her over the next few weeks, and I have every reason to believe you will become fast friends. But should you ever need an escape, I recommend the nursery or a ride on Belle."

"And if I run into you in here or on Blaze, am I to assume you're escaping too?"

He should have guessed she would see through his means of evading disquieting thoughts. "That is a distinct possibility."

She sighed. "I'm sorry for dragging you into this. If I were more capable, I wouldn't need someone to guide me through everything."

"Miss Crawford—"

She set her hand on his arm, effectively stopping him before he could say anything more. "Please," she said. "If we are to behave as if we're engaged, would you call me Isla? People tend to go by their first names in the twenty-first century, and it would help me feel more normal."

"Isla," he said. It was an unusual name, but it suited her. "Very well." He paused. "Would it help if you called me Simon?"

"Yes." She smiled, and he was struck yet again by how much the simple gesture lit her entire countenance. "But if you'd like me to keep up my horribly awkward curtsies when we run into each other, I can do that too."

He laughed. "Martha will have you curtsying gracefully within a day. She will tell you who should be greeted that way. If my name is on the list, however, you may remove it."

"Given that you are a titled gentleman, I'm not sure that she will agree with that decision."

"Probably not," he admitted, "but I believe we can persuade her that it is what we would both prefer whilst at Copfield Hall, even if we must reinstate obligatory bows and curtsies when we are in London."

She released a heavy sigh. "Okay."

"Ah." She'd spoken without thinking, and Simon was disinclined to let it pass without teasing her. "The word that means you wish to go riding again."

She clapped her hand over her mouth.

He grinned. "I believe more riding can be arranged."

"You know that's not what I meant," she said, and then she groaned. "I really think keeping my mouth closed the whole time is safer."

"And horribly tedious," he said. "I would rather be betrothed to someone who speaks her mind—even if I do not fully comprehend it."

Isla shook her head helplessly. "I will try harder. Really, I will."

"Of that, I have no doubt. Besides, Martha will not rest until you are speaking as a true Jacobean young lady."

"I don't think she fully realizes what she's taken on."

"Do not take that burden upon yourself. Martha is extremely capable and remarkably fearless." He gestured toward the door. "And to that end, I should probably take you to her chambers before she comes looking for you."

Isla nodded but did not immediately move. "Do you think she would mind if I came to the nursery on my own occasionally?"

Memory of Maidstone's mandate concerning restricting Isla's access to his sons flooded Simon's mind. To the best of his knowledge, Isla had not been left alone in the house since Maidstone had issued it. After their recent meeting in the parlor, however, Simon thought it likely that his brother-in-law's stance would soon change. "As long as Miss Tomlinson is with you, I do not think Martha would mind at all." He glanced at the boys' nursemaid, who was currently watching the twins from the comfort of the nursery rocking chair. "And I speak from personal experience when I say that Will and Sam are always pleased to have visitors."

Relief filled Isla's eyes. "When I'm here, it doesn't seem so important that I have the wrong vocabulary or don't know how to use a quill."

"Indeed," he said. "How fleet of foot you are and how well you spin a peg top are far more important."

"I think I'd better add practicing turning a peg top to my list of things to do."

"Very wise," Simon said, offering her his arm. "And if you also choose to add riding to your schedule, you will find me at the stables most mornings at sunrise."

CHAPTER 10

Guy stood in the small square in the center of York, his gaze
focused on the tollbooth a few yards distant. Memories
assaulted him. Painful, loud, and full of hate. He gritted his
teeth, willing himself to keep his feet planted. As unpleasant as
it was to relive the day Margaret Clitherow had died, it was a
good reminder of why he had returned to England. Of why he
was so eager to light the fuse under the House of Lords.

Two women walked by, and he pulled the brim of his hat a
little lower. Coming to York had been a risk. He'd been gone for
a decade, but the young Guy Fawkes was known in this community, and it would take only one person calling out his name
to end his anonymity. Worse, a person who knew his childhood
associates might ask about Kit and Jack Wright. They'd been his
closest friends at school and were his coconspirators now. The
fewer who made that connection, the better.

His thoughts drifted to their headmaster, John Pulleyn.
The venerable gentleman had been more than a teacher to Guy.
He'd been a mentor—a father figure when Guy's own father
had died at the young age of forty-five. And though Guy had
been raised in a Protestant home, John Pulleyn had opened his
eyes to the evil that Henry VIII had spawned when he'd broken from the Catholic church. Pulleyn had made it his mission

to educate the boys at St. Peter's School on the harsh reality of living life as a devout Catholic in a country run by those whose pride and avarice had turned them from the right path. And that tutoring had included bringing his students to this very square to witness the cruel death of Margaret Clitherow, a woman who had been killed for openly teaching Catholic doctrine to others in her home.

Guy had been sixteen years of age. Old enough for the horrific experience to permanently sear itself into his mind. Old enough to know that he would never be as the craven adults in the crowd that day who had stood by, doing nothing while a woman's anguished cries had filled the air.

His stomach roiled, fueled by the hate that festered there. There would be vengeance for Margaret Clitherow and the other Catholics in the country who had suffered a similar fate. And it would come far sooner than England's tyrannical monarch could possibly imagine.

The bells of York Minster chimed, drawing Guy from his heavy thoughts and reminding him that he must be on his way. Turning his back on the tollbooth and his memories, he started down the narrow lane that led to his childhood home. A few more days and he would return to London, and then there would be little over a week before he and his comrades set things right. Anticipation hummed through his veins, the promise of vengeance dispelling his earlier frustration. His mother would undoubtedly consider a fortnight in York not nearly long enough to make up for his having been gone for so long, especially as he'd expressly forbidden her from gathering friends and neighbors to celebrate his return. But two weeks was all he could offer her. There were more important things at hand than a lengthy mother-and-son reunion, and his role in the coming events was pivotal. Straightening his shoulders, he increased his pace. Once the king and his ineffective government were destroyed, his mother would understand his need to leave—and his reason to stay away afterward.

————·•✳•·————

Isla exited Copfield Hall's front door and hurried down the stone steps. A little over two weeks ago, she'd slipped out of the house at a similar time, desperate to find answers—or even a way back to McQuivey's Costume Shop—at the woodshed. Now she barely glanced at the distant structure as she followed the gravel path toward the stables, intent upon reaching it by the time Simon returned from his morning canter.

A robin sang in a nearby holly bush, and Isla smiled. Somehow, despite the craziness of her situation, her life at Copfield Hall had fallen into a comfortable routine with people she now considered friends. A morning ride with Simon, followed by penmanship practice in the parlor and a midday meal at which Martha reviewed seventeenth-century dining etiquette. The afternoon began with an hour spent with Sam and Will and then moved into another lesson with Martha that usually revolved around clothing, dated vocabulary, and approved subjects of conversation. Finally, Lord Maidstone and Simon joined them for an evening meal, where Isla was required to practice what she'd learned. They were each unfailingly patient with her efforts, but Isla chafed at how often she made mistakes and how slowly her calligraphy was improving.

Most nights, when she was alone in her bedchamber, she was beset by doubts that she would ever be able to pass herself off as a Jacobean lady. Those feelings had further intensified three days ago when Lord Maidstone had informed her that he had received an official invitation for them all to attend Lord

Monteagle's dinner. Her role at that event had immediately become more real—and ever more daunting. But somehow, after each night's sleep, morning brought with it new hope and the opportunity to spend time with Simon.

She rounded the corner of the house. No one was in the yard outside the stable, but the doors to the large building were open. As she approached, Ezra emerged, drawing Belle behind him.

"Good morning, Ezra," she called.

The stableboy looked up and grinned. "'Mornin', Miss Crawford. Looks as though we timed it just right t'day."

"Yes." Isla stepped closer and ran a hand down Belle's long neck. "We're getting rather good at this, aren't we?"

He chuckled. "Well, I reckon Belle must 'ear ya comin' 'cause she starts shufflin' in 'er stall. If I don't get 'er out fast enough, she lets me know."

Isla smiled. She couldn't deny that after almost a dozen rides together, she and Belle had developed a fondness for each other that Isla would not have believed possible when she'd first tried mounting the horse. "I think she knows that I'm as anxious as she is to be outside." She glanced over her shoulder at the path Simon usually took. "Did I beat Lord Bancroft back today?"

"Yes, miss," Ezra said. "Would ya 'ave me get the stool?"

Isla hesitated. Even though she always left her ridiculous farthingale in her bedchamber when she planned to ride, situating herself in the sidesaddle was much trickier without Simon's help. On the other hand, if she were mounted when he arrived, they could leave straightaway.

"I suppose you'd better bring it out," she said.

"Right ya are, miss." Ezra handed her Belle's leather straps and hurried into the stable.

He'd barely disappeared through the doors when Isla heard the pounding of hooves. She looked to her right and immediately spotted Simon and Blaze galloping across the pasture toward them. Isla's heart rate quickened. At her side, Belle lifted her head, her ears twitching, alert to the return of her stablemate.

"They're almost here, girl," Isla whispered.

Belle nickered softly, and Isla smiled. She wasn't the only one pleased to see the handsome pair return.

Blaze entered the yard just as Ezra reappeared. Without a word, the stableboy set the small stool he was carrying on the ground and stepped forward to take Belle's reins from Isla. Moments later, Simon brought Blaze to a halt a few feet from them.

"Forgive me," he said, dismounting in one swift movement. He stepped toward her, the bright sparkle in his eyes only enhancing his windswept good looks. "Have you been waiting long?"

"Not at all," Isla said, wishing she still had access to mascara or had at least taken a few minutes longer to do something with her hair. It wasn't right that Simon could look so good this early in the morning. "How was your ride?"

"Marvelous. The weather is perfect." He glanced at Belle. "Are you ready to go?"

"Absolutely," Isla said.

He smiled and extended his arms. "May I?"

At her nod, he placed his hands on her waist. Awareness pulsed through her, but without a word, she set her hands on his shoulders, and with practiced ease, he lifted her onto the saddle. She shifted slightly, anchoring her leg around the pommel.

"Okay?" he asked.

She laughed at his use of the modern expression. "Yes. In my sense of the word and yours."

With a chuckle, he mounted Blaze again. "Would you open the gate for us, Ezra?"

"Right away, m' lord." Ezra handed Isla the reins and was across the yard in a flash.

Isla tapped Belle's side with her heel, and the obedient horse moved to Blaze's left. Blaze offered her an acknowledging snort. The stallion probably knew what was coming. At Belle's decorous pace, the short ride to the lookout each morning offered Simon's horse little more than a cooldown after his more demanding morning run.

"So," Simon said after Ezra had closed the gate behind them. "What miraculous twenty-first-century contraption are you going to tell me about today?"

Isla gave him an amused look. On their second ride to the lookout, Simon had asked her what she missed most from her life in the future. The question had been the beginning of a unique portion of their morning ride. Every day, she told him about something new. Describing flushing toilets and indoor plumbing had not been nearly so difficult as explaining a computer or electricity, but Simon's fascination over future inventions had yet to abate.

"You believe I will run out of things, don't you?" she asked.

"Will you?"

"I don't think so. At least, not for a very long time."

He appeared thoughtful. "You are missing a great deal."

"Yes. But I'm experiencing some amazing things too. I'd never have the opportunity to ride sidesaddle every morning if I were still at home."

"That is completely foreign to me," he said. "I can scarcely imagine a world without a daily ride."

They had almost reached the fallen tree, and the beautiful dale below was coming into view.

"Truthfully," Isla said, "my time is louder and faster and lacks the many peaceful moments you enjoy." Memories of her long hours at work and stressful deadlines filled her mind. "Or maybe they're there if you search for them, but I didn't take the time to find them."

"Well then," he said, "I am glad the seventeenth century has offered you something of worth."

"Many things actually." If she were torn away from this life as quickly as she'd been sent here, there was no doubt in Isla's mind as to what—or who—she would miss most, but she wasn't going to admit to that now.

Simon guided Blaze to a halt at their usual stopping spot, dismounted, and walked to Belle's side. "I would like to hear what you have come to consider to be of value," he said, raising his arms to her.

"Time spent with Sam and Will," she said without hesitation. It was a safe answer and one that he could not refute. He knew how much she enjoyed being with the twins.

"Of course. I miss them when I am elsewhere." He set his hands on her waist, and a familiar spark crackled to life between them. "Anything else?"

He wasn't playing fair. Steeling herself against the warmth in his eyes, she slid her leg over the pommel and reached for his shoulders. "Bread pudding."

"Bread pudding!" He shook his head. "I am twice amazed. I was quite certain you were going to say braised eel."

She pulled a face. A week ago, when Martha's attention had been diverted by something her husband was saying, Isla had braved asking Simon if he'd like her portion. His initial surprise had quickly turned to collusion, and they'd managed to transfer Isla's helping onto his plate with no one the wiser. More to the point, they'd managed the same feat twice since then. Simon could have no doubt as to Isla's feelings about the dish.

"Braised eel may stay firmly in this century," she said.

He lifted her off Belle and set her on her feet beside him. "I agree," he said. "I would be quite put out if one of my favorite foods disappeared with you." He smiled, his teasing tone enabling Isla to find her footing in more ways than one.

"You only like it because you haven't tasted fish and chips yet."

"Is that so?" He appeared dubious. "What exactly is fish and chips?"

Isla laughed and pulled away. "I'll save that one for another day. Today's marvelous twenty-first-century invention is medicine."

"Medicine is in existence here." He shuddered. "It is quite awful."

"If the little I've read about it is true," Isla said, "*awful* is a euphemism." She walked to the fallen log and sat down, glad when he followed her there and took a seat beside her. Over the last few days, the distance he'd placed between them had shrunk.

"Tell me about your medicine," he said.

"I'm not qualified to explain much to you," she admitted. "But I can tell you that modern doctors can do miraculous things. They've learned that most illnesses are caused by viruses or bacteria, which are so small they can't be seen by the human eye. When they enter the body, they cause myriad diseases."

Simon gave her a skeptical look. "How?"

"I don't know, but those tiny things are real. And discovering them has done away with the belief in humors and evil spirits and has led to new and improved medicines, safer surgeries, and all sorts of life-saving medical techniques." She paused. It wasn't her place to share too much, but if a little information could protect Simon and his family from contracting the Black Death, she had to say it. "The bubonic plague is caused by one of those viruses. It's being spread by rats and lice."

He stared at her. "You believe if London were free of rats and lice, it would also be free of the plague?"

"Yes. It may take a while for the disease to fully disappear, but if people were to couple the removal of those two things with improved hygiene, it would happen."

"I would have great difficulty persuading others of this."

"I know. But even if you and Martha and her family are the only ones to benefit from that knowledge, it was worth telling you."

He rubbed the back of his neck. "This situation—you being here and knowing so much about so many things—is disturbingly complicated."

"Yes, it is."

"I shall warn Maidstone and Martha about the rats and lice." His smile was strained. "Thank you for your concern for us."

Isla's chest ached. *Concern* was not the word she would use to describe her feelings. The friendship she'd developed with Martha, the bond she had with the twins, the connection she felt to Simon. Those relationships engendered far more than a nebulous concern for their welfare. She gazed out at the view before her, struggling to know what to say.

The silence stretched on a few seconds too long. Simon cleared his throat. "I imagine there are many gentlemen desiring to court you in your London," he said. "I assume that since you mentioned no one in particular when the subject of our counterfeit betrothal was first mentioned, you remain unattached at present."

Isla had been ready for a change in subject. Unfortunately, this one was no better than the last. "Totally unattached," she said. "Our courtship rules aren't nearly as strict as yours, and we call it 'dating' or 'going out' rather than courting. There was someone I dated while I was at uni, but we parted ways several months before I left York." She darted a glance at him. "With no negative repercussions to either of our reputations."

"I am glad to hear it," he said, although the lines on his forehead belied his supposed pleasure. "What was his name?"

"Jeremy Robinson," she said, a vision of Jeremy sitting at a table in the small coffee shop where they'd often studied together rising in her mind. He'd been the one to call things off, and although it had been gutting to hear him say the words, it hadn't been completely unexpected. He'd been making excuses for why he couldn't meet up with her for weeks.

She sighed, grateful that the memory of the breakup no longer brought with it any pain. She had seen Jeremy with a stunning brunette several times after he'd walked out of the coffee shop without looking back that day. The first instance had hurt. Badly. But the passage of time and moving to London had helped immeasurably. "Jeremy was studying law at the same university as me," she said. "We were together for about a year, but then he met someone else who he felt was a better match."

"Because of her finances or her family?" Simon asked.

"Actually, I'm pretty sure it was more about how pretty she is and that she enjoys listening to rock music more than I do."

Simon shook his head. "The fellow must be demented. I have yet to hear rocks make any form of music, and it is all but impossible to believe that he found anyone else so attractive as you."

Isla probably should have taken the time to instruct Simon about modern music and Jeremy's favorite bands, but how was she supposed to do that when his seemingly involuntary compliment hung in the air between them?

"You didn't . . ." She swallowed. It might be better to simply accept his kind words graciously and move on. "Thank you."

He released a tight breath. "Forgive me. I am usually better at controlling my tongue."

"There's nothing to forgive," she said. "It was very nice of you."

"Honest rather than nice." He paused. "I hope this Robinson fellow did not hurt you badly."

Was the emotion in his dark eyes empathy?

"At first, it was hard," she admitted, "but now I realize that it was for the best. Jeremy may be wrong about some things, but he was correct about us not being right for each other." Keeping her eyes on him, she tested her hunch. "What about you? Why is the handsome Lord Bancroft not already married or truly courting someone?"

Half expecting him to tease her about her use of the word *handsome* or to blow off her question with a superficial response, Isla was taken aback when Simon looked away.

"I'm sorry." Regret filled her. Her words had obviously hit a nerve. "I didn't mean to be flippant or to pry."

He shook his head. "It is only fair that I answer the same question I posed to you."

"Maybe. But you certainly don't have to."

"I believe I do." His gaze flitted to the right and the distant chimneys of Greenbriar Manor before returning to her. "Despite our differing circumstances, our experiences are similar. Our sham betrothal is not my first. I was betrothed once before, but the young lady ultimately chose another over me."

Isla's unsettling pang of jealousy was tinged with indignation. "But I thought that was severely frowned upon."

"It is. However, in the case of that particular young lady, the allure of being a duchess was enough to offset the stigma of broken vows."

Simon's opposition to Martha's suggestion that he and Isla pose as an engaged couple suddenly made sense. He had been forced to reenter Society with a black mark to his name already. What on earth would two do to him?

"A second broken betrothal, Simon?" Without thinking, she reached for his hand. "If I'd known, I never would have agreed to our charade."

"Then, it is well that you did not know," he said. "Martha is fully aware of my situation, and she would not have suggested our role-play if there had been any other way to accomplish what must be done. Those who know me may offer their condolences at my lack of good fortune in acquiring a wife, but I daresay I shall eventually rise above the blight on my manhood."

Simon had fallen back on his teasing again, but Isla didn't feel like smiling. Not when she was the one who could shatter Simon's reputation once and for all. "There has to be another way."

"Not unless we wish to introduce a significant risk of failure," Simon said.

"But your good name—"

"Isla, this is not your burden to bear." He squeezed her fingers lightly before releasing her hand. "My reputation may be sullied for a short time, but eventually, the stigma will fade. Besides, the blame for any besmirchment that comes my way does not lie with you. It can be placed firmly at the feet of Catsby, Fawkes, and their coconspirators—and, perhaps to a lesser degree, Lydia."

"Lydia?" Isla asked. "Is that the name of the young lady you were courting?"

"It is."

Isla pulled a face. "I've never liked that name much."

As she had hoped, the anxiety in Simon's eyes was replaced by amusement. "Is that so?"

"Yes. It's the name of an obnoxious, self-centered character in a wildly popular book written in the late 1700s."

"Ah, so you are employing perfectly logical reasoning for your aversion of the Greek name given to one who is beautiful and noble."

"That's right." Isla rose, and Simon immediately followed suit. "Perfect logic coupled with feminine intuition. It can't be faulted."

Simon chuckled, and with a smile, Isla led the way back to their waiting horses. Her apprehension over what lay ahead had yet to abate, but this morning's outing had taught her that she and Simon could navigate a difficult conversation and emerge strengthened. That knowledge lifted her spirits and brought new hope for the challenges that awaited them in London.

CHAPTER 11

Simon stood at the edge of the front lawn, waiting for Isla's signal.

"Are you ready?" she whispered. At Simon's right, Sam nodded enthusiastically. At his left, Isla smiled. "Very well. On the count of three."

Simon listened as she counted down, marveling at how far she'd come under Martha's tutelage. He was quite sure that if they'd been playing this game a fortnight ago, Isla would have used the word *okay* rather than *very well*. Now, however, the vocabulary he was familiar with flowed naturally from her.

Her counting ended, and in unison, he, Isla, and Sam chanted, "What time is it, Mr. Wolf?"

On the other end of the lawn, Will stood with his back to them.

"Six o'clock," the little boy yelled without turning around.

Simon, Isla, and Sam took six steps toward him.

"Again," Isla whispered.

"What time is it, Mr. Wolf?" they cried in chorus.

"Twelve o'clock!" Will yelled.

Simon grinned. Will was playing with fire. Simon's stride was considerably longer than the others, and another twelve paces would have him within three arm lengths of the boy.

The trio took the obligatory twelve steps, then said again, "What time is it, Mr. Wolf?"

Will must have sensed that Simon was nearby, and he was ready. "Dinnertime!" the little boy cried, swinging around and lunging for Simon.

With a squeal of laughter, Isla and Sam ran for safety. Simon pivoted, darted right, and then slowed his steps just enough to give Will a chance to catch him. His nephew made a wily wolf, but he deserved a turn on the other side of the game Isla had taught them.

"I caught you, Uncle Simon!" Will lunged for Simon's left leg and wrapped his arms around it.

"Ah!" Simon feigned distress. "I am the wolf's dinner!"

Will giggled, and from the safety of the other side of the lawn, Isla's and Sam's laughter reached him.

"You're it, Uncle Simon!" Sam called. "You're the wolf now!"

Conceding defeat at Will's hands, Simon took his place at the far side of the lawn, with his back to the others.

Moments later, the chant began again. "What time is it, Mr. Wolf?"

"Eight o'clock," he replied, angling his head slightly so as to listen for the gentle swish of Isla's skirts.

They repeated the chant three more times before Simon caught the rustle of fabric at his right. She was close, and when they asked the question again, he was ready.

"Dinnertime!" he called, swiveling around as the other three scattered.

Isla had lifted the front of her gown a couple of inches and was racing across the grass. She was unbelievably fast, but Simon was undeterred. Lengthening his stride, he tore after her, closing the gap between them in seconds. She spun on her heels, dashing right. Adjusting his direction, he followed after her. She turned her head to glance over her shoulder. The slight movement was enough to check her speed, and moments later, Simon's arms were around her.

"Caught you!" he panted. "You, Miss Isla Crawford, are it!"

With winded laughter, she spun to face him. "Well raced, Lord Wolf."

He laughed, his arms around her still. "If it weren't for my longer stride, you would have beaten me across the lawn."

Her blue eyes sparkled. "I was close."

She *was* close. To the edge of the lawn, certainly, but more to the point, she was pressed against him and had yet to pull away. His gaze dropped from her captivating eyes to her up-turned mouth. Heaven help him. She surely had no idea how much he wished to touch the lock of hair that had fallen from her pins or run his fingers across her soft skin, or kiss her enticing lips. He took a steadying breath.

"Simon?" She lifted her arms to place her hands on his chest.

"A carriage is coming!" One of the boys called out a warning, and the other took it up.

"It's black with two white horses."

Sanity returned in a rush. Simon released Isla and took a step back. Confusion clouded her eyes.

"Are you o—" She caught herself. "Are you well?"

"Yes." He ran his fingers through his hair. He could do better than this. He *must* do better than this. "I was obviously more winded than I thought, but I am well."

"Come quickly." Sam arrived at his side and grabbed his hand, towing him toward the drive. "Who do you think has come?"

In his present befuddled state, Simon would be hard-pressed to recognize his own stallion, let alone the horse and carriage belonging to one of Maidstone's or Martha's acquaintances.

"Their carriage is shinier than ours," Will said, joining Sam.

It was, indeed. And the crest on the door was gleaming equally brightly in the autumn sunshine. Simon studied it uneasily as the vehicle followed the bend in the drive.

"Do you recognize it?" Isla stepped up beside him and watched the approaching vehicle curiously.

The carriage slowed, coming to a stop opposite Copfield Hall's front doors. Hobbes immediately descended the steps and opened the carriage door. An exceptionally wide, yellow, silk skirt appeared in the opening, and as the young lady descended from the vehicle, awareness of who had come fell upon Simon in the form of a boulder in his stomach.

"It is the Whitelys' carriage," he said. "It appears that Lady Whitely and her daughter have come to visit Martha."

"The Whitelys who live in the house we can just about see from the fallen tree?"

"Yes. Although their daughter is now married and no longer lives there." He squared his shoulders. "She must be visiting whilst her husband awaits the opening of Parliament."

"The daughter married a peer, then?"

"She married a duke."

Vaguely aware that Isla was staring at him, Simon kept his attention on the two women now standing outside the carriage.

A little shorter and plumper than her daughter, Lady Whitely had changed very little since the last time he'd seen her. Neither had Lydia, he supposed, although her wardrobe was even more elegant today than it had been eight months ago. She was positively resplendent in her embroidered yellow gown. Her Medici collar was tall and trimmed with wide, stiff lace. A large, deep-red gemstone and a string of pearls hung from her neck, and her dark hair was ratted to perfection. She was, in fact, a picture of flawlessness.

Sam tugged on Simon's jacket. "Uncle Simon?"

Shaking off his torpor, Simon gave his attention to the little boy. "Yes, Sam?"

"Can we play What Time Is It, Mr. Wolf, now? It's Miss Crawford's turn to be the wolf."

"It may be time to end the game, Sam," Isla said, answering before Simon voiced a reply. "But I would be happy to be the wolf when we play next."

Sam's face fell, but his twin was not willing to give up.

"One more time?" Will begged. "Miss Tomlinson has not yet come for us."

Simon looked at Isla. "What do you think? Did that last run wear you out?"

"Not at all." She lowered her voice slightly. "But if you wish to avoid an awkward reunion, you will need to act quickly."

He raised an eyebrow. He would do well to remember that Isla was more preceptive than most. "Martha's guests will wish to avoid that as much as I do."

"I would not be so sure."

Isla had scarcely finished speaking when Simon heard the crunch of gravel beneath approaching feet.

"Good afternoon, Lord Bancroft."

Schooling his features, Simon turned to face Lady Whitely and Lydia. He bowed. "Lady Whitely. Your Grace. What an unexpected surprise."

Lady Whitely looked rather too pleased with herself. Lydia, Simon was gratified to see, appeared more uncomfortable.

"Our thoughts precisely, my lord," Lady Whitely said. "Neither Lydia nor I had any notion that you were currently at Copfield Hall."

"I imagine my reason for being here is similar to that of the Duke and Duchess of Tunstow. A delayed opening of Parliament has doubtless impacted most members of the House of Lords."

"But of course." Lady Whitely's haughty gaze slid over Isla, and Simon felt his hackles rise. Isla's natural beauty was undeniable, but her windswept appearance and grass-stained hem was far removed from the ideal the Whitely ladies held.

"Please introduce us to your companions, Lord Bancroft." It was the first time Lydia had spoken. He would know her voice anywhere, but whereas it had once filled him with pleasure, its overly sweet tone now left him irritated. She had no need to be presented to Sam and Will, but by adding them to her request, she had effectively lessened the importance of Isla's introduction.

"Forgive me," he said. "Lady Whitely, Your Grace, you will remember Master Samuel Winslow and Master William Winslow. Gentlemen, your mother's guests, Lady Whitely and the Duchess of Tunstow."

The little boys bowed politely.

"Goodness," Lydia said. "They are quite grown up since last I saw them. I hardly recognize them."

It did not escape Simon's notice that Lydia talked *about* the boys, even though they stood before her, whereas Isla had spoken *to* them from their very first meeting. Of course, Lydia would never deign enter into a spinning-top competition or chase a five-year-old across a lawn either. The tension in Simon's shoulders eased, and with unforeseen pleasure, he placed his hand gently on Isla's elbow and drew her forward. "My lady, Your Grace, may I present Miss Isla Crawford."

Isla dropped into an elegant curtsy. "A pleasure to meet you, my lady, Your Grace."

"Crawford, you say." Lady Whitely's brow furrowed. "Where does your family hail from, exactly?"

"From the north, my lady," Isla said. "Not far from York."

The older lady sniffed. "Well, that would explain our lack of connections."

"I have heard it can be very wild in that part of the country," Lydia said.

"Some may consider it so," Isla replied. "For myself, I am grateful to have an unspoiled place where I may go to escape the clamor of the city." She paused. "I imagine you find the same to be true for Little Twinning."

"There are few places so lovely." Lady Whitely offered Lydia a knowing smile. "Except, perhaps, the grounds at Tunstow Castle."

"Where is Tunstow Castle located, Your Grace?" Isla asked.

Lydia's eyes widened with surprise. In truth, she had probably never met anyone who had never heard of her husband's extensive property.

"It lies on the southern edge of Dartmoor," she said.

"Ah, yes, of course." Isla assumed a concerned expression. "I hope you have not suffered greatly from taking your outings over boggy soil and in misty weather? I visited the Dartmouth area once in the winter, and it was very bleak."

Biting back a smile, Simon released Isla's elbow. She had no need of his support. Her subtle jab at Lady Whitely's prideful comment was masterfully done, and her language usage was faultless. He did not have to look at Martha's neighbor to sense her displeasure. It simmered in the air between them. Lydia, however, appeared taken aback.

"I confess," Lydia said. "I have been married only a few months, and so I have yet to spend a winter at the castle."

"You have no need to fear the shorter days or colder weather, Lydia. The duke will take good care of you." Lady Whitely's chin rose a fraction. "An affluent husband is a great blessing."

It seemed that the lady wished her barbs to penetrate more than Isla alone. Attempting to maintain a placid expression, Simon flexed his fingers. The movement would do little to alleviate his mounting headache, but it was a better way to release some of the pressure building in his chest than was speaking his mind to the woman who had likely held a great deal of sway in Lydia's decision to choose a duke of significant means over a baron with modest holdings.

"That may be true," Isla said, "but affluence is certainly not the greatest blessing to be offered a bride. I believe that honor is held by unconditional love, which includes faithfulness, decency, and sacrifice."

In the stunned silence that followed, Isla's fingertips brushed against Simon's fist. Acting instinctively, he opened his hand and curved his fingers around hers.

"As you can see," he said, "I have a great deal to live up to."

Lydia gasped. Her mother's eyes narrowed.

"Do you mean to say that you are betrothed?" Lady Whitely asked.

Isla's fingers tightened around his, but Simon did not hesitate. "We are."

"What is 'betrothed'?" Sam said, his eyes wide.

Simon ruffled his hair affectionately. "Nothing either you or Will need to worry about for some time, young man."

"Good," Will said. "Can we play What Time Is It, Mr. Wolf, now?"

"Good heavens!" Lady Whitely said, although whether her exclamation was directed at the twins' interruption, the news of his betrothal, or his and Isla's willingness to entertain the boys, Simon could not tell.

Lydia had yet to lose her stunned expression, but Simon could not summon any feelings of regret. The sense of loss he had expected to feel upon setting eyes on her again had never materialized, and the dread over their first meeting was gone. So, too, were the remnants of bitterness and hurt that had plagued him for months. With genuine relief, he inclined his head to both ladies.

"If you would excuse us, ladies, Miss Crawford and I have a prior engagement with my nephews. Enjoy your time at Copfield Hall. I have no doubt Lady Maidstone will be anxious to hear all your news."

And then, before Lady Whitely could find her tongue, he led Isla back across the lawn to the sound of Sam's and Will's whoops of delight.

Finally. Isla leaned back in her chair and studied the piece of paper on the writing desk before her. It was free of ink splotches, the lines were straight, the spacing even, and the words legible. Relief mingled with accomplishment, and she allowed herself a grateful smile. Her penmanship was nowhere near as elegant as Martha's, but this was her best work to date, and it might just be good enough.

Setting down her quill beside the two others she'd worn through, Isla rose to her feet and stretched. She wasn't sure how long she'd been working on the letter. Long enough for the sun to lower in the sky and for her back to ache from being hunched over the small table.

She'd heard Lady Whitely's carriage roll down the drive some time ago but had opted to remain in her room rather than relocate downstairs. Martha's forethought in placing paper, ink, and quills at the writing desk in Isla's bedchamber, along with the one in the parlor, where she usually practiced, had been a blessing. Isla would have resorted to staring at the walls in her room rather than enter the parlor before Lady Whitely and the Duchess of Tunstow had left. As it was, she'd made significant progress and was excited to share it.

Moving over to the small wash basin on the other side of the room, Isla picked up the piece of lye soap and rubbed it across her ink-stained fingers. She winced at the now-familiar zing. The caustic bar was as likely to take off a layer of skin as it was to remove the black marks. She should add moisturizing soap to the list of twenty-first-century advancements she shared with Simon.

For the first time since they'd parted at the nursery door, Isla allowed her thoughts to settle on the gentleman. They'd played two more rounds of What Time Is It, Mr. Wolf, before Miss Tomlinson had come for the boys, and at no time during the game or the walk back into the house had she or Simon brought up their interactions with Lady Whitely or her daughter. It had to have been difficult for him to see Lydia again. Truth be told, it had been surprisingly unpleasant for Isla too. Lady Whitely was waspish, and Lydia was stunningly beautiful. The latter detail should not have bothered Isla so much, but feeling like a rag doll standing beside a porcelain doll hadn't been the most enjoyable experience.

Isla rinsed her reddened fingers and dried them off on a small towel. She hadn't expected Simon to take her hand in front of Martha's visitors. Or to announce their betrothal. Perhaps both things had been a defense mechanism after all the unkind darts Lady Whitely had thrown their way. Or maybe he'd thought it better for word to get out that they were betrothed before they arrived in London. There was no doubt that Lady Whitely would take great pleasure in being the one to spread that news.

Isla sighed. The snarky noblewoman would probably include something about Isla's untamed appearance being a fitting match for her remote northern background.

Setting down the towel, she opened the nearby wardrobe. With a handful of Martha's altered old gowns to choose from, Isla couldn't have hoped to outshine Lydia's appearance this afternoon, but she could at least make some effort to clean up for dinner. She may not be able to help Simon through the aftermath of another broken betrothal, but when he'd taken her hand today, Isla had made herself a promise that she would do everything in her power to make the time they were together a good memory rather than another painful one.

A soft knock sounded at the door.

"Come in," Isla called.

The door opened, and Maggie appeared. "Good evenin', miss," she said, bobbing a small curtsy. "I've just come from Lady Maidstone's chambers an' wondered if you were needin' any assistance afore you go down t' dinner."

"Oh, Maggie, you are an answer to an unuttered prayer. If you can make my wind-snarled hair presentable, I'd be most grateful."

The maid smiled. "I can 'ave it lookin' lovely in no time at all."

Maggie was as good as her word. Less than half an hour later, Isla descended the stairs holding the letter she'd penned and wearing a royal-blue Jacobean gown with white lace and an elaborate updo.

Feeling unaccountably nervous, she approached the door to the dining room. Martha's voice reached her from within. Was she the last person to arrive? Crossing the threshold, she looked around the wood-paneled room. The table was set for four, but Martha and Lord Maidstone were standing beside the fireplace, goblets in hand, obviously waiting for their guests.

"Good evening, Miss Crawford." Lord Maidstone inclined his head. He had yet to call her by her first name, and Isla felt strangely reluctant to forgo addressing him by his title.

"Good evening, my lord. Martha. I hope I am not terribly late."

"Not at all," Martha said. "As you can see, you have arrived ahead of Simon."

"But, thankfully, only just." Simon's voice reached them from the doorway. "I beg your pardon, Martha," he said as he entered the room. "I took Blaze out again this afternoon and lost track of time."

Isla's heart sank. A second long ride after having spent a considerable amount of time with the twins meant that Simon's interaction with Lady Whitely and Lydia must have affected him far more deeply than he'd let on.

"It must have been an enjoyable ride," Lord Maidstone said.

"Indeed." Simon did not elaborate. Instead, as though anxious to change the course of the conversation, he turned to Isla and pointed to the paper in her hand. "What do you have there?"

"Oh!" Isla held it out. "My latest attempt at a letter for Lord Monteagle."

His eyes widened. "May I read it?"

"Please do," she said. "I brought it to dinner so that each of you could offer me your feedback." His brows drew together in a look that was all too familiar. Mentally replaying the vocabulary she'd used, she hurriedly offered an alternative for the problem word. "I mean, your assessment."

Simon studied the paper. "The improvement in your penmanship is remarkable," he said. "Well done."

A glow, warm and bright, filled her chest. "Thank you. But it's Martha who deserves the praise, not me."

"Nonsense," Martha said. "I have lost track of the number of hours you've devoted to this project."

"Read it out loud, would you, Bancroft?" Lord Maidstone said.

"Of course." Simon cleared his throat.

My Lord, I have a care for your preservation; therefore, I would advise you to devise some excuse to shift your attendance at the opening of this Parliament. God and man have concurred to punish the wickedness of this time, and you would be best served to retire to the country, where you may later learn of the events to come. For though there shall be no appearance of any stir, Parliament shall receive a terrible blow, and none shall see who hurts them. May God give you the grace to make good use of this warning.

He ended his reading and slowly lowered the letter.

"Merciful heavens!" Lord Maidstone breathed.

Simon stared at her. "Isla, this is a masterpiece!"

"You really think so?"

"I know so." He glanced at the paper again. "How did you manage to articulate the warning so perfectly?"

"One of my political science reference books included the text of what was believed to be in the letter Lord Monteagle received. I've spent the last few nights desperately trying to remember what it said."

Simon shook his head slightly. "Your memory is truly extraordinary."

"May I?" Martha reached for the letter, and Simon relinquished it. She read it and then handed it to her husband. "I believe this is exactly what we need. Would you seal it and keep it safe until we attend Lord Monteagle's dinner?"

"I shall take it directly to my office," he said. "Have the staff bring in the first course. I shall return momentarily."

He disappeared through the door, and Martha moved to take her seat at the table. "Lady Whitely was agog with the news of your betrothal this afternoon," she said. "I confess, I had not expected that to be her first and most pressing topic of conversation upon entering the parlor." She eyed Simon with a hint of concern. "It was unfortunate that you happened to be outside when she and the duchess arrived. I hope your meeting was not horribly uncomfortable."

"It was sufficiently uncomfortable that I was glad when Sam and Will drew us back to our game," he said. "But I would contend that Isla and I came through the experience remarkably unscathed."

"Did you speak with the ladies, Isla?" Martha asked.

"I did." Isla caught the twitch in Simon's lips. Was he remembering Lady Whitely's poorly veiled insult about her wild background, or was he mildly amused at her less-than-subtle retort about Dartmoor's misty bogs?

"Well, you must have fared well under their scrutiny," Martha said. "If Lady Whitely had had any suspicion that you were not exactly who you said you were, she would never have ceased her hounding."

"Isla managed the situation perfectly," Simon said. "And it is probably for the best that word of our betrothal reaches London ahead of us."

"Will it?" Isla asked. How did people spread news that fast without mobile phones or email?

"If you remember," Simon said, "we are speaking of Lady Whitely. Her love of gossip is surpassed only by her penchant for arrogance. I cannot tell you how it will be done, only that it shall be."

"Really, Simon." Martha's tone held reproof, but Simon chose to ignore it, setting his sights instead on the footman entering the room with a steaming platter in his hands.

Lord Maidstone followed immediately behind the servant, and as the nobleman took his place at the head of the table, Isla leaned a little closer to Simon. "Is there braised eel on the menu this evening?" she whispered.

"I have not heard." He raised his goblet and gave her a knowing look. "But if there is, my answer is yes."

Isla smothered a smile. Maybe Simon's long ride actually had helped erase any angst he may have felt over seeing Lydia again. If he was willing to eat a double helping of braised eel, at least the experience wasn't affecting his appetite.

CHAPTER 12

Guy guided his mount into the stables attached to the Bell Inn in Daventry, grateful to be out of the drizzling rain at last. The deepening darkness of evening had dropped the temperature, making his sodden state all the more miserable. If Catsby had not reserved a room with a roaring fire, they would be relocating forthwith.

"Give her a good rubdown," he told the stableboy, who appeared out of the gloom. "It has been a long, wet ride."

"Yes, sir." The boy took the reins and led the horse to a nearby stall. "I'll see t' 'er right away."

"Very good." Guy hesitated. He avoided sharing his plans with anyone unless absolutely necessary, but the lad had best be told that he would not be staying long. "I shall return within the hour. My horse must be ready."

"Yes, sir," the boy repeated.

The lad likely thought him mad to be going back out in such inclement weather, but he would not stay here. Not if other members of the conspiracy had rented rooms. He would find another inn. One closer to London and the safety of his well-established position as Percy's manservant. Besides, the sooner he reached the city, the sooner he could check on the gunpowder.

Opening the stable door, he lowered his head against the rain and cut across the small yard to the inn's back door. Once inside, he assessed the passage beyond. Empty. Although, if the voices and laughter coming from the front room were any indication, the inn was busy tonight. Turning his back on the sounds of merrymaking, he took the narrow staircase to the upper floor. At the top, he stopped, listening. No voices. No footsteps. Catsby's letter, which had arrived mere hours before Guy had departed his mother's home, had given him a time and a very specific location: third door on the right, upper floor, Bell Inn, Daventry. Cautiously, Guy moved down the passage. When he reached the third door on the right, he knocked. Two taps, a pause, two taps. Seconds later, the pattern was echoed on the other side of the door. It was safe to enter.

Guy walked into the room and closed the door behind him. Four gentlemen sat around the fire: Wintour, Bates, Catsby, and Kit Wright. A fifth gentleman, Jack Wright, stood beside the door. He had obviously been assigned to give the all-clear knock.

"Welcome, Fawkes," Catsby said, rising to greet him. "We wondered if you were coming."

"Daventry is a considerable distance from York," Guy said, removing his hat and shaking off the water before doing the same with his cloak. "And traveling on horseback in this weather is less than ideal."

"You would have been better served to take a coach." Catsby pointed to a row of hooks on the wall, where the other gentlemen had hung their outerwear.

Tamping down his irritation, Guy hung his cloak and hat on the farthest peg. Catsby's comment deserved no response. The fellow knew full well that Guy did not own a carriage. Traveling by stagecoach would have exposed his journey to far too many witnesses and would have taken him twice as long. "I am here now," he said, claiming a stool close to the fire. "But I am not of a mind to stay long. What is the reason for this gathering? I assume you have news of some import."

"We are in need of money," Catsby said bluntly. "Percy has paid no rent on the property across from the Palace of Westminster, and Ferrers is hounding him for payment. We cannot afford such attention."

"I will see that he is paid," Guy said. One payment was all that would be needed before he left the country.

"That is not all," Catsby continued. "The captain of the ship scheduled to take you to Spain after the gunpowder blows is requiring advanced payment for his services. The extra horses Rookwood acquired for those of us who must ride north to reach Lady Elizabeth and Duke Charles must be purchased." He paused, likely knowing that he had already made his point. "I have approached my cousin, Francis Tresham. He has taken the oath of secrecy and is willing to assist us. Not only is he a friend to the Catholic cause, but he is also in possession of a fortune in land and coin."

"He is also known to be unpredictable and untrustworthy," Wintour said, the scowl on his face expressing his displeasure as unmistakably as his verbal censure.

"He has vowed to help us," Catsby said.

"And you believe him?" Kit Wright's voice held a concerning level of skepticism.

"He is my cousin, and he gave me his word."

"Tell me more about this fellow," Guy said. His decade on the continent had proved advantageous in preparing him for this assignment, but it had left him without vital connections in Society or a working knowledge of those who wielded significant influence among England's nobility.

"He was imprisoned for assaulting a man and his expectant daughter," Kit growled.

Catsby waved the accusation away with a flick of his hand. "They owed Tresham money, and he went after it." His eyes hardened. "Perhaps you also remember that he was imprisoned for his participation in the Essex rebellion. That, amongst other things, should prove his dedication to the Catholic church. For a gentleman of his position to openly oppose the Protestant queen took courage and devotion."

"He did not die for the cause, nor stay incarcerated for long," Jack Wright argued.

"For which we should all be thankful," Catsby said. "Had either of those things happened, he would not have been in a position to now aid us in bringing an end to our devilish government and king."

Catsby's final argument was impossible to refute, and he appeared to know it. Reaching for one of the flagons of ale on a nearby table, he poured some into a goblet and handed it to Guy. After refilling his own goblet, Catsby offered the flagon to Bates. Catsby's longtime servant topped off the goblet of each of the gentlemen in the room, and when he set the flagon back on the table, Catsby raised his cup. "To the unqualified success of the gunpowder plot," he said.

"To the gunpowder plot." The chorus of male voices, though low, brimmed with passion and conviction.

Guy took a swig of the pungent drink, the desire to see the successful culmination of their plans burning within him. The scheme had taken overly long to reach fruition. If Tresham's money ensured speedy and efficacious results, he would not fault Catsby for bringing him into their circle. Guy may never meet the gentleman himself. And that was just as well. Even now, he itched to be gone from this gathering and on his way to London. He would remain in this private room long enough to eat a hot meal and catch up on any updates these gentlemen had to share, but that was all. The rainy weather notwithstanding, he would linger no longer.

———— ·· ✳ ·· ————

Three days of rain had left the road to London pitted with puddles. Mud coated the wheels of the Maidstones' carriage, causing the vehicle to occasionally slide in a rather alarming manner. Isla sat on one side of the carriage, across from Martha and Maggie, but although they were protected from the damp, chilly weather, it was proving to be the most uncomfortable ride Isla had ever experienced.

The carriage rolled over another rut in the road, and Isla lurched right, hitting her elbow on the side of the vehicle. She winced from the instant pain, and for what seemed like the hundredth time, she wished that she could have made this journey in the comfort of a twenty-first-century car. Attempting to ignore her throbbing her arm, she wiped the fog off the window and peered outside. The glass was slightly opaque, and twilight was falling, but she could just make out the forms of Lord Maidstone and Simon riding their horses alongside the vehicle.

The greenery that had been their backdrop for most of the journey had disappeared. Buildings now lined their path. Dogs barked. The babel of voices coming from the crowded, narrow street was muted inside the carriage, but Isla could hear the louder cries of those hawking their wares on the street corners. Oysters, pies, and chestnuts. Isla's unsettled stomach rebelled at the thought.

"Are we getting close to our final destination?" she asked. Standing upright in some fresh air was the only thing that might save her.

Martha took her turn peering out through the rudimentary glass. "Once we have crossed London Bridge, it will not take long to reach the house."

London Bridge in 1605. It had been the only bridge across the Thames, and the tall, timbered structures that lined it had served as kindling when the Great Fire had swept through the city six decades later. Isla wiped at the window again, hoping for a better view. Lord Maidstone and Simon must have moved ahead of the carriage because the road was even narrower now, barely wide enough for the carriage to pass by. The buildings pressed in on them, leaving little room for sunshine or fresh air. Isla could smell the chimney smoke even though the carriage was enclosed. Perhaps it was smog obscuring her view.

"I do not like bringing the boys to London," Martha said. "They are curious and eager to see the sights, but the chaos, the squalor, and the stench . . ." She shook her head. "If I am able, I shall spare them from experiencing those things a little longer."

"I understand," Isla said. "Though it must be difficult to be apart for so long."

"It is." Martha managed a brave smile. Along with missing her sons, she was probably feeling the negative effects of the juddering ride too. "But they will be well cared for at Copfield Hall, and we have important work to do here."

Isla's queasy stomach did a slow roll. The closer they'd come to London, the harder it had become to ignore the primary purpose of their journey. Lord Monteagle's dinner was tomorrow night. A full eight days before the opening of Parliament. With the twins far away, Simon had better come up with a good alternate diversion for the meantime, or she was going to go crazy.

She closed her eyes and pictured the boys as she'd last seen them, playing with their tops in the nursery. It had been hard to say goodbye, not knowing exactly what her future held. But no matter what happened to her, they would have their parents and Simon. Protecting them—and the hundreds of other people who would be in the vicinity of the House of Lords on November 5—had to be her focus.

Their progress was slower now. The carriage stopped occasionally, only to jerk forward again a few moments later. With the oncoming darkness, it seemed as though the congestion on the roads might clear. The lack of street lights probably made for an early night for merchants and shoppers alike. Occasionally, Isla spotted a candle flickering in the window of a building. It should have been a comforting sight, but as the shadows deepened, she found herself growing more and more uneasy at the strangeness of it all.

At last, the carriage came to a stop outside a tall building. Large timbers framed the house, and each of the windows on the upper level glowed warmly with candlelight.

Martha gave a heartfelt sigh of relief.

"We've arrived?" Isla guessed.

"Thankfully, yes." She smiled. "Welcome to Maidstone House."

Before Isla could respond, the door to the carriage opened, and Lord Maidstone appeared. He extended an arm toward his wife.

"It appears that the servants are ready for us, my dear."

Martha took his hand and eased herself out. "Thank goodness for that. Let us hope there is a warm fire burning in every room."

Isla waited for Martha to exit and then shuffled along the bench toward the opening. She had just reached the doorway when Simon materialized out of the darkness.

"May I assist you?" he asked, offering her his hand.

Moving slowly and stiffly, she accepted his help. "Thank you."

Once she was standing, he studied her with a concerned expression. "How are you faring?"

"A bit rocky." She took a hesitant step forward. Remarkably, her legs cooperated.

"Which is more similar to a rock? Your limbs or your stomach?" he asked.

She grimaced. "Neither. They're both like a wobbly jellyfish."

"I fear that long carriage rides are not for the faint of heart—or stomach."

"You should have warned me. I might have persuaded Martha to let me ride Belle."

"Had you managed that remarkable feat, you would assuredly be extremely saddle sore and significantly chilled."

He was right. But if they'd been riding together and talking like they'd done at Copfield Hall, he might have been able to ease her burgeoning worries.

"I should probably go in," she said. "Martha will be wondering what's become of me."

"Undoubtedly." He didn't move. "Isla?" She sensed his scrutiny. "Is there something more than physical discomfort ailing you?"

"We're in London, Simon." Her voice caught, and she lowered it to a whisper. "And it's a little over a week until November 5."

He had yet to release her hand, and now his fingers tightened around hers. "True, but remember, you are not facing any of the things that lie ahead alone."

"I know. And I'm grateful. It's just that . . ." She faltered. "The outcome is so important."

"It is." He lifted her hand to his lips and pressed a kiss to her fingers. "And you shall manage it. We all shall."

She could barely put one foot in front of the other, and now her fingers were tingling as though she'd received an electric shock, but she nodded.

"Okay?" His teeth gleamed in the darkness, and she knew he was smiling.

"Okay," she repeated. "And that will have to be the last modern word I use until this madness is over."

His smile disappeared, and he released her hand to grasp her elbow. "Come," he said. "I shall walk you to the door."

"There you are, Isla." Martha appeared, silhouetted in the faint light coming from inside the house. "Come in out of the cold." She turned to Simon. "I assume you plan to ride with us to Lord Monteagle's gathering tomorrow?"

Isla knew a moment of panic. Simon was leaving. She'd known he would be staying at his own lodgings, but she didn't want him going there now. Something was off, and she didn't want to part like this. In a matter of seconds, he'd gone from treating her as though he really cared to being all business.

"I think that would be best," he said, responding to Martha's question. "When would you like me to be here?"

"Isla and I shall be busy all day," Martha said. "We have a great deal to do and much to review before the dinner. I imagine six o'clock will suit."

As much as Isla liked Martha, a day full of lessons on social protocols sounded awful. She touched Simon's arm. "Please come early," she whispered.

He gave no indication that he'd heard her, but after offering them both a polite nod, he moved to stand beside his horse. "Until tomorrow, then," he said, mounting in one graceful movement. "I shall aim to be here by five o'clock."

Isla's relief and accompanying smile was instant, but Simon was already wheeling Blaze around and probably didn't see it.

——— · * · ———

Thin slivers of sunlight traced lines upon the wooden floor in Simon's bedchamber. He rolled over, the mattress beneath him rustling noisily. It was a new day, and outside, Londoners were going about their business. The pie man who stood on the nearby corner every morning was in fine fettle, his insistent voice cutting over the sounds of wagon wheels, barking dogs, and the thud of shutters and doors opening and closing.

Simon groaned. He'd been gone from Copfield Hall for less than a day, and already, he missed the tranquil mornings, his invigorating gallops across the countryside, and the anticipation of seeing Isla waiting for him outside the stables. Mostly, he missed Isla. And that was a highly disconcerting realization. Particularly after her poignant reminder last night that she considered her present situation to be madness.

It had taken him under ten minutes to traverse the short distance from Maidstone House to his rented rooms a few streets north of the Strand. Not long by any means but just enough time to reclaim his equilibrium after he'd so manifestly lost his footing. He'd sensed Isla's distress when she'd exited the carriage. The depth of his desire to relieve her of her discomfort had taken him by surprise. Holding her hand, kissing her hand—they had been instinctive. Token attempts at comforting her. Thankfully, she would never know how tempted he'd been to draw her into his arms and kiss her lips instead.

No matter Martha's plans for the day, if Belle were stabled with Blaze, he'd be tempted to invite Isla to go out with him this morning. Simply to calm her nerves. Unfortunately, betrothed or not, such an outing would go against every act of decorum Martha was trying to instill in Isla. It was one thing for Isla to join him on a leisurely amble across a pasture; it was quite another to ride side by side through the streets of London. If the stablehands had wished to watch them, he and Isla would have been within their sights all the way to the log and back. Such was not the case on the meandering city streets, however. And if Lady Whitely and her ilk caught sight of them without a chaperone, they would fuel London gossip for weeks.

The easy solution, of course, was the inclusion of a chaperone. But the presence of anyone other than Martha or Maidstone would prevent them from speaking of the true reason they were in London, and any reassurance Simon might have offered Isla ahead of the dinner would be severely diminished. As much as he wished it were different, it would be better for Isla if he kept his distance today and allowed her to focus on her preparation.

Climbing out of bed, Simon walked to the window. He drew back a portion of the curtain and pushed open the shutter. The outside noise instantly increased in volume.

"Pies! All 'ot! Eel, beef, and mutton pies! Penny pies! All 'ot!" The pie man on the corner appeared to be doing a good business already.

Simon dropped the curtain back into place and crossed to the chair where he'd set his breeches and jacket. Following a familiar routine may be the only way to survive the next few hours. His manservant, Anson, had arrived at his lodgings before him and had unloaded his trunk and set the place to rights. Indeed, everything was exactly as it should be. Anson could not be blamed if the sense of peace and homecoming that Simon was accustomed to experiencing upon returning had been replaced by a feeling of loneliness.

He'd send Anson out for a pie, and once Simon had eaten, he would take Blaze for a ride. Lack of fresh air and rolling hills notwithstanding, a long ride was exactly what he needed to take his mind off this evening's critical events and the young lady at the center of them all.

CHAPTER 13

T here now." Maggie stepped aside to allow Isla a clear view of herself in the mirror.

Isla gazed at her reflection. She scarcely recognized the person staring back at her. Gone was the smartly-dressed government employee she usually saw there. The casually attired twenty-four-year-old she occasionally saw on a Saturday was also missing. In their place was a young woman who belonged in an oil painting at the National Gallery.

"You have worked wonders, Maggie."

Maggie smiled. "The gown looks lovely on you, miss."

The pale-blue skirt and waistcoat were covered with white embroidered flowers. A wheel-shaped farthingale held the skirt in a wide dome and was topped with a ruffle of extra fabric. Narrow sleeves ended a couple of inches above her wrists, and a tall Medici collar encircled the back of her neck. Her neckline in front was lined with lace and white ribbon rosettes, and her hair was piled high over cloth pads that the maid had placed on top of her head. Teased and braided, her hair was studded with tiny pearls that sparkled in the candlelight.

"You are kind to say so, but I think your workmanship would look beautiful on anyone."

Maggie's cheeks flushed at the praise. "Thank you, miss."

"And you even managed to insert a pocket for me." Isla ran her right hand down the skirt's side seam. The many layers of fabric hid the narrow opening where Maggie had attached a hidden but marvelously deep pocket.

"Ever so clever, it is. I'd never 'eard of such a thing afore, but I'm of 'alf a mind t' put them into every skirt I make from now on."

Isla smiled. "If you did, I believe you would win over every lady who was fortunate enough to wear something you made. Where I'm from, ladies are always wanting pockets in their clothing."

There was a light knock on the door. Moments later, a man-servant walked in. He bowed.

"I beg your pardon, Miss Crawford," he said. "Lord Bancroft asked that I inform you that he has arrived."

Isla's pulse tripped. Her thoughts had turned to Simon more often than she cared to admit today. Martha had kept her busy from the moment she'd first emerged from her bedchamber, but without her morning ride and conversation with Simon, nothing about the day had seemed quite right.

Running her fingers down her skirt's heavy fabric, she took one last look in the mirror. She, Martha, and Maggie had done all they could to prepare for this evening. She was dressed for the part. The time had come to act it.

Emulating Martha's polite incline of the head, she acknowledged the servant with a small smile. "Please tell His Lordship that I will join him shortly."

"Very good, miss." The servant bowed a second time and slipped out of the room.

Maggie gathered up the few ribbons and pins remaining on the nearby table. "If you 'ave no further need o' me, miss, I'd best see if there's anything more I can do for 'Er Ladyship."

"Yes, please do," Isla said. "Thank you for all your help, Maggie. I'm very grateful."

Martha's lady's maid bobbed a curtsy. "My pleasure, miss."

Maggie exited the room, and Isla eyed the narrow doorway uneasily. Over the last few weeks, she had become used to wearing the farthingale Mrs. McQuivey had given her. The one she was now wearing, however, was significantly wider. It might have been wise to add practicing sitting and navigating doorways in excessively wide skirts to the many things Martha had reviewed today. Pressing down on the billowing fabric, Isla shimmied through the narrow opening. Her skirts brushed the doorframe, but the farthingale shifted to allow her through. Grateful to have that minor obstacle behind her, she hurried down the poorly lit passage to the stairs that led to the ground floor.

The wooden stairs creaked as she descended, but as far as Isla could tell, the sound forewarned no one of her arrival. The small entryway at the base of the stairs was empty. She paused, listening. Male voices reached her from the nearby parlor. She moved toward the half-open door, stopping when she was close enough to see inside. Simon was standing with his back to her, talking to Lord Maidstone. Both gentlemen were elegantly dressed, Simon in maroon with gold trim and Lord Maidstone in black with silver and red embellishments. Each wore a white ruff collar and hose.

"Did Monteagle give you any indication as to who else has been invited to this dinner party?" Simon asked.

"None," Lord Maidstone said. "Miss Crawford was unable to recall any details regarding the size of the gathering, so even the numbers are unknown at this point."

Isla winced. Truth be told, almost everything about this evening was unknown. Including whether or not she would need to orchestrate the delivery of her letter. Wishing she could roll some of the tension out of her shoulders but knowing that her stays and fitted bodice made such movement almost impossible, she gathered her courage and entered the room with a swish of her skirts.

"Good evening," she said.

Simon swung around. His mouth opened, but whatever response he had intended to give appeared to die on his tongue. Snapping his mouth closed again, he stared at her.

"Miss Crawford." Lord Maidstone inclined his head. "You look most elegant this evening."

Lord Maidstone's comment seemed to rouse Simon from his stupor. "Indeed." He cleared his throat. "You are truly stunning, Isla."

"Thank you." His compliment brought an unexpected rush of pleasure. "Martha and Maggie deserve all the credit."

"Nonsense." Martha swept into the room behind her, a vision in lavender and lace. "I grant you that Maggie is a marvel with a needle, but I know of few young ladies who could model her creations so well."

If the warmth in Isla's face was any indication, over the last couple of seconds, she had gone from pleasantly pink to red as a beetroot. It was time to deflect everyone's attention. Lowering her head, she fumbled for the hidden opening in her skirt. "Allow me to show you just how talented Maggie is," she said. "I told her I needed a pocket large enough to contain a letter, and she sewed one into the seam." Isla's fingers found the opening, and she turned slightly so as to show the gentlemen. "You see? A protected fold of fabric in which I can hide the letter to Lord Monteagle, and no one will know it is there. Nothing in my hands and no purse at my waist."

Simon stepped forward. "You call it a 'pocket'?"

"Yes." She tucked her hand inside. "Pockets hidden in garments are another wonder of future clothing."

"Ah! This is the innovation I would have learned about had we taken a morning ride today."

Isla smiled. "Yes."

"Do you have the letter, Hugh?" Martha asked.

"I do." Lord Maidstone crossed to the fireplace and removed a folded paper from behind a candlestick. "It is sealed and ready for Monteagle."

"Will it fit in that small cavity in Isla's skirt?" Martha asked.

Lord Maidstone handed it to Isla. Under everyone's watchful eyes, Isla slid it into the pocket and then turned to show them that it had disappeared.

"Remarkable," Lord Maidstone said.

Martha clapped her hands. "That is perfect. Now, before we leave, we must devise a plan for the evening."

Simon leaned a little closer to Isla. "Has she been issuing commands all day?" he whispered.

Isla shook her head. "She's been marvelous. Without her, I may not have been brave enough to rise from my bed." She met his eyes. "I missed our morning ride."

His expression softened. "As did I."

Isla pressed her hand to her bodice, wishing the fluttering internal butterflies away. No matter how much she enjoyed being with Simon or how handsome he looked this evening, she needed to remember that their time together was limited. Like Lord Maidstone and Martha, he was attending Lord Monteagle's dinner for the greater cause.

"Isla," Martha said, "would you tell us what you recall about this evening's events once more?"

"Of course." Isla pushed aside her muddled thoughts to focus on those few details. "When one of Lord Monteagle's servants leaves the house to take some air, he will be handed a letter by a stranger. The stranger will request that he take it to his master immediately. Lord Monteagle will be at the table, his hands sticky, and so he will request that the servant read the missive aloud. All in attendance will hear, and its contents will fuel a discussion that ultimately leads Lord Monteagle to take the note to Cecil."

"How long should we wait before we act?" Lord Maidstone asked.

Martha appeared thoughtful. "I would surmise that the Monteagles will serve at least six courses. If the servant has not produced a letter by the end of the fourth course, I believe it would be wise to delay no longer."

"I shall escape the room to deliver the letter," Simon said.

"You cannot, Simon," Isla said. "None of you can. It has to be me. I am the only one who would be a stranger to the servant."

"You will not be a stranger if he sees you enter the house to attend the party," he said.

"Do you have an old cloak I may borrow, Lord Maidstone?" she asked.

"Why, yes," the gentleman responded, clearly startled at the sudden change in topic. "Although, I fear it will be far too large."

"All the better," Isla said. "If we take an extra cloak and hide it somewhere near the door, I can don it upon exiting. An oversized hood will hide my face, and I can also draw heavily on my Yorkshire accent when called upon to speak." After a few sleepless nights, it was the best idea she'd come up with.

"How do you hope to explain leaving the table?" Simon asked.

"I will remain as quiet and inconspicuous as possible during the meal. It is quite possible that I shall leave and return without anyone noticing."

"Dressed as you are this evening," Simon said, "that is highly improbable. The eyes of every gentleman in the room will be upon you from the moment you walk in."

Isla experienced a moment of panic. She hoped he was joking. "I am attending as your betrothed. As far as everyone else knows, I am spoken for, and no one need engage me in conversation."

Simon ran his fingers through his hair, appearing unconvinced. "A pleasant thought, to be sure, but unlikely to occur."

"Even if Isla's absence is noted," Martha said, "no one would suspect Lord Bancroft's betrothed of being outside in the dark on her own."

"For the simple reason that she should not be," Simon muttered.

Isla attempted a reassuring smile. "I'm not afraid of the dark."

"The dark is not what worries me," he said.

"Come, now, Bancroft," Lord Maidstone said. "Monteagle lives in an affluent area of town. Footpads will not be lurking at his doorway." He must have taken Simon's lack of disagreement as a good sign because he continued. "It may be that the all-important letter arrives without our involvement. We shall hope for that. But if not, I believe it must be Miss Crawford who delivers it."

Simon glared at his brother-in-law. "Why would you send a young lady on an errand such as that?"

"Because I agree that she is the only one of us who can manage it. With political unease and distrust rampant amongst our peers, neither you nor I could leave the table only to return moments before or after the reading of the letter without arousing the suspicion of all."

Simon's jaw tightened, his expression grim. "But Isla is—"

"An extraordinarily resourceful young lady," Martha supplied. "Look at how much she has overcome and accomplished since she arrived." She stepped closer and placed a comforting hand on Simon's arm. "I appreciate your wish to spare her, but if we are right, she was sent here for a reason. For *this* reason. It is her role to fulfill."

"And if something goes wrong?"

"We assist her," Martha said.

"How?"

"We will all need to do what we can to deflect attention away from her—and her absence."

"And what of her safety when she is gone from us?" Simon asked.

"If she has not reappeared by the time the servants bring in the last course, one of us shall go after her," Lord Maidstone said.

"Can you manage the assignment in that amount of time, Isla?" Martha asked.

It was an impossible question to answer.

"That is my hope," Isla said.

Simon's concerned eyes met hers. "You are sure of this?"

Sure that she could manage it? Not at all. Sure that she must be the one to try? Absolutely. "Yes," she said.

"Very well." His verbal agreement notwithstanding, he had yet to relax his stance. "What more need we discuss?"

"Nothing," Martha said, a hint of pride in her voice. "Isla is ready. Not only does she look the part, but she has not used an unfamiliar word since she walked into this house. For her own peace of mind, however, I have suggested that she remain close to you or me for the duration of the evening."

"Good," Simon said. "That portion of the plan I can wholeheartedly endorse."

———··✳··———

Twilight was the perfect time of day for work of a clandestine nature. There was sufficient light to allow Guy to see his way, yet the oncoming darkness concealed his features from any possible passersby. He preferred to roam the city streets at this tenebrous hour on most occasions, but it was especially important when he was approaching a building he intended to demolish.

A young man drew closer, two small dogs at his heels. His rapid footsteps and occasional yank on the leads in his hand suggested that he felt no particular affection for the creatures. A servant tasked with walking his mistress's pets, Guy surmised. The poor fellow was undoubtedly anxious to complete the assignment and return to the warmth of his master's house. Just as well. With a fixed destination in mind, the servant would pay little attention to Guy.

Regardless of the young man's seeming disinterest, however, Guy angled his face away as they passed each other. Cecil's spies were everywhere. If Guy could pass as Percy's manservant, one of Cecil's men could most certainly assume the role of a dog walker. Guy turned the corner, grateful when the echo of footsteps continued in the other direction. One of the dogs yapped. Guy sneered. The poor sap. If walking spoiled pets was a regular assignment, he should look for another position.

Another few yards and Guy had reached the first structure in the jumble of buildings that made up the Palace of

Westminster. The London landmark had been a symbol of political power for centuries, yet he would level it. Guy's pulse quickened. With one small flame, he intended to bring the English government to its knees.

A feeling of power, hot and heady, licked through his veins. He picked up his pace, passing the shadowy form of two more buildings before reaching the one that housed the House of Lords. Voices reached him. He stopped. Where were they coming from? Keeping his steps steady and even, he continued forward. It must not appear that he had any particular interest in the building ahead. Or in the two men conversing near the main door.

A muttered curse passed Guy's lips. He had been gone from London long enough that it was imperative that he check on the condition of the gunpowder. Coming here alone had been a risk—one he had been willing to take for the sake of expediency—but he could not access the undercroft beneath the Lords' Chamber without alerting the men to his activity. No matter the inconvenience, he would have to return later. The last thing he needed was one—or both—of them asking what he was about.

Tugging the brim of his hat another half inch lower, he continued past the two men, past the other palace buildings, and on to the road that led to the docks. If the men had noticed him at all, they would assume he was heading for the bawdier nightlife beside the river. Few gentlemen who frequented the docks at night wished their identity known. His lack of greeting would likely be accepted and shrugged off.

The exhilarating buzz of expectancy defused inside him, leaving him angry. There was no way of knowing how long those gentlemen would loiter outside the House of Lords. Guy would need to circle around to reach Percy's rented house by another route. It was one more in a seemingly never-ending stream of precautions and aborted efforts. He uttered a grunt of frustration. The razing of the palace buildings could not come soon enough.

CHAPTER 14

Candles illuminated the windows of Monteagle's manor. Up ahead, another carriage pulled forward, stopping opposite the front doors. Simon watched as a couple descended. It was too dark to identify them, but based on the gentleman's bearing, Simon judged him to be older than those riding in the Maidstones' carriage.

The journey to Hoxton had been excruciatingly long. Simon could have traversed the thirty furlongs to the Monteagles' elegant house on the outskirts of the city in less than half the time had he been riding Blaze. But he'd had no desire to exchange his place beside Isla in the carriage for his saddle. The two of them sat opposite Maidstone and Martha, and although Martha had done an admirable job of maintaining small talk for most of the journey, they had now lapsed into a silence born of anxious anticipation.

Isla's voluminous skirts covered a great deal of the seat. If her stiff posture was any indication, she did not find her attire overly comfortable. Simon, however, could find no fault with it. Her appearance in the parlor this evening had quite literally taken his breath away. If Maidstone had not unwittingly given Simon a moment to collect himself by greeting her first, Simon would have been proved a complete simpleton. Even now, he marveled that he had managed to string more than two words together so soon after his lungs had suspended their normal operation. He shook his head slightly. Perhaps the greater wonder was that Isla seemed completely oblivious to her exquisite appearance.

He glanced at her. Moonlight coming in through the window painted her face paler than usual, but she wore a look of quiet determination.

"Martha is correct, you know." He kept his voice low, knowing that the rumble of the carriage wheels was enough to mask a private conversation.

She turned to him. "Correct about what?"

"You are truly remarkable."

Her smile was strained. "I have offered up more than one prayer that I do not prove myself a remarkable failure this evening."

The carriage rolled to a stop, swaying unexpectedly. Isla set her hand on the seat between them to steady herself.

"I am confident that you can accomplish whatever you set your mind to," he said.

"I wish that were true."

"Believe it." He reached for her hand and squeezed it gently. "All that you've learned in preparation for this evening notwithstanding, the way you have so masterfully altered your speech is proof enough."

Isla gave him a knowing look. "You may tempt me all you wish, my lord. I shall not break down and say okay."

Simon grinned. He had missed their bantering. "As we are without mounts at present, that might be for the best."

She shook her head at the weak jest, but he noted that the tension in her fingers had lessened.

A servant opened the carriage door. Maidstone exited first, the extra cloak he'd brought with him tucked beneath his arm. He reached back to assist Martha. Simon followed, glad that he had the opportunity to reclaim Isla's hand to help her out immediately afterward.

She barely had her feet under her when Maidstone stepped closer. "The cloak is beneath the shrub to the left of the front steps," he said. "I took advantage of the servants' preoccupation with unloading the carriage to place it out of sight."

Isla strained to see the small bush in the darkness. "Thank you, my lord. I shall find it."

He nodded and then offered Martha his arm. "I believe the time has come, my dear."

They started toward the door.

Simon turned to Isla. "Are you ready?"

"Not remotely," she said, and then she set her hand upon his arm. "But seeing as I likely never will be, we'd best go in anyway."

Attempting to smother his own apprehensions, Simon summoned an encouraging smile. "As you wish."

The Monteagles' house was much like the other manors that had been built in Hoxton over the last few decades. Tarred wooden frames and limewash-painted wattle and daub gave the house a clean, black-and-white appearance. Inside, the wood-paneled entrance hall led directly into the great hall, where, if the sound of chatter and laughter was any indication, many people were already gathered.

"It sounds like a big group," Isla said.

"We may be surprised. Voices tend to echo through the rafters in larger rooms." He led her through the open doors. A fire burned brightly in the enormous fireplace. Two long wooden tables had been set end to end and were lined with cushioned stools. Goblets, knives, and trenchers marked the place settings. Simon made a rapid, silent count of the seats. "The table is set for sixteen."

"And I know only three people," Isla said. "That might make it easier if I'm called upon to slip out."

A titter of forced female laughter sounded at Simon's left. Without turning his head, he knew its source. The sound had inspired dread and frustration in the past, but this evening, those emotions did not come. With an unexpected feeling of release, he offered Isla an apologetic look. "You may be acquainted with more than three. I believe Lady Whitely is here, and if she is here, it stands to reason that her husband and perhaps even her daughter and son-in-law are also in attendance."

Isla's eyes met his, and by the light of the many candles in the room, he saw the concern shining there. "I am very sorry."

"There is no need. My meeting with Lydia at Copfield Hall taught me that whatever feelings I had for her were superficial at best, and I can now face her—and her family—with polite indifference. Indeed, if I am being completely honest, I must own to some relief." He lowered his voice. "Lady Whitely would have been an extremely trying mother-in-law."

Isla's soft laughter warmed his heart. It had been too long since he'd heard it.

"It seems that mother-in-law problems transcend the centuries," she said.

"Would your mother be similarly challenging?"

She pondered the question for a moment. "Given that my brother-in-law and sister-in-law seem to enjoy visiting my parents, perhaps not."

"Is she very like you?"

"In some ways, I suppose. She's a far better nurse than I could ever be. On the other hand, she's never ridden a horse."

It was Simon's turn to laugh, and he was hit by a completely irrational desire to meet Mrs. Crawford. "Given the opportunity, I would be happy to teach her."

Isla's smile held a hint of sadness. "I think you would get along very well."

"Lord Bancroft!" Lady Whitely's grating voice interrupted their conversation, and moments later, the older woman stood before him. "And Miss Crawford! What an unexpected surprise."

Simon bowed, and Isla executed a polite curtsy.

"Lady Whitely," he said. "Always a pleasure."

"Miss Crawford," the older lady said. "May I introduce my husband, Lord Whitely."

The gentleman approached with a slight limp. He acknowledged Simon with a nod. "Miss Crawford, is it?"

"Yes, my lord," Isla said.

He eyed her curiously. "Betrothed to Bancroft, I hear."

"Yes, my lord," she repeated.

"Hmm. I daresay you shall be comfortable enough."

Mentally expanding his gratitude over escaping any relationship with Lady Whitely to include her disdainful husband, Simon was spared from defending himself by Isla's swift response.

"More than comfortable, my lord. Lord Bancroft has ample means and has already proved himself to be extraordinarily solicitous. To be quite frank, I cannot imagine marrying anyone finer or more well suited to me." Lord Whitely's skeptical snort would have been sufficient to silence most young ladies. Unfortunately for the gentleman, Isla was built of sterner stuff. Her chin rose a fraction. "What would you consider to be your strongest attributes, my lord?"

"Why, I have never given it any thought," he blustered.

"Perhaps you have an especially open mind, thoughtful disposition, and uncommon civility," she said. "Those would be praiseworthy indeed and would mean that you share *some* of Lord Bancroft's honorable traits."

It was the closest Simon had ever come to seeing Whitely sputter. The gentleman's face turned an unpleasant shade of purple. Lady Whitely, on the other hand, was uncommonly pale, her lips pressed together in a disapproving, thin line.

"Good evening, Lord Bancroft. Miss Crawford." Blissfully oblivious to her parents' state of displeasure, Lydia approached them, her husband at her side.

Simon bowed, grateful for the diversion, regardless of its source. "Your Graces." He waited for Isla to rise from her curtsy. "Isla, may I introduce the Duke of Tunstow. Tunstow, Miss Isla Crawford."

"A pleasure, Miss Crawford," Tunstow said, inclining his head.

"Thank you, Your Grace." Isla smiled politely, but Simon sensed a shift in her mood. For some reason, she was more on guard with Tunstow than she had been with Lydia's parents. He found that curious, but he had no desire to extend this meeting any longer than courtesy demanded, and if Isla felt similarly, he was happy to make their excuses.

"It was good of you to join us," Simon said, "but out of deference to our hosts, I had best introduce Miss Crawford to Lord and Lady Monteagle before we are called to the table."

"Of course," Tunstow said, stepping aside to allow them passage.

A flicker of regret touched Lydia's eyes, but her smile was understanding. Lady Whitely offered them a curt nod. Lord Whitely ignored them. Simon took Isla's elbow and guided her away from the small group and toward their hosts.

"Tell me your father is more agreeable than Whitely," he said.

"Infinitely," Isla said. "I can think of two politicians and one university professor who might match Lord Whitely's discourtesy, but my father would be more likely to offer you a drink and then invite you to watch a football game with him."

"A football game?" Simon asked.

"I shall tell you about it the next time we go for a ride."

With the promise of another outing together, the evening seemed suddenly brighter. "Come," he said. "Monteagle and his wife are looking this way."

He led Isla toward the portly man wearing an elaborately embroidered blue doublet and jerkin with a wide ruff around his short neck. The fair-haired lady beside him was wearing pale green, and the ruff at her neck was even wider than her husband's.

"Lord and Lady Monteagle," Simon said, executing a low bow. "May I introduce my betrothed, Miss Isla Crawford."

Isla curtsied. "It is an honor to meet you," she said. Her eyes lingered on Lord Monteagle, and Simon was struck with the unsettling thought that for the first time since she'd arrived in this time period, Isla was meeting someone she had read about in her history books.

"The pleasure is ours, Miss Crawford," Monteagle said.

"Yes, indeed," his wife concurred. "I was thrilled to learn that Lord Bancroft is to be married. May I offer you both my congratulations."

"Thank you, my lady," Simon said. "I am a most fortunate gentleman."

Even as he spoke the words, the truthfulness of the statement struck him. It was possible that his good fortune would last only another week or so, but he was grateful for the time he had been given with Isla.

Lady Monteagle smiled. "I daresay Miss Crawford feels the same, my lord. We are glad that you could both join us for dinner."

"And with that said, I believe we should take our places at the table." Monteagle's jovial voice carried across the room, and the hum of multiple conversations dimmed. All eyes turned toward their hosts. Monteagle gestured at the long table. "Ladies and gentlemen," he said, "please be seated."

---- · ✳ · ----

Lord Monteagle sat at the head of the table in the only chair. His wife and guests were seated on stools. Lady Monteagle was at his right, with the Duke of Tunstow and Lydia beside her. Across from them, Lord Maidstone and Martha were seated beside Lord and Lady Whitely. Upon taking her place next to Simon farther down the table, Isla had been offered a brief introduction to the other guests seated near them: Lord and Lady Byrdsall, Mr., Mrs., and Miss Ellerson, and Mr. Tanner. They all seemed pleasant enough, and she couldn't help but be glad that the Byrdsalls and Ellersons separated her from the Whitelys. Not only had she developed a strong dislike for the couple, but it would be far easier to slip out of the room if Lady Whitely's attention were directed elsewhere.

Surprisingly, Isla's impression of Lydia was more positive. She hated the way the young lady had treated Simon, but under different circumstances, she thought it likely that she and Lydia might have been friends. In an odd sort of way, Isla was glad. It meant that Simon's judgment was not skewed. Lydia would probably have made him a very good wife—if the Duke of Tunstow had not interfered.

She glanced at the tall, thin gentleman now. His fair hair fell to his shoulders and was thinning on the top of his head. His goatee was scraggly and his teeth crooked, but despite her reluctance to be introduced or to think well of him, Isla had to admit that he had a ready smile and appeared genuinely interested in those around him. She hoped he would be good to Lydia, because there was no doubt in her mind that without his title and money or Lydia's parents' avarice, he would not have won the young lady's hand. Simon was a better man—in all respects.

"You must eat something, Isla."

At Simon's gentle urging, Isla shifted her attention to the trencher in front of them. They had eaten meals at the Maidstones' house on pewter plates. Isla hadn't realized at the time that Martha's passion for the latest fashions extended beyond clothing. Apparently, her table was one of the few that had embraced the individual plates and two-tined forks now used in France.

Isla stabbed a piece of meat with the small dagger in her hand and slid it into her mouth. She hoped it was chicken but couldn't be sure.

"I don't think I can manage much more," she said. Nerves and unfamiliar foods were poor companions.

"Try some bread," he said, tearing a piece off the loaf in the basket at the center of the table and handing it to her.

Isla accepted it but didn't take a bite. "The next course will be the fourth."

"It will."

She glanced at the people sitting closest to her. Mr. Tanner was making a valiant attempt at maintaining small talk with

Miss Ellerson, but most were intent on eating. Isla had made an effort to discourage conversation by averting her gaze whenever she caught someone's eye. It was a shame because she would have loved to learn more about these people and their lives, but this evening, it was more important that she be forgettable.

"I will slip out with the servants after they bring in the platters," she said.

He nodded, his expression serious. "I wish you were not the one tasked with this errand."

"I know. But it must be me."

Simon set the bread in his hand on the edge of the trencher and slid his arm under the table. Moments later, his fingers found hers. He'd held her hand a few times now, and each time, she'd drawn comfort and strength from it. But that was not all. The simple act engendered something else. Something she'd only ever experienced with Simon. It was harder to identify but incredibly powerful. A sense of connection as rare as it was wondrous.

"Given that an unexpected missive has yet to appear, I fear Martha may have the right of it: you were always meant to deliver the letter." His jaw tightened. "But that does not mean I have to like the notion."

Isla didn't like it either, but now was not the time to admit to it. She glanced down the table. Lord Monteagle was speaking with the Duke of Tunstow, a large piece of meat dripping from his knife. If the history books were right, he would allow a servant to interrupt his meal and his conversation. Her stomach churned. Could she really count on the accounts in those centuries-old records? Movement at the left of Lord Monteagle caught her eye. She shifted her attention only to meet Lady Whitely's critical gaze.

"I confess, Miss Crawford, though I have asked around amongst many of my friends and acquaintances, I have yet to find anyone familiar with your family." The lady's strident voice carried across the table, effectively silencing everyone else. "Perhaps you would be good enough to tell us more about them."

Simon's fingers tightened around hers, but Isla met Lady Whitely's look without flinching. "My father was raised in a small community in north Yorkshire, my lady. It is not an area familiar to many."

"And your mother?" Lady Whitely pressed.

"Another village, not more than ten miles from my father's home. They met when they were quite young."

"Why did they not stay there? You did tell me you hailed from the city of York."

"I was raised in York, yes. My father is a second son," Isla said. It was true, even if it meant nothing in the modern world. "It was not his place to inherit my grandfather's property."

Lady Whitely sniffed. "So he became a merchant of some sort, I imagine."

"He is a much-sought-after teacher." That was also true. Lady Whitely didn't need to know that his popularity was manifest in his classes at secondary school consistently filling up first rather than in a steady stream of nobles wanting him to tutor their sons.

"Good heavens!" Lady Whitely's exclamation was followed by a murmur of surprise that circled the entire table.

From her position near Lord Monteagle, Martha shot her a worried look, and as the small army of servants arrived to exchange the empty platters on the table for the ones containing the meal's next course, Isla realized that in a few short minutes, she had gone from being almost invisible to being the center of attention.

"Blast the woman!" Simon's frustrated whisper told her that he'd come to the same conclusion. "If she keeps up her infernal prying, I shall come up with another way of facilitating your escape."

"Does your father consider himself an expert in any particular subjects?" the Duke of Tunstow asked.

"The sciences, Your Grace."

"By Jove, in my youth, I would have benefited greatly from a tutor with that expertise."

Under the circumstances, it was a generous thing to say, but Isla would have much preferred to end the discussion. In fact, she *had* to end the discussion. If she was going to leave with the servants, it would have to happen in the next minute or two.

"Forgive me," Simon whispered. "I can think of no other way."

Isla darted him a puzzled glance, but a servant standing between their stools blocked her view of his face. The maid was raising the pitcher in her hand, but before she could pour more mead into Simon's empty goblet, he shifted, bumping her arm. Giving a startled cry, the maid staggered back, her grip on the pitcher slipping. Reddish-brown mead spurted upward, landing on Isla's shoulder and running down her sleeve. The women at the table gave a cumulative gasp.

Lord Monteagle rose to his feet. "What is the meaning of this careless behavior?"

"Forgive me, miss, m' lord." The maid turned her stricken face from one to the other. "I didn't mean t' do it. The jug. It just slipped out o' me 'ands."

"I must take the blame, my lord," Simon said, speaking out quickly to absolve the maid of responsibility. "Your servant deserves no censure. She could not have anticipated my sudden movement."

"It is quite all right." Isla stood. Simon had orchestrated the spill as a means of getting her out of here, and she meant to seize it. "There was no harm done."

"But your beautiful bodice is ruined," Lady Monteagle moaned.

"Not at all." Isla moved away from the table. "If—" She paused to face the quivering maid. "What is your name?"

"A-Agnes, miss."

"If Agnes would be so good as to take me somewhere where I might make use of some water," Isla continued, "I shall simply mop off the worst of it and then return."

"Yes, of course," Lord Monteagle said, the relief in his voice suggesting that he was more than happy to accommodate her proposal.

Interpreting her master's agreement as her cue to leave, the perceptive maid bobbed a hurried curtsy, and with the empty pitcher in her hand, she turned toward the door. "This way, if you please, miss."

Needing no second bidding, Isla hurried after her.

CHAPTER 15

Isla followed the maid down a narrow hall, her thoughts racing. They were moving away from the front of the house, but maybe that was for the best. If she were to be seen leaving through the front door, it might raise questions she was unwilling to answer. Surely there would be a back door associated with the kitchen or the servants' quarters.

They passed three or four closed doors before the smell of roasting meat and baking apples signaled that they'd reached the kitchen. An older woman stood in front of an enormous fireplace. A cauldron-like pot hung over the flames, and as Isla entered, the woman drew a peeled apple out of the pot with a long-handled ladle and set the fruit on a platter beside a dozen others. A younger servant girl then proceeded to pour some kind of syrup over them.

"This way, miss."

Unaware that she'd slowed her steps to watch, Isla turned to see Agnes standing at the entrance of another smaller room.

"This 'ere's the scourin' 'ouse," she said.

The narrow space lived up to its name. Two maids knelt beside a large metal tub, their arms elbow-deep in water. They were scrubbing trenchers, pots, and platters clean.

"Lord Monteagle's guest is needin' some fresh water," Agnes announced from the doorway.

The two girls looked up with a start. The one who looked to be the oldest immediately rose to her feet, and drying her hands on her apron, she crossed to a wooden pail in the corner. "We just dumped th' last of it int' th' tub. I'll fetch some more." She eyed Isla's gown. Even with the room's faint candlelight, the stains were obvious. "Might ya be needin' a rag as well?"

"That would be wonderful," Isla said. "But don't trouble yourself to go for water. I can do it myself."

The maid's eyes widened in shock. To have a member of the upper class offer to do such a menial task was probably unheard of, but Isla had just been gifted a way out of the house, and no matter how many protocols she was bending, she was determined to take it. She reached for the pail. The girl's hesitation was so slight, it was almost unnoticeable, but as she relinquished the pail to Isla, the concern on her face remained.

"Think nothing of this," Isla said. "It will take me only a moment. You have your work to do, and Agnes needs to return to the great hall with more mead."

"As you say, miss." The maid offered her a small rag. "You'll find th' rainwater barrel on th' left, just outside th' back door."

"Thank you." Isla exited the scouring room. "Which door takes me outside, Agnes?"

Agnes pointed down the passage. "That one, miss. It's right after th' cheese room an' bake'ouse."

"Perfect. You've been most helpful, but I can manage now."

Agnes's anxious expression was a mirror image of the scullery maid's. "If you're sure, miss."

"Absolutely. I am perfectly capable of mopping up a spill, and I shall find my own way back to the great hall."

By now, the cook would have the platter of apples ready for Lord Monteagle's guests. She'd heard nothing to suggest that it had already left the kitchen, but she had no doubt it would happen soon. Mentally willing Simon and the Maidstones to slow their enjoyment of the food already on the table so that the delivery of the next course was delayed, Isla hurried toward the exit.

A gust of cold air accompanied the opening of the door. Dropping the rag into the empty pail, Isla slipped outside and closed the door behind her. Moonlight painted the back garden in shades of black and gray. Trees and shrubs appeared in ghostly silhouettes, and at her left, a large barrel partially blocked her view of a gravel path—a path that undoubtedly led to the front of the house. Setting the pail on the ground beside the barrel, Isla lifted her frustratingly wide skirts a few inches higher and started running.

The gravel crunched loudly beneath her feet. Too loudly. She turned the corner of the house and stepped onto the grass. If Lord Monteagle's servant was already outside, he would hear her approach. He must not know that she'd come from within the house. Staying on the grass and moving as quickly as she dared, she followed the silver-ribbon path as far as the next corner. Here she paused to listen. In the darkness, every sound was magnified: the rattle of tree branches in the breeze, the distant hoot of an owl, and the rhythmic thud of footsteps drawing steadily nearer.

Pressing herself against the wall, she peered around the corner. Dark shadows marked the shrubs lining the front of the house. She was within a couple of yards of the spot where Lord Maidstone had hidden his cloak, but did she dare hunt for it now? The footsteps sounded closer. Could it be the servant she was supposed to meet? If so, she had to find the cloak straightaway.

Bending low, she scurried past the nearest bush, aiming for those that grew closer to the steps. A branch caught on her skirt. She tugged at it, and it snapped. She froze, but the footsteps kept coming. Dropping to her hands and knees, she extended her arms, groping in the darkness for the cloak. Rocks, sticks, dirt, thorns. Her fingers encountered everything except what she was looking for. She inched a little closer to the steps. Candles burning in lanterns on either side of the front door partially illuminated this area. It was probably only a matter of seconds before the person approaching the house was close enough to catch sight of her. Offering up a silent prayer for divine help, she thrust her arm around the base of the nearest bush. Thorns scratched her fingers. She pressed her lips together to prevent a cry from escaping, and then she felt it. The soft pile of fabric was pressed against the base of the rosebush. She drew the cloak out, backing away from the illuminated stairs as soundlessly as her voluminous skirts allowed.

She'd almost reached the corner of the house when the front door opened. She held perfectly still. A man exited. Short but broad shouldered, he stood on the top step, gazing out across the front garden. Perhaps he heard the approaching footsteps, too, because he appeared to stiffen.

"Who goes there?" he called.

"You know full well who I am," a man's voice replied. He must have stopped within the shadow of the large ash trees that lined the front lawn because he remained invisible.

The man near the door descended the steps. "No matter that I expect a visit whenever Lord Monteagle entertains, I cannot be too careful."

"Most wise."

The two men were close enough to each other that they could converse in whispers. Isla strained to hear.

"What news?" the newcomer asked. "Any hint that your master is hosting one of Cecil's spies?"

Isla tensed. Lord Maidstone and Simon had warned her of the men who infiltrated Society, gathering information for Sir Cecil. Surely no one at the table this evening fell in that category.

"No mention has been made of the king or the delayed opening of Parliament," the servant replied.

"Any whisper of frustration or hint of defiance?"

"No, sir."

"Hmm." The visitor paused as though thinking through the information. "My friends and I are most appreciative of your allegiance to the Catholic cause, Ward. With good men such as you keeping an eye on the evil and misguided course Protestant nobles intend to pursue, we better know how to counteract their actions."

Isla pressed her hand to her mouth, her thoughts spinning. Ward. That was one of the names she'd been unable to recall. Thomas Ward. He was the servant who read the letter to Lord Monteagle. He was also the man who would inform Catsby that a warning had been sent to his master. It seemed that Sir Cecil was not the only gentleman in London employing spies. The Catholic conspirators had some of their own.

"I aim to do my part with full diligence, sir," Thomas Ward said, his voice low.

"I am glad to hear it." There was the sound of a slap—perhaps a hand on a back or arm. "I trust that you will send word should you learn of anything that might be of value to us."

"I shall."

"Good man."

The visitor was leaving, and that meant Ward would return to the house. Isla fumbled with the cloak, throwing it across her shoulders and raising the hood. Her farthingale held the fabric in a wide circle, but it was long enough to cover all but the bottom few inches of her gown. If she remained in the shadows, Ward might not notice, and if she masked her voice well enough, he might be tricked into thinking she was a short, stout man.

She looked toward the trees. The stranger had chosen his location strategically. Close enough to the house to attract the attention of someone on the front step without raising his voice, yet far enough away to remain anonymous. Isla would do well to follow his example. Ward still had his back to her. A rustle of footsteps suggested that the stranger was already heading back across the lawn to the road. Hoping the retreating man had no further interest in what was happening behind him, Isla darted out from behind the corner of the house. She crossed to the other side of the narrow path in one leap and ran for the closest tree. Sliding her hand into the pocket in her skirt, she pulled out the letter.

Ward stood waiting. Isla inched closer, listening for the distinctive sound of footsteps on the hard-packed road. Moments later, she heard them. The visitor was off the Monteagles' property. Ward must have reached the same conclusion. He turned toward the steps.

"Ward!" The rasp in Isla's voice was partly intentional and partly breathlessness.

The servant swung around. "Who goes there?"

"A friend of your master's."

Ward took a step back, but his gaze remained fixed on the tree that obscured Isla from view. "A friend of my master's would not come to his house only to remain in hiding."

"At times such as these, the very best of friends choose to conceal themselves," Isla croaked. "You know this."

"Why have you come?" Ward asked.

"I bring a message of vital import to Lord Monteagle. You must take it to him this very night. There can be no delay. His very life depends upon it."

"Why should I believe you?"

Isla grasped the tree trunk with tense fingers. Somehow, she had to motivate him to act. "Why should you not?"

Ward's laugh was hollow. "Half of what is spoken abroad these days should not be believed."

"True. But the other half—the half that hints at a change that will impact all true believers—should be taken seriously."

For an agonizingly long three seconds, there was complete silence.

"I will give your letter to Lord Monteagle," he said. "What he chooses to do with it, however, is his concern."

Relief left Isla's knees weak, but she took an unsteady step forward and thrust the sealed message at Ward. "There is no time to lose," she said. "Take it to him directly."

"That is not possible. He is at dinner with guests at present."

"Do not underestimate the urgency of this message," Isla said. "The danger to Lord Monteagle increases with every minute that passes. He must be notified immediately."

The servant grunted his displeasure at her injunction, but he accepted the letter. "You'd best leave here," he said. "No matter whose errand you are on, there is no safety to be had in these parts."

"A well-deserved warning," Isla said, retreating farther into the shadows. "You shall not see me again."

That, it seemed, was the very assurance Ward had wanted. Without another word, he turned and strode across the short distance to the front steps without a backward glance. The moment he entered the house and closed the door behind him,

Isla tore the cloak off her shoulders and tossed it to the ground. Raising her skirts, she raced across the lawn toward the back of the house. Dunking her hands in the rainwater barrel would be enough to wash off the dirt on her fingers. A few splashes on her clothing would give the impression that she had attempted to soak the stains. A modern-day stain-remover stick would have been really helpful right now. Instead, she would simply have to hope that the candlelit grand hall was shadowy enough to mask the new grass stains on her skirt and scratches on her hands.

Simon did not know exactly how long Isla had been gone. He knew only that he could not sit at the table pretending to enjoy his meal much longer. The maid who had led her out of the great hall had returned long ago, her pitcher refilled. But there had been no opportunity to surreptitiously question the servant about Isla's whereabouts, and he was quite sure that Isla would not wish him drawing any attention to her prolonged absence.

He'd told her that he would wait until the sixth and final course was served before going after her, but he'd been rethinking that vow from the moment she'd disappeared. So many things could go wrong. He knew full well that her focus was on seeing the letter delivered to Monteagle and preventing a tragedy of catastrophic proportions. He desired those things just as badly, but he also desperately wanted Isla returned to him safe and uninjured. The depth of that desire was uncomfortably revealing. Their betrothal might be a sham, but his feelings for her were not.

He glanced at Martha. She and Simon were the only people at the table who had yet to finish their poached apples, and he had the distinct impression that she was fully aware of it. He watched her take a tiny bite and then pause to exchange a few words with Lydia. His sister was either suffering from the same lack of appetite that he was, or she was deliberately delaying the servants' removal of the remains of the fifth course.

Across the table, Mr. Tanner set his spoon in his dish with a clatter. An echoing thud sounded from without the great hall. Had that been the front door closing? Simon pushed his half-eaten apple aside, wishing he could do the same for his mounting anxiety. Isla had been gone too long. Something must have happened to prevent her from passing along her letter. His gaze darted to the top of the table again. This time, he caught Maidstone's eye. His brother-in-law's shrug was almost imperceptible, but Simon noticed and understood. The final course would likely be cheeses and would be consumed in no time at all. If a servant was truly meant to make an appearance during the meal, he should have done so by now.

Simon pushed his stool back and had just begun to rise when a servant he hadn't seen before entered the room. Dressed more grandly than those who had served the food, Simon guessed this was Monteagle's personal manservant. Simon dropped back onto his stool, his pulse quickening. The fellow had a sealed letter in his hand.

"Ward?" Monteagle had spotted him. "What are you doing here?"

"I beg your pardon, my lord." The manservant bowed. "A letter was just delivered, and I was told that it must be given to you without delay."

Monteagle frowned. "I am not in any position to read a letter at present." He raised his hands, and even though Simon sat some distance away, he could clearly see the meat juices and apple syrup coating his host's thick fingers.

"Of course, my lord." The servant took a reluctant step back.

"Blast it all, Ward, you cannot come barging in here and wave a mysterious letter beneath my nose only to take it away again unread."

"No, my lord." Ward appeared distinctly uncomfortable. "What would you have me do instead?"

"Why, read it, of course. You can hold it and read it out loud for all to hear. I daresay it might be quite amusing."

Simon swallowed against his suddenly dry throat. He did not dare look at Maidstone or Martha. It was happening. Just as Isla had said it would.

An expectant silence fell across the table. All eyes were on Monteagle's manservant. The fellow straightened his shoulders and broke the seal on the letter. Simon attempted to maintain an air of mild interest even as his chest tightened. He may be one of the only ones in the room who knew what the letter contained, but he could not be sure of the response it would receive.

Ward cleared his throat. "*My lord*," he read. "*I have a care for your preservation; therefore, I would advise you to devise some excuse to shift your attendance at the opening of this Parliament. God and man have concurred to punish the wickedness of this time, and you would be best served to retire to the country, where you may later learn of the events to come. For though there shall be no appearance of any stir, Parliament shall receive a terrible blow, and none shall see who hurts them. May God give you the grace to make good use of this warning.*"

Some of the ladies gasped. Monteagle appeared temporarily dumbfounded.

Whitely issued his signature contemptuous snort. "What rot!" The arrogant gentleman dismissed the message with a shake of his head. "You are being played for a fool, Monteagle."

"How can you be so sure, Whitely?" Maidstone countered. "The letter was exceedingly well written, and everyone in this room is well aware that the king and his policymakers are despised by many powerful men."

Monteagle dipped his fingers into the small washbasin on the table and reached for the cloth beside it, his expression grave. "Who gave you this missive, Ward?"

"I cannot say, my lord. The gentleman wore a hooded cloak and remained in the shadows. I did not recognize his voice."

A heady blend of relief and gratification flooded through Simon's veins, and it was all he could do to prevent a smile from forming. Isla had managed to pass along the letter without divulging her identity—or even that she was no gentleman.

"You see!" Whitely was on his self-important pedestal once more. "No honorable gentleman would send a message in such a secretive, disreputable way. It can only be the work of ne'er-do-wells."

"If you believe that, my lord, you must be wholly unfamiliar with the methods of Cecil's men," Simon said.

Whitely scowled, but before he could respond, the Duke of Tunstow spoke. "Cecil's spies are well known for their clandestine behavior. Could this message have come from one of them?"

"There is only one way to find out." With the passage of time, Monteagle's confidence was returning. "I am well enough acquainted with Cecil; I shall raise the question with him myself."

"Given that his men do not own to being spies, Cecil is unlikely to admit to it," Tunstow pointed out.

"True. But I am not in need of knowing the identity of the deliverer or his master. I simply seek to know if there is any truth behind this warning. If Cecil is aware of the threat, he will surely tell me that much. If he is not, then I shall leave it up to him to determine how to proceed."

"No matter Sir Cecil's response," Lady Monteagle said anxiously, "after so specific a warning, I would wish you to be absent when Parliament reconvenes."

Monteagle leaned over and patted his wife's hand. "Have no fear, my dear. If I am unable to get to the bottom of this myself, I shall insist that Cecil investigate."

"Do you think he will?" Lydia's face was pale, her eyes wide.

Monteagle cast a silencing look at her father. "Yes, Your Grace. Cecil has reached his current position because he is ruthlessly thorough in all that he does. I see no reason to believe he will ignore so troubling a message."

A hum of assent hung over the table. Everyone present was aware of Cecil's unpopular draconian methods. He was more likely to accuse an innocent than allow an innocent to go free. If Whitely thought otherwise, he was wise enough to hold his tongue. No matter what his wife thought of his opinions, it appeared—in this instance, at least—that his daughter had been swayed the other direction.

Monteagle waved his hand, and the servants, who must have been awaiting some kind of signal at the door, flooded forward, platters of cheese and flagons of mead in their hands.

"We shall finish our meal," Monteagle announced, "and then, if you will pardon my discourtesy, I shall ride to Westminster to meet with Cecil. At this juncture, I believe it would be foolishness to ignore the message or the messenger, and so I must act upon the warning with haste."

"Hear, hear." Lord Byrdsall voiced his approval.

"Most wise, my lord," Maidstone said, adding his approbation to Byrdsall's and bringing a gratified smile to Monteagle's face.

"Yes, well, one must do what one must to maintain the law, I always say." Their host waited until the servant at his elbow had refilled his goblet, and then he raised it. "To King James."

All around the table, goblets rose, and a chorus of voices echoed the toast. "King James."

Simon took the obligatory sip of mead, his elation that Monteagle was willing to act upon the warning tempered by the fact that Isla had yet to reappear. She had obviously delivered the letter some time ago. What had become of her?

One of the many servants exchanging empty platters for those covered in a variety of cheeses appeared at his elbow. She leaned forward to remove the trencher containing his half-eaten apple. "May I take this for you, m' lord?"

"You may." Another mouthful of food was beyond him at present.

"Actually, would you be so good as to leave the apple a little longer?"

Simon swiveled at the request and was on his feet before the servant had fully retreated empty-handed. "Isla!" Barely remembering to lower his voice, he seized her hand. "Are you well?"

"I am."

The stains on her gown seemed to have multiplied, and a few strands of hair had fallen free of their pins.

"I was concerned for you," he said. A small leaf was caught on her Medici collar. He reached for it, brushing his fingers against her neck as he pulled it free.

Her cautious smile was a good reminder that they were not alone and could not speak freely.

"Come." He took her hand, straightway noticing the angry scratches that had not been there earlier. "I deeply regret that you were unable to remove the stains from your gown after all this time."

"And I regret that I have been gone for so long." She took her seat, and he did the same. "The scouring house had no fresh water."

"Oh, you poor dear." They had been wise to refrain from speaking plainly. It seemed that Mrs. Ellerson had been eavesdropping, and now her expression was full of sympathy. "You should have returned directly. None of us would have minded your stains."

"That is very good of you," Isla said. It was a ridiculous response to an equally ridiculous comment, but Isla must have gauged Mrs. Ellerson's temperament better than he had because it seemed to please the older lady.

"Well, I have been told that I have a very compassionate nature." Mrs. Ellerson smiled serenely. "I find that it is helpful to remember that we all have to endure such discomfitures at one time or another."

Discomfitures? Simon could scarcely believe the lady's empty-headedness. Lord Monteagle had just received an anonymous threatening note, had chosen to curtail the evening's activities so as to take it directly to Sir Cecil, and the lady was extolling her own empathetic virtues.

Isla took a small bite of the apple on their trencher. "This delicious fruit dessert aside, what more did I miss whilst I was gone?" she asked.

"Lord Monteagle received a rather ominous warning regarding the opening of Parliament," Simon said, jumping in before Mrs. Ellerson could offer any more words of commiseration.

"Oh my!" Isla's voice was filled with concern even as her eyes brimmed with questions.

"He has decided to take the missive directly to Sir Cecil this evening," he told her.

The tension fell from her shoulders as though it were melting butter. "Then, I pray Sir Cecil will know how to act."

"I believe we all entertain the same hope." *Even Whitely.* Simon did not say the words out loud, but he spared the insufferable gentleman a brief glance. It seemed that the arrival of the cheese platter had been enough to redirect Whitely's attention, even if it had not done the same for his daughter. Unlike all the other guests at the head of the table, Lydia was watching Simon intently. Why? Had she seen him take the leaf from Isla's collar and suspected that Isla had been farther than the scouring room? A trickle of unease skittered down his spine. This event could not end soon enough.

As though Monteagle fully concurred with Simon's desire, the gentleman rose from the table. "Ladies and gentlemen, I beg you would excuse me. Lady Monteagle and I invite you to stay as long as you wish, but due to my pressing need to reach Westminster before Sir Cecil retires, I must take my leave."

There was a general murmur of appreciation, and everyone rose. Martha exchanged a quiet word with Maidstone, and as Monteagle strode out of the great hall, they turned to speak with Lady Monteagle.

Guessing that his sister and brother-in-law were as anxious to depart and hear Isla's report as he was, Simon leaned a little closer to Isla. "I believe Maidstone and Martha may be offering Lady Monteagle their thanks and preparing to leave," he whispered. "Shall we do the same?" He sensed her nod and took her elbow. "If you will excuse us." He included all those standing near them. "It appears that Lord and Lady Maidstone are preparing to depart, and as we rode together, we must do the same."

"What a shame," Lady Ellerson said. "Miss Crawford and I were just getting to know one another."

"We shall enjoy it all the more next time, my lady," Isla said.

The older lady gave a gratified smile. "Just so," she agreed.

After inclining his head politely, Simon guided Isla toward the head of the table.

It seemed that Monteagle's withdrawal had prompted the departure of every one of his guests. They milled around the table, expressing thanks to their hostess and farewells to each other. Simon readjusted his course, steering Isla toward Martha.

"I am very sorry, Isla." His sister eyed Isla's soiled gown with concern. "You must be as cold as you are uncomfortable in that wet gown."

"Are you?" Simon asked, chagrined that he hadn't even thought to ask.

"I shall manage very well in the carriage if I have a cloak," she said.

"Do we have an extra cloak available?" Maidstone asked.

Isla shook her head. "No, my lord."

Her message was clear. She had discarded it and had no plans to retrieve it.

"You must wear mine," Simon said.

"Thank you, Simon." Martha claimed Isla's arm. "If you would express your appreciation to Lady Monteagle on Isla's behalf, I shall ensure that Isla is warmly clad in your cloak by the time you join us in the entrance hall."

With no small amount of reluctance, Simon let Isla go and crossed to where Lady Monteagle was taking leave of her guests.

"Lord Bancroft!" Lydia broke away from speaking with her mother and approached him.

Simon hesitated. More than anything, he wished to offer his thanks to Lady Monteagle and be gone from here. With

Isla. But no matter their complicated past, he could not bring himself to snub Lydia. Stifling a sigh, he inclined his head. "Your Grace."

"I need only a moment of your time, my lord." Her hesitation was so fleeting, he wondered if he had imagined it. "I simply wish to offer you an apology."

Simon stared at her. He had not known what to expect, but it was certainly not this.

"You have always treated me with the utmost respect and kindness." Her hands were clenched, and there was a look of determination in her eyes that he had never seen before. "But I am ashamed to admit that the same cannot be said of me. I should have spoken to you—explained my situation more fully—before dissolving our betrothal."

"I . . . I see."

"You deserved better," she continued, "and although I had nothing whatsoever to do with your change in fortune, I am happy that you have been offered it now."

Simon felt quite certain that he should know what Lydia was referring to, but his head was spinning too fast to grasp it. "Offered what exactly?"

Sadness tinged her smile. "You gave me no reason to doubt that you cared for me all those months ago, and had circumstances been different, I truly believe we would have been content together. But I have watched you with Miss Crawford. You never looked at me the way you look at her. It is quite obvious that the two of you share something far more rare and lovely than we ever experienced."

"I . . ." Simon shook his head as if to clear it. Did Lydia have the right of it? Was this why she had been studying him so intently? "I hardly know what to say."

"You do not need to say anything," she said. "My apology stands regardless of whether or not you accept it."

For months, Simon had dreamed of this moment, of the satisfaction he would feel if Lydia ever deigned say those words. But he had never considered that his foremost reaction to her admission would be relief or gratitude.

"Please consider your apology accepted." He could have said more—likely *should* have said more—but the words escaped him.

"I am most thankful, my lord." She smiled, and this time, he caught a glimpse of the carefree Lydia he'd once known. "You have lifted a burden I have carried for too long."

He understood the sensation. On the day he'd walked out of the Whitelys' front parlor in gutted despair, he could never have imagined being fully free of the anguish he'd known then. "I wish you well, Your Grace." He could say that in all honesty now.

"And I, you, my lord." Her smile faltered slightly. "Miss Crawford is lovely. I am sure you shall be very happy together." She bobbed a curtsy and turned to go, unaware that her parting words had pierced him with more pain than joy.

With an all-too-telling ache in his heart, Simon crossed the short distance to Lady Monteagle. He was twice the fool. He had overcome past hurt only to set himself up for even greater injury. If his desperate concern for Isla this evening was any indication, he was well on his way to being fully in love with her. He smothered a groan. Given that Isla could disappear at any moment, never to return, he was in no better position now than he had been when he'd exited the Whitelys' manor alone and for the last time.

CHAPTER 16

S imon sat in the carriage, fighting a silent but torturous inner battle. On the one hand, for the sake of self-preservation, he desperately wished he could remove himself from Isla's captivating presence. On the other hand, he did not want to be anywhere but beside her. Especially while she was recounting her experiences escaping the house, recovering Maidstone's cloak, and confronting Thomas Ward. Her ingenuity and bravery astounded him, but he was aghast at the number of things that could have gone wrong.

"You were marvelous, Isla." Martha spoke from the other side of the carriage. "I cannot think of anyone else who could have managed it. And to have Lord Monteagle respond just as we'd hoped is most encouraging." She paused. "I do wish we were privy to Lord Monteagle's meeting with Sir Cecil though. Or at the very least, had some way of knowing whether the gentleman will act upon the written warning."

"We should not need to worry on that score," Simon said. "If Isla's history books are to be believed, the letter will motivate Cecil to undertake a search of the Palace of Westminster."

"Well, not exactly," Isla said. "Sir Cecil could be swayed either way, but ultimately, he should bring up the matter with the king when he returns to London. It is the king who will order an investigation."

"Regardless of who issues the command," Simon said, "it will surely happen."

"It is unlike you to make so sweeping an assumption, Simon," Martha said. She was peering at him across the shadowy carriage. "I would have thought you would have been as anxious for inside information as I am."

"Inside information would be welcome, but I do not think it is necessary. Everything Isla predicted—from Ward's appearance at dinner to Monteagle's sticky hands to His Lordship's response—occurred just as she said it would. That should give us no reason to doubt that her memory of what happens next is equally sound."

"That may be sufficient for you, Bancroft," Maidstone said, "but I have been married to your sister long enough to know that the same cannot be said for her. She will be pacing the floors until she knows that the threat to the king and England's noblemen is fully defused."

"I most certainly shall," Martha said with feeling. "And regardless of how things went this evening, I am quite sure Isla will do the same. We are relying upon you gentlemen to provide us with adequate reassurance that Sir Cecil has done what he must."

"If that is the case, my dear," Maidstone said, "I believe I shall make a visit to the Earl of Suffolk in the near future."

"You believe Cecil will confide in Suffolk?" Simon asked.

"I do," Maidstone said. "Cecil is the Principal Secretary of State and wields more influence with the king than any other gentleman in the country, but Suffolk is Lord Chamberlain. With the king gone, it is all the more likely that Cecil will consult with Suffolk."

"Then, by all means, go," Martha said. "If he is available tomorrow morning, so much the better."

Her husband chuckled softly. "I believe an afternoon visit in two or three days may be more reasonable."

Martha sighed. "Very well. But the wait will be interminable."

"Do you plan to visit the Maidstones' house again soon, Simon?" It was the first time Isla had spoken since she'd corrected his assumption about Cecil. He had become used to her quiet observance of others, but he sensed that her recent silence had more to do with exhaustion than anything else.

"My plans are not fixed," he hedged. It would be wiser for him to stay away, to become used to being without her. "Are you in need of a day of rest after the events of this evening?"

"Probably. But I don't suppose my body will comply, and I have a horrible suspicion that I will not know what do to with myself now that I no longer need to spend hours studying seventeenth-century comportment."

"I hope it was not as awful as it sounds," he said.

Isla laughed. "Not at all. I shall miss it."

"So shall I," Martha said. "And there is no reason why we need curtail it. We could fill hours discussing menu options for the week or the fashions on display at the Monteagles' event."

Simon cringed on Isla's behalf.

"We could," Isla said with sufficient forced enthusiasm in her voice that Simon knew he would be the worst sort of friend and gentleman if he did not come to her rescue.

"As stimulating as that activity sounds, might I suggest taking a ride past the Palace of Westminster as an alternate pursuit?"

Isla almost covered her mouth fast enough to mask her gasp of delight. But not quite. He grinned. Gone was the young lady who scarcely knew one end of a horse from the other. She may not yet be ready for a spirited mount, but she had developed a love for riding.

"Is that even possible?" she asked.

"If it is something you would enjoy, I am quite sure I can acquire a mount for you for the afternoon." He caught sight of her smile in the moonlight, and whatever defenses he had remaining to him crumbled. "Be warned, however, if you agree to this outing, you owe me a full explanation of a football game."

"I did promise you that, didn't I?" She turned to Martha. "Would you be very disappointed if we saved discussing food and fashion for another time?"

"Not at all. You deserve an outing after all you did this evening, and time spent with Simon is exactly why we contrived your betrothal."

"Yes, I suppose it is."

Isla lapsed into silence, and Simon could not help but wonder if Martha's reminder had hit her as forcibly as it had him. When his sister had first suggested a betrothal between him and Isla, he'd been completely opposed to the notion. He'd acquiesced only for the good of the nation and the safety of his colleagues in the House of Lords. But it had been weeks since he'd considered that aspect of his fabricated relationship with Isla. It had been a critical motivator at the start, and it remained so. But at some point, his primary focus had shifted from saving the king and government to supporting Isla. To being with Isla. And now, with most of the key moves to save England's political structure made, he was trapped in a bizarre world where he had been granted access to the future in one area of his life while he looked to lose all in another.

"Simon?" Isla's whisper brought him back to the present with a start. Martha must have taken the quiet to mean that they were all in agreement, and she was now engaged in a softly spoken conversation with Maidstone. The steady grind of the carriage wheels masked their voices.

Simon shifted to face Isla. "Yes?"

"Thank you."

"For saving you from having to agree to have braised eel for dinner and a discussion of the height of ladies' heels?"

"Yes. And for knowing me so well." The moonlight caught her small smile, and his heart responded.

"In truth, it is quite a remarkable feat, given that we barely speak the same language."

"Yes." She hesitated. "Although I am trying."

Blast it all. Why did she have to be so charming?

"You are doing marvelously well." Seemingly of its own volition, his hand reached for hers, and when her fingers closed around his, he knew he was sunk. He would not let go until he absolutely had to.

———— · ✴ · ————

Guy closed the door of Percy's lodgings and studied the scrap of paper in his hand with a frown. The urchin who had delivered the unsigned note was long gone. Not that he needed to know who had paid the boy to drop it off. There were very few people who considered it their place to give Guy orders and even fewer who knew where to find him. He read the message once more.

> Urgent. Survey for any sign of disturbance, and then meet at WSI at noon to receive update and report on findings.

Irritation smoldered within his chest. Catsby knew Guy sufficiently well to assume that he would have checked on the contents of the cellar at the Palace of Westminster as soon as he'd returned to London. It was equally possible that Catsby had been informed the moment Guy had entered the city. A request for another visit to the site of their gunpowder stockpile so soon afterward—especially one conducted in broad daylight—was pushing the boundaries of Catsby's authority. Guy clenched his jaw. Another meeting, also done during daylight hours, suggested something unforeseen had arisen. Something that could not be delayed. Concern surfaced above Guy's annoyance. What did Catsby know that he was not telling him?

Guy moved to the window and stared down the street. An old man dressed in threadbare clothing pushed an empty cart across the road. Two dogs—strays by the lean, hungry look of them—followed close behind. A woman passed by carrying a basket of flowers. She was likely coming from Bedford House. More than one flower seller gathered there in the mornings before finding a busy corner in the city from which they could peddle their wares. The sun was barely up. Working people were about, but it was too early for members of the nobility. Which might make it the best time to venture into the cellar beneath the House of Lords.

His decision made, Guy donned his hat and cloak and left the house. He walked briskly and with purpose; the sooner he reached his destination, the better. Once there, however, he would employ more caution. His attention to detail had saved him on more than one occasion in Spain. This would simply be one more instance in which his natural wariness proved providential. His lips twisted into a cynical smile. All it would take was opening the door to the storage room and he would instantly know if anyone else had been there.

It took very little time to reach the Old Palace Yard. Much as he'd supposed, there were fewer people here than on the nearby streets. The empty courtyard notwithstanding, Guy slowed his pace, studying the windows and doorways in the buildings across from the undercroft. Shutters covered all but two windows, and there was no sign of life at the open windows. The doors were closed; the only occupant on any of the steps was a solitary mangy cat. Guy continued walking until he turned the corner around the House of Lords. There he stopped to survey the path ahead. It was clear. Satisfied that no one would enter the courtyard for the next minute or two, he retraced his steps until he reached the entrance to the undercroft. With one more careful look around, he withdrew the key from the purse at his belt and hurried down the three steps that led to the solid wooden door.

The lock drew back with a loud thud. Guy waited, his ears strained. Nothing. Pushing the door open, he stood at the threshold and studied the floor. The undercroft had been used as a storage room for years, and the hard-packed dirt floor was pressed smooth. Except at its entrance, where a fine layer of sand coated the floor. An unsuspecting visitor to the room would be hard-pressed to notice, especially in the poor light. But Guy was no unsuspecting visitor.

He studied the floor with a critical eye. The small pail of sand he'd brought to the undercroft weeks ago had proved perfect for his needs. Dusting the area nearest the door with sand every time he left the room was almost as good as employing a watchman. There was no semicircular scrape made by the opening of the door, scuffs left by shoes, or exposed dirt where significant movement had displaced the sand. He gave a gratified nod. No one had entered this way since he was last here.

Stepping sideways to avoid displacing much of the sand, Guy entered the room. He lit the lantern and gently pushed the door closed, then raised the light as he moved toward the far wall. The barrels filled with wine, cider, and gunpowder appeared just as he'd left them. He noticed no displacement of wood, and the small table and chair he had placed in the room in preparation for his long wait on the evening of November 4 had accumulated a thin layer of dust. As far as he could ascertain, fresh rat droppings at the foot of the chair were the only addition to the room.

With a scowl, he kicked the droppings away from the furniture with the toe of his boot. He was tempted to bring a piece of bread laced with hemlock the next time he came. One or two fewer rats might be worth the effort. Then again, he had to endure them only a short time longer, and dead rats were almost as repugnant as live ones. He sneered. Rats and the gentlemen comprising the king's cabinet. They were one and the same. And they would soon come to the same ignominious end.

Satisfied that all was as it should be in the undercroft, he returned to the door and opened it a crack. He tilted his head to listen. No voices. No footsteps. Snuffing out the candle, he set the lantern on the ground and took a fistful of sand from the pail. He then pushed the door open and stepped over the threshold. A quick sprinkle of sand covered the footsteps he'd made before he closed the door and locked it. Grateful to exchange the dank, stale air of the undercroft for the crisp morning air outside, he climbed the steps and surveyed the empty courtyard. No one was visible, but someone was whistling nearby. It was a timely reminder. Once he left the courtyard, there would be more people about.

Lowering his chin, he started to walk. Even if he took a circuitous route to the rendezvous location at the White Swan Inn, he would arrive before the noon hour. But that was just as well. Catsby was known at the White Swan, and although members of the conspiracy had met there often, up until now, it had been done under the cover of darkness, and they had entered through the back door. It was safer for everyone if those at the inn believed Guy was having a chance encounter with Catsby rather than a scheduled meeting.

———·•✳·•·———

Guy had been nursing his goblet of mead in the shadowy corner of the inn's front room for over an hour when Thomas Wintour entered the establishment. Wintour perused the room, his eyes settling on Guy before moving on to assess the other three occupants: two old men already well into their cups and unlikely to have noticed his arrival, let alone his identity, and a young maid wiping down tables and chairs on the other side of the room.

Exhibiting no outward indication that he had recognized Guy, Wintour walked up to the bar just as the innkeeper appeared from the back. Keeping their voices low, the two men exchanged a few words, and then Wintour walked around a few tables to disappear through a door that led to the upstairs rooms. Guy waited, listening for the soft thud of Wintour's footsteps ascending the stairs. Above Guy's head, the wooden floor creaked and then fell silent.

Guy leaned back in his seat, swirling the liquid in his goblet thoughtfully. So, this meeting was to involve more than Guy and Catsby. And it would surely lead to discussion, else why the need for a private room? Frustration seared his chest once more. And with it came a generous dose of resentment. Given his pivotal role over the next few days, if something had arisen that might impact their plans, he should have been informed privately and straightway.

Coming to his feet, Guy tossed a few coins on the table beside his half-empty goblet and made for the door. No matter the innkeeper's seeming willingness to allow known Catholics to meet secretly within the walls of his establishment, Guy would find his way to the upper rooms through the back entrance.

Under three minutes later, he issued the preassigned knock on the door of an upper room.

Wintour opened it almost immediately. "You took your time."

"I could say the same." Guy brushed past him to stand before Catsby near the fire. "I have been listening to those two drunkards downstairs discuss London's bear-baiting pits for the best part of two hours. Sending word that you planned to meet upstairs would not have gone amiss."

Catsby acknowledged his complaint with an inclination of his head. "Wintour and I arrived within minutes of each other. You would have been waiting just as long."

Guy eyed him dourly. Remaining out of sight in his own room would have been preferable to his situation downstairs, and Catsby knew it. "Be that as it may, I assume you have good reason for summoning me in the middle of the day."

"Aye. And for having you visit the undercroft." He hesitated. "You went, I assume."

"I did. It was unneedful. The place was just as I left it two nights past."

Relief eased Catsby's tense expression. He pointed to a stool. "You'd best be seated. We have much to deliberate."

"I thought the time for deliberation was long past."

"As did I." There was a hardness to Catsby's voice. "But you may wish to reconsider after you hear Wintour's report."

Guy's impatience was mounting. Wintour was here to report? So much the better. He would rather hear the bad news for himself than receive it through numberless channels. "What have you to tell me, Wintour?" he asked.

The tall, dark-haired man took a seat on one of the other stools. "Thomas Ward came to me late last night with an alarming account."

"Thomas Ward?" Guy looked from Wintour to Catsby. "Who is that?"

"Manservant to Lord Monteagle and a reliable source," Catsby said. "He's been known to share valuable information with Catholic loyalists in the past."

"Very well," Guy said. "What did he have to say?"

"A stranger approached him outside Monteagle's manor and gave him a missive for his master," Wintour said. "Monteagle was hosting a dinner party and had Ward read the message before the entire group. It was a warning. No details were given, but Monteagle was told that if he valued his life, he should refrain from attending the opening of Parliament and remove himself to the country instead. It further said that no one would know the source of the upcoming blow to Parliament."

Guy stared at Wintour, a cold chill coursing down his spine. "How did Monteagle and his guests respond?"

"According to Ward, there was a mixed reaction, but it ended with Monteagle leaving posthaste to inform Cecil of the anonymous message."

Guy swore. "And Cecil? Has he acted?"

"We have heard nothing more," Catsby said. "But Cecil is not known for sitting idly by."

The reason behind Catsby's pressing request to check the contents of the undercroft suddenly became glaringly clear. As did the danger inherent in accomplishing the task.

"You thought to give me no warning of this ahead of my visiting the undercroft this morning?" Guy said.

"There was no need." Catsby was infuriatingly nonchalant. "I knew full well that you would employ the same caution with or without the additional information. And committing such intelligence to paper only invites disaster."

Under present circumstances, Catsby's argument could hardly be refuted.

"Who wrote the missive?" Guy asked bluntly. "The number who know of our plot is limited, and you have had time to ponder upon each man's innocence—or lack thereof."

"It has to be Tresham," Wintour said. "His sister Elizabeth is married to Monteagle, which gives him reason to warn the nobleman."

Catsby visibly bristled. "You think he would break his oath so quickly?"

"Tresham has not been with us long enough to prove his worth or his loyalty," Wintour retorted.

"It does not follow that those traits are lacking," Catsby said. "His joining us at this late juncture was my choice, not his."

"Who would you accuse in his stead?" Wintour asked.

"I am accusing no one," Catsby said. "Least of all you, Wintour. I believe it safe to say that no one in this room is culpable, and so I suggest that before we leave, we determine who amongst our group cannot be trusted and whether or not our plans must irrevocably change."

"Agreed," Wintour said. "But surely, to move forward now, with Cecil forewarned, would be sheer foolishness."

"Not at all," Guy said. "If the note was as cryptic as you suggest, Cecil knows nothing of substance. Regardless of whether his suspicions have been heightened, he has no reason to suspect a cache of gunpowder lies beneath the House of Lords." He stood and began pacing. "The months of preparation, the gathering of gunpowder, horses, and men, the carefully formulated timetable for each part of the scheme—from the capture of the heirs to the throne to the commissioning of a ship to facilitate an escape. This groundwork cannot be abandoned on a whim."

Catsby sat forward, his gaze unwavering. "You are willing to enter the undercroft and light the fuse alone, as planned, despite the warning Cecil has received?"

"I am." An unquenchable fire burned within him. "The opportunity to bring an end to King James, his government, and all those who support their evil works is worth the risk."

A satisfied smirk appeared on Catsby's face. "Cecil will be left fumbling in the dark for clues."

"In the dark and in the rubble," Guy said. "There will be little left when our work is complete."

"And the traitor?" Wintour asked. "You would go forward knowing he might warn another?"

"He must be stopped. There can be no reservation about that." Catsby rubbed his bearded chin. "You truly believe it is Tresham?"

"I have thought on little else since Ward gave me the news," Wintour said. "My earlier arguments aside, Tresham is in London, whereas most of our men remain in the country."

"And those who are in the city?" Catsby asked.

"Can all be accounted for last night," Wintour supplied.

With a muttered oath, Catsby came to his feet. "If Tresham has double-crossed me, he shall pay for it with his life."

A flicker of excitement warmed Guy's hardened heart. Action. At last. First, with Tresham, and then with the king. "When and where?" he asked.

Catsby squared his shoulders. "Two o'clock in the afternoon, three days hence, in the Royal Forest of Epping Chase," he said. "I shall send word to Tresham to meet me at Barnet. We shall enter the forest from there. Fawkes, I would have you join us. What shall begin as a pleasant walk amongst the trees shall become a private inquisition. If he answers false, we shall know it, and he shall lose all."

"Very well." Guy stood. "Until then, Catsby." Turning to Wintour, he touched the brim of his hat. "I would have you inform me directly if you hear anything more regarding Cecil's response to Monteagle's note, Wintour."

Wintour's expression was grim, but he inclined his head in agreement. "As you wish."

It was obvious that Catsby wished for answers and revenge. Wintour may be troubled by what had transpired, but he would not abandon their cause. Satisfied that he need say or do no more at this meeting, Guy made for the door. He had an undercroft to watch.

CHAPTER 17

Outside the Maidstones' townhouse, a distant church bell rang to mark the two o'clock hour. It was time. Isla smoothed a minute wrinkle off her gown. Her nervousness was ridiculous. She had ridden with Simon almost every morning for weeks at Copfield Hall. But no matter how often she repeated that thought, her heart refused to listen. For some reason, riding with Simon through London this afternoon felt different. The most logical explanation to her inner turmoil was that seventeenth-century protocols were finally rubbing off on her. To be seen accompanying a gentleman in the city was a big deal. Then again, it could also be that Simon had held her hand at least half the way home the evening before and had seemed as reluctant as she had been to part when the carriage journey had ended.

She reached for the cloak Martha had loaned her and set it around her shoulders. Her fingers fumbled with the clasp, and she groaned. She needed to get a grip on her emotions. Simon was becoming far too adept at reading them. This outing was merely an educational trip to see sites of historic significance—nothing more. That must be her focus. Not the gentleman riding at her side.

She took one last look in the mirror hanging on the wall of her bedchamber. The cloak covered most of her pale-blue gown, which was probably a good thing since she had dispensed with the all-important farthingale for the ride. As far as she was concerned, horses and farthingales did not belong together. If she and Simon happened to pass any of his acquaintances, she would have to hope that none would notice that she was missing such a vital part of a Jacobean lady's wardrobe.

Slipping out of the bedchamber, she hurried to the top of the stairs. Male voices reached her from below, and despite her best efforts to remain calm, her pulse tripped. Simon was here. She started down and had almost reached the narrow entry when the servant who must have answered the door to Simon stepped aside, and Simon looked up to see her there. The worry on his face dissolved, and he smiled. Isla's heart responded immediately. What on earth was wrong with her? Just because he looked dashingly handsome, it didn't mean she had to become completely unglued. She tightened her grip on the banister.

"Good afternoon, Simon," she said.

"Good afternoon." He stepped closer. "I am glad to see you. Grantham was just telling me that Maidstone and Martha are away. He was unclear about your whereabouts."

"Lord Maidstone had business to attend to," she said. "And Martha had an appointment with her haberdasher."

"I see." He ran his hand across the back of his neck, and Isla received the distinct impression that something was not quite right.

"Did you need to speak to one of them?"

"No, not at all." He smiled again, but it did not quite reach his eyes. "Are you ready for our outing?"

"I am. Were you able to find a docile mount for me?"

"So docile, she barely puts one hoof before another." He offered her his arm. "Come. My manservant, Anson, is waiting outside with all three horses."

A servant and an extra horse. It was a timely reminder that they would be chaperoned on this trip. Isla wasn't sure how closely Simon's servant would follow them, but if they were to have a private conversation, now might be their best opportunity.

She placed her hand on his arm, but instead of moving toward the door, she looked up at him. "Is something wrong?"

"Why would you ask that?" His voice hinted at surprise, but his troubled eyes confirmed her suspicions.

"Simon," she lowered her voice. "If sharing whatever is bothering you would help, you can tell me."

He looked away. Isla waited, her anxiety mounting. Any minute now, another servant would appear. In a house so well staffed, that was the way of things.

"I may be limited in what I can do to help," she added, "but I can listen."

"You do a great deal more than simply listen, Isla," he said, turning back to face her. "I can offer you a rather extensive list of remarkable things you have done since your arrival. But this is not the time or place to discuss my present concern. If I may, I should like to postpone that conversation until after our outing."

"You are sure?"

He nodded. "I am sure. It will wait until you have experienced London as it is today." He raised an eyebrow. "Okay?"

She smiled at his use of the word. She wished he had chosen to talk now, but she would not force him to confide in her. Instead, she would play along with his teasing, and perhaps that would be enough to remove the lines on his forehead—at least for a while.

"Okay," she said. "Take me to the barely moving horse."

With a chuckle, Simon led her outside. Anson was standing on the side of the road, holding the reins of three horses. Blaze stood half a head taller than the gray horse at his right and the brown horse at his left.

"Which one is mine?" Isla asked.

"The gray." Simon ran his free hand along the animal's nose. It gave a contented snort. "The gentlest mare in the stable, is what I was told."

"I like the sound of that." Isla reached up to pat the horse's neck. "What is your name, young lady?"

"Stormy," Simon said.

Isla gave him a dubious look. "Stormy? My confidence in your choice of mount just dropped a few notches."

Simon grinned. "She's the same color as today's skies, and there's scarcely a breeze. I daresay someone named her before her placid disposition manifested itself."

"Hmm." Isla was far from convinced, but with her "okay" in the house, she was committed.

"Are you ready?" Simon asked, releasing her arm so he could place his hands at her waist.

"Yes," she said.

Moments later, she was in the saddle, and his hands were gone. Anson handed her the reins, and as Simon took charge of Blaze, Anson mounted the brown horse.

"We will follow the Strand to Charing Cross, Anson," Simon said.

"Very good, my lord."

Anson waited until Simon and Isla were several paces ahead of him before bringing up the rear, and it wasn't long before Isla all but forgot he was there.

"The place names are the same as the ones I know," she said, gazing at the row of timbered Tudor houses lining the road on either side of them. "But everything looks completely different."

"How is it different?" Simon asked.

"In the twenty-first century, the dirt roads are covered with a hard, black coating and are painted to help the vehicles stay where they're supposed to be. The wooden buildings are gone, replaced by tall structures made of stone, brick, and concrete."

"Concrete?"

"It's a man-made substance that revolutionized construction of all kinds—from houses to bridges to walkways."

"What color is it?" Simon asked.

"Gray, usually."

They entered a square where three roads converged. A large stone monument topped with a cross stood in the center of the open area. Isla studied it with interest.

"Is this Charing Cross?" she asked.

"Yes," Simon said. "And that is the memorial to Eleanor of Castile."

"How amazing." The monument was smaller and simpler than the one that stood outside Charing Cross Station, but it was the first thing Isla had seen that bore a resemblance to something she knew.

"And this," Simon said, taking the road at his left, "is King Street. The high-pitched roofs may prevent you from seeing beyond the buildings, but the street runs parallel to the Thames on the left and St. James's Park on the right."

"Does it run down toward Westminster?" Isla asked.

"It does."

Notwithstanding the vast differences in scenery, dress, and transportation around her, an odd sense of familiarity washed over her. The raucous seagulls overhead, the distant lap of water, and the glimpse of St. James's Park's greenery were just as she'd always known them.

"In the London I know, this road is called Whitehall," she said.

"Whitehall," he repeated. "Named after the king's residence, the Palace of Whitehall."

"Yes." This was probably not the time to tell Simon that the royal palace no longer existed.

"Then, you must also be familiar with the Palace of Westminster," he said.

Familiar, yes, in a vague sort of way. "Westminster Abbey still stands, but most of the other buildings associated with the palace you know have either been destroyed or rebuilt."

Simon kept Blaze at a steady walk, his expression thoughtful. "And yet, we are fighting to keep that very thing from happening within the week."

"True. But this time, our concern is not just for the buildings or upholding the law of the land. It's also about saving countless lives." Particularly, the lives of people she had come to care for deeply.

They were approaching a wall, and beyond it, a cluster of buildings surrounded what Isla guessed was the original portion of Westminster Abbey.

"No matter what happens," Simon said, "the king will be protected."

"But not the other innocents." A sickening blend of dread and panic welled within her. They were mere days from the culmination of Guy Fawkes and Robert Catsby's elaborate conspiracy, and they had no idea whether any steps had been taken to prevent its implementation. "Promise me that no matter what happens, you will not come here on November 5."

"Hush," he warned, his voice low. "We have reached New Palace Yard. It is the entrance to the House of Commons. Beyond the archway is Old Palace Yard and the House of Lords." He paused to look up at the venerable structure ahead of them. "Within these walls, men linger longer than is needful, listening for conversations not meant for their ears."

A chilling frisson skittered up Isla's spine. Weeks ago, Simon and Lord Maidstone had warned her of Cecil's spies. Was this where they gathered? And was it possible that at least one of Catsby's accomplices was also in the vicinity, watching over their cache?

"Will you show me the House of Lords?" Isla asked softly.

With a nod, Simon led the way beneath the archway and into a second courtyard. "It is the building immediately to your left," he said, giving no indication that he meant to stop.

Isla understood. The prickly sensation that she was being watched had begun the moment they'd entered the second courtyard. Attempting to ignore it, she gave the structure at her left a brief glance and then forced her attention to linger on the other buildings they were passing. Built of stone, with arched windows and tall chimneys, there was a similarity to the structures. She dropped her gaze from the rooflines to the ground level. How would one enter an undercroft? In this era, it would have been like a cellar or crypt accessed from outside the building.

Near the corner of the farthest building, Isla noticed a set of shallow steps leading down to a door partially visible above the ground. Her pulse quickened. If that led to an undercroft, the chances were good that there was a comparable door in the building that accommodated the Lords' Chambers. Steeling herself not to turn around and look, she kept her eyes forward and her expression passive. Once she was safely back at the

Maidstones' house, she would pass along her observation to Simon and Lord Maidstone. Perhaps they, in turn, could pass it along to Lord Suffolk.

Simon was unprepared for the relief he felt when he guided Isla out of Old Palace Yard and back onto King Street. In his many visits to the House of Lords, he had never before experienced the sense of foreboding that had hovered over the palace grounds today. Not even the foul stench wafting on the light breeze from the alleys that led to the humbler dwellings near the river could compare to the malicious aura that had seemed to hang over the palace buildings. He chanced a brief glance over his shoulder. All appeared as it should. And that was particularly concerning. Where was Cecil? Had he taken Isla's note seriously? Would he act upon the clue he'd been given?

Simon tightened his jaw. He could not remember a time when he had felt less in control. Not only could he learn nothing more about whether any effort was being made to foil Catsby's plot until he and Maidstone had spoken to Suffolk, but he also had no way of knowing how long Isla would remain in the seventeenth century. With his burgeoning desire to have her forever in his future, the unknown was eating him up one painful bite at a time. And if Isla's gentle probing at Maidstone's house was any indication, he was doing a very poor job of hiding his inner turmoil. She deserved an explanation. But exactly what he should say and when he should say it, he did not know.

"Simon. We must stop."

With a start, Simon reined Blaze to a halt. He was every kind of blockhead. He'd been so consumed with weighty thoughts about his current situation, he'd all but ignored the young lady at the center of them. And now she was half a dozen paces behind him, attempting to free her foot from the stirrup. Wheeling Blaze around, he moved his horse to stand beside hers.

"What are you doing?" he asked.

"Getting off." Isla dropped the reins to untangle her skirts from around the pommel.

Unprepared for the unexpected movement, Stormy nickered and sidestepped. Isla wobbled.

"Steady." Keeping one hand firmly on his own reins, Simon reached for Isla's arm. "If you wish to dismount, you need only ask and I will assist you."

"I want to," she repeated, this time with more urgency.

"Very well." Thanking all the saints that Blaze had chosen to remain unruffled, he slid from his saddle. "Anson," he called. "Take the reins, would you?"

His obedient servant edged his mount close enough to grasp the straps, and Simon lifted Isla from her saddle and onto her feet.

"Are you well?" he asked, searching her face for any sign of illness. Her complexion was a becoming and healthy shade, but she was clearly distressed.

"I am fine, but that little girl is not." She pointed to the other side of the road, where a child who looked to be similar in age to Will and Sam was lying in the dirt at the entrance to one of the alleys. "I noticed her when she was a little way off because her steps were so unsteady. But then she collapsed." She caught hold of his arm. "We must go to her, Simon. She is obviously alone and in need of help."

Simon stood completely still. From his position behind Stormy, he could clearly see the child's ragged clothing and tangled hair, but his gaze glossed over those things to settle on the girl's hands. Blackened skin tipped every finger. "No, Isla."

She swung around, shock shining in her eyes. "No?"

"No." He reached for her, but she backed away.

"Is it because she is poor?"

"Of course not." Alarm consumed him. They had to leave. Now. "The child has the plague."

"The plague!" Isla stared at him. "How can you possibly know that?"

"She has blackened fingers, her neck is swollen, and she appears to be feverish."

Isla looked across the street once more, and when she turned back to him, her eyes were filled with tears. "But she's only a child."

"I know." The anguish on her face cut him to his core.

"Can we truly do nothing for her?"

He did not answer her question. He could not bring himself to tell her that with such evident symptoms, the child would likely be dead by nightfall.

"Come," he said. "We must leave here immediately."

She was openly weeping now, but she offered no resistance when he lifted her back into the saddle.

"Can you manage?" he asked softly.

She nodded mutely.

"Once we are away from here, we shall stop again," he promised. She nodded again, and he leaped into his saddle. "Make haste, Anson," he said, reclaiming his reins. "We must put some distance between us and this place."

When Simon saw the tops of the trees signaling the edge of St. James's Park, he veered off the road and onto the grass that surrounded the royal estate. Isla followed his lead, her mount remaining at Blaze's side as they approached the fringes of the park. Without an invitation from the king, they could not go beyond the first line of trees, but the solid oaks would offer Isla the privacy she deserved to grieve for the little girl she did not know.

A quick glance over his shoulder reassured Simon that Anson was near. He brought Blaze to a stop and dismounted. Then he reached for Isla. Wordlessly, she set her hands on his shoulders, and he lifted her off Stormy's back.

"I am leaving the horses in your care, Anson," he said. "Miss Crawford needs a moment to recover her equilibrium. I daresay our mounts will be glad of the opportunity to graze."

"Of course, my lord." Anson had dismounted and was already gathering the various straps.

Taking Isla by the hand, Simon led her to a break in the trees. There he stopped and met her sorrow-filled eyes. "Can you ever forgive me?"

"There is nothing to forgive." Her lips quivered. "You had nothing to do with the little girl contracting the plague and everything to do with protecting me from the illness."

"I should not have taken you out. I knew full well that the city has been overrun with the disease. It is the very reason I escaped to Copfield Hall."

"You told me as much, but I didn't think . . ." Her voice broke. "I didn't think I would actually see . . ." She covered her face with her hands. "She was so young."

His heart aching, Simon wrapped his arms around Isla and held her close, fighting back his own tears as she sobbed into his shoulder.

When she finally pulled away, she ran her hand across the damp patch on his cloak. "Now it is my turn to ask forgiveness. I have made your cloak wet."

He took her hand and pressed her palm to his lips. "You may cry on my shoulder whenever you feel the need. I only pray that I am never again the cause of your sorrow."

"You were not the cause."

"Perhaps not directly," he said, "but after you have heard me out, you may realize that you have been overly generous with me."

Her brows came together, and though he longed to wipe the puzzlement away with a brush of his finger, he knew this was the opening he had been waiting for. "Over the last few weeks, I have come to discover that I am a far more selfish creature than I had supposed. Notwithstanding the many wonders of your modern world, if the choice were mine, I would have you stay here with me in an era afflicted with plague and treachery."

"You . . . you want me to stay?"

He sighed. "Earlier today, when you asked if something was amiss, Maidstone's servant had just informed me that you had not been seen downstairs for some time. For one full minute, my worst fears appeared to have been realized: with your letter to Monteagle successfully delivered, you had finished your assignment in this century and had returned to your own." He ran his thumb over the back of Isla's hand as the memory of that supposed loss returned. "I have always known that you are as likely to leave as to stay, but it seems that my head neglected to fully communicate that to my heart." He managed a wry smile. "I had thought that I was strong, that I had already successfully weathered disappointment in love with Lydia, but I was wrong. On both counts. My determination to distance myself from you lasted only from the end of our time at Monteagle's manor to the moment I took your hand in the carriage. And the disillusionment I felt at Lydia's rejection was nothing compared to the heart-shattering loss I experienced in the entryway when I thought you were gone."

"Simon," Isla whispered. He had never felt more vulnerable, yet he braved meeting her eyes. Hers were moist, but she raised her free hand to gently touch his face. "You and I have very different views of selfishness. To open up one's heart the way you have just done is the very opposite of that trait. And if I have given you the impression that the twenty-first century is without problems, I have led you astray. The challenges there are different, but they are as big if not bigger and more troubling than the ones here." She paused. "Turning away from that suffering child this afternoon may be one of the hardest things I've ever done, particularly since I know that centuries from now, she could be cured, but if I'm forced to leave you to return to that future world . . ." Her fingers had found his hair. "I think that might be even harder."

"Then, you are willing to consider staying?" It was something he had hardly dared hope.

"Do you think I will be given that option?"

"Perhaps," he said. "If my prayers are heard."

Her expression softened, and for the first time, he saw a longing in her eyes that mirrored his own. "Our betrothal could be real."

His arms encircled her. "The most real, love-filled betrothal anyone has ever known," he said, lowering his head until his lips were within a breath of hers.

"Yes," she murmured. And then their lips touched, and he was kissing her, sharing his heart in a way no words could express.

Above their heads, the branches trembled, clicking softly in the strengthening breeze.

Slowly, reluctantly, Simon raised his head and looked upward. While they had been under the trees, the gray skies had darkened. "A storm is coming," he said. "We must leave if we wish to avoid a soaking."

A scattering of brown leaves fluttered by.

Removing one of her arms from around his neck, Isla brushed a leaf off his shoulder and then extended her hand outward, palm up. "I felt a drop," she said.

Simon groaned. Pressing another brief kiss to her lips, he released her only to immediately take her hand. "Are you willing to try coaxing Stormy into a canter?" he asked, already making for the spot where Anson was waiting with the horses.

"Yes, as long as you catch me if I bounce right out of the saddle."

He grinned. "Falling off is not permitted."

"If you would tell that to Stormy, I would appreciate it."

"I am quite certain she already knows it," he said, lifting Isla onto the horse as he spoke. "And I am equally certain she would rather increase her speed than be caught out in the rain."

"Okay, then," Isla said, grasping the reins with fresh determination.

Simon mounted Blaze and turned him toward the road, love for the beautiful and astonishingly brave young woman at his side washing over him. "Okay, then," he repeated. "To the Maidstones' house without delay."

———— · ✴ · ————

Night had fallen. From beneath the covers of her rustic bed, Isla listened to the fading sounds of life in old London through the closed window shutters. The glowing coals in her bedchamber's fireplace emitted just enough light to make out the shadowy features of the small room. Rolling onto her back, she gazed up at the dark wooden beams traversing the daubed ceiling and tried to visualize the smooth white paint and electric light fixture on the ceiling of her bedroom in her Knightsbridge flat.

"This one has more character," she whispered to herself. And it was true, even though flipping a switch to fill the room with light seemed very appealing when compared to tiptoeing across the cold floor to light a candle on the mantel with a flint.

Grasping the woolen blanket at her chin a little more tightly, Isla gazed around the simply furnished room. Did she truly have what it would take to live in this century for the rest of her life? This afternoon, while wrapped in Simon's arms and melting beneath his fervent kisses, the choice to stay had seemed easy. He was the best man she'd ever known, and she had fallen hopelessly in love with him. But to stay meant never seeing her family again, or her friends, or the places she called home. She would be without access to modern medicine, technology, or even the most rudimentary indoor plumbing and central heating. It was a commitment of epic proportions, and she wasn't afraid to admit that it scared her.

Of course, there was the distinct possibility that the decision was not hers to make. It had been Martha who had first suggested that Isla had arrived in the seventeenth century to perform a specific task and that once it was completed, she would return to her former life. Before then, Isla had assumed that she had entered some kind of time warp never to return. It had been a terrifying concept. It still filled her with trepidation, but now her apprehension was offset by the knowledge that Simon would be beside her every step of the way.

The very thought of Simon filled her chest with warmth, and she allowed herself to drift through the memories they'd made together that day. The ominous aura surrounding the House of Lords and the heartbreaking encounter with the child suffering from the plague had made for a difficult start to their outing, but the ending had brought unexpected joy. Even their canter home through the drizzle could not be faulted. Isla had managed to remain in her saddle, and afterward, Martha had insisted that she sit beside Simon in front of the fire until their clothing was dry. A small smile touched Isla's lips. She could still hardly believe that Simon had confessed his love for her, but he had kissed her so convincingly, she did not doubt his earnestness for one moment.

He had promised to return to the Maidstones' house in the morning. He'd told Martha it was necessary because Isla had yet to explain a football game to him, but Isla suspected that it was really that he knew how hard it was going to be for all of them to wait for news from Sir Cecil's office. It might take days before they learned anything new, and time would pass more quickly and far more pleasantly if they were together.

She closed her eyes, picturing Simon standing at the doorway immediately before he'd left for the night. Her stomach fluttered, and she pressed her hand to it in an attempt to subdue the butterflies. As hard as it was to contemplate giving up the life she'd once known, she could not imagine being truly happy in a life without him. Perhaps it was time for him to tell her more about his home in the Peak District.

CHAPTER 18

The wind was cold. Guy pressed his stovepipe hat more firmly onto his head and eyed the tree line up ahead. Once they were within the Royal Forest of Epping Chase, they would be better protected from the elements. And from curious onlookers.

Tresham had accepted Catsby's invitation to meet at Barnet. He'd surely thought it was a friendly meeting of cousins, with Catsby footing the bill for whatever victuals they consumed. Indeed, there was a good possibility that Tresham had actually looked forward to it. Unfortunately for the gentleman, that positive outlook had likely not lasted long after his arrival at the local inn.

Guy's presence would have been Tresham's first warning that this was not merely a social gathering. His suspicions had undoubtedly redoubled when, after perfunctory pleasantries had been exchanged, Catsby had suggested a walk to the forest. Given that Catsby had been resting his hand on the hilt of his sword at the time, it could not have escaped Tresham's attention that both Catsby and Guy had weapons hanging from their belts. Tresham did also, but Guy thought it possible that his was more a statement of fashion than a threat.

Guy studied the man walking directly ahead of him. Anxiety radiated off his stiffened shoulders, but to his credit, he had yet to balk at their steady pace or the peculiar nature of the outing. Catsby had taken the lead and was guiding them toward the forest entrance. Tresham followed, with Guy close behind. It was an odd sight, to be sure, but Tresham had to be questioned—and if this silent march was any indication, Catsby desired a setting that offered both privacy and an opportunity for intimidation.

The breeze tugged at Guy's cloak. It flapped noisily. Guy snatched the fabric and pulled it closer. He wished to know who had sent the traitorous letter to Monteagle as much as Catsby and Wintour, but with the damage already done, his concern centered on whether Cecil would unravel the cryptic clues rather than on listening to the confession of a cowardly betrayer. Guy had carefully monitored activity at the House of Lords for the past three days. No one had shown undue interest in the building or the undercroft, and he was beginning to think Cecil was not quite so clever as the gentleman would have his associates believe.

Up ahead, the snap of a twig underfoot marked Catsby's arrival at the forest's edge. Moments later, Tresham and Guy were also under the cover of tall, almost-leafless branches. Catsby did not pause. He continued into the forest, past dense bushes and evergreen trees that served as barriers to the wind and the outside world, until, at last, they reached a smallish clearing. There he took a position with his back to the trunk of a tall ash tree and turned his eyes on Tresham.

"Why are we here, Catsby?" Tresham asked.

Guy owned to being surprised. For someone who was facing an accusation of disloyalty, Tresham had more courage than Guy had supposed.

"I believe you know," Catsby replied.

"Then, you credit me with more intelligence than you should." Tresham's gaze flashed to Guy. "I would suppose that since Fawkes has joined this woodland party, it has something to do with your plot to change the face of English politics." He shrugged. "That is all the intelligence I can muster."

"A letter was delivered to Monteagle some four nights ago," Catsby said. "Did you pen it?"

"Why would I write to Monteagle?"

"He is your brother-in-law, is he not?"

"Of course. Which makes your question all the odder. If I wished to speak to the fellow, I have only to stop by his house. To the best of my knowledge, I am welcome there at any time."

"I am not speaking of a trivial letter containing material suitable for a social call, Tresham." Catsby's voice had become menacing. "This particular missive was written by someone who broke a solemn oath made before God and men."

Guy caught Catsby's subtle nod and withdrew his sword. The blade left its sheath with a zing of grazing metal.

Instantly, Tresham swung around, his face pale. "If you are accusing me of betrayal, you must know that you are sorely mistaken."

"I know no such thing." In one practiced move, Catsby removed his sword from its sheath. "But because of our familial ties, I shall offer you three minutes to prove it to me."

"We are cousins!"

"Indeed. And your sister is married to one of the very nobles who should be in attendance at the House of Lords when Fawkes plans to light the fuse. Which of those loyalties is the strongest, Tresham?"

"How can you ask such a thing when you know full well that we have enjoyed a unique bond since childhood?"

"So I thought." Catsby took a step toward him, his eyes narrowing. "But you have yet to persuade me that it remains intact."

"This is monstrous! Do you not recall my service during the Essex rebellion? I was jailed for my dedication to the Catholic cause. Why would I forsake that now, when we are on the cusp of making real and lasting change in this country?"

"Why indeed?" Catsby circled him, the tip of his sword pointed at Tresham's chest.

Tresham pivoted, setting his desperate gaze on Guy. "I am innocent, I tell you. Whatever was shared with Monteagle did not originate with me." He waved his arms. "You must believe me!"

"Who else would have written it?" Guy asked. "You are the newest member of our group and have yet to fully prove yourself."

"Then, allow me to prove myself now!" Tresham cried, dropping to his knees. "If I am lying, may God strike me down before you."

His plea ascended upward through the trees. A bird took flight in a flutter of wings, and then there was nothing but the hiss of wind cutting through branches.

Guy looked to Catsby. He was eyeing his cousin narrowly. Tresham's head was bowed, as though awaiting his end. Was this merely theatrics, or was the man's faith in God so great that he would commend his soul to Him in this way? Guy did not know him well enough to make a fair assessment. But Catsby did.

Guy waited, watching Catsby for a signal. A creature shuffled through a bush behind him, and the sound seemed to rouse Catsby from his pondering. He squared his shoulders and met Guy's questioning gaze with another slight nod.

"Get up, Tresham," he ordered, sliding his sword back into its sheath.

Tresham's head bobbed up, the look in his eyes a mixture of doubt and relief.

"Up, I said." Catsby moved forward and offered his cousin his hand.

Tresham took it and staggered to his feet. Not bothering to brush the twigs and dead leaves from his knees, he stumbled back a pace. "You have judged fairly," Tresham said. "You need never fear my breaking my oath."

"If you hear of anything that would lead us to the traitor, I would have you come to me straightway," Catsby said.

"Understood." Tresham took another step back, and Catsby grunted.

"You are free to go, cousin."

Tresham needed no second invitation. He swung around and hurried away through the trees. Catsby and Guy watched him go.

"You believed him?" Guy asked.

"I did." Catsby's jaw tightened. "But if I am correct, that means there is another deserter amongst us."

"It matters not." Guy sheathed his sword. "We move forward regardless of the whispers abroad. No one has visited the undercroft since Cecil read Monteagle's note. We have only four days more until it is over."

Catsby clapped a hand on Guy's shoulder. "Four days and you shall be hailed as the man who saved England."

A spark of pride lit Guy's chest. He would light the fuse and then disappear. Until the government was fully overturned, it was the way it must be. But when word spread of what he had done, no one—not even a king—would have the power to prevent his name from being spoken in awe-filled whispers.

————· ✦ ·————

Simon entered his sister's London townhouse with new-found eagerness. It had been three days since he'd kissed Isla at St. James's Park. Three days since she'd given him reason to hope that his feelings for her were reciprocated. And three days of coming to love her even more than he had before. Allowing himself to nurture rather than suppress his feelings had some-how seemed to encourage Isla to do the same. And although the fear that she would suddenly disappear still lingered, it was muted by the knowledge that if Isla were given the choice, she might yet stay.

"Good day, Grantham." Simon handed his hat and cloak to Maidstone's manservant. "Is Maidstone about?"

"No, my lord. Although I believe he is expected back within the hour."

Simon was fairly certain that his brother-in-law had gone in search of Suffolk. Martha continued to be the most vocal regarding her desire to know that Cecil was acting upon the information hidden within Isla's letter, and so Maidstone had pledged to obtain answers today. His assurance had cut Martha's pacing to a minimum last evening, but if it were to stay that way, the gentleman would need to deliver.

"What of my sister and Miss Crawford?" he asked.

"I believe Miss Crawford is in the parlor, and Lady Maid-stone is abovestairs, my lord. Would you have me send some-one to fetch Her Ladyship?"

"Thank you, but that won't be necessary."

A few moments alone with Isla would be welcome. If he knew his sister—and he did rather well—she would not give them long before she made an appearance.

"Very good, my lord."

Leaving Grantham to take care of Simon's outerwear, Simon moved swiftly down the narrow passage to the parlor. The door was open, so he walked in. Isla was standing at the window, gazing out at the rainy day. She was dressed in a green gown with lace at her neck and the ends of her sleeves. Her hair was piled atop her head in tiny ringlets, and as he watched, she absently reached up to tuck an errant curl behind her ear.

"I believe you may be the most beautiful young lady in London," he said.

"Simon!" She swung around, her lips curving into a welcoming smile. "When did you arrive?"

"Just now." He crossed the short distance between them in a few long strides and wrapped her in his arms. "I missed you."

"You were here until late last night." She laughed.

"I was indeed, and yet that was almost twelve hours ago." He ran his forefinger gently across her cheek. "Which, in case you were unaware, is altogether too long."

"It is rather," she whispered.

"I am glad you agree," he murmured, and then he lowered his lips to hers.

Her arms rose to wrap themselves around his neck, and he pulled her closer, drinking her in as he deepened the kiss. Footsteps sounded in the hall, but he gave them no heed.

"Ahem." Someone cleared her throat at the doorway. Someone who sounded remarkably like Martha.

Slowly, Simon raised his head and looked over his shoulder. "Good day, Martha."

She was standing with her hands on her hips, glaring at him. "*Good day, Martha?* You enter my house without so much as a 'by your leave,' accost Isla, and then have the audacity to greet me with 'Good day'?"

Smothering a grin, Simon turned so that he was standing beside Isla with one arm firmly around her small waist. "First, I was under the seemingly erroneous assumption that I did not need an invitation to enter your house. That is how we have functioned since you were first married. Second, I was not accosting Isla; I was kissing her. And third, given that you interrupted said kiss, I thought it was remarkably decent of me to greet you so politely."

"Isla," Martha said, ignoring Simon completely. "Do you wish me to throw him out?"

"Not really."

Simon pulled a face. "Not really?"

Isla's lips twitched, and he knew she was battling laughter. "Very well. Not at all."

"Better," he said.

"Enough, Simon," Martha said. "I wish to hear Isla's side of this, and if need be, we shall have the conversation without you."

It was the best threat she could have used, and Simon knew that if he were wise, he would wait for her fondness for ordering people around to pass. He tightened his hold on Isla's waist and closed his mouth.

"I know proper young ladies don't conduct themselves this way in the seventeenth century," Isla said, "but I'm afraid I regressed to the twenty-first century for a few minutes. Please, don't be too cross with Simon. He did kiss me, but I kissed him too."

It may have been his imagination, but Simon thought he caught a flicker of amusement in Martha's eyes.

"Am I to believe that you have developed real feelings for one another?" she asked.

"Yes," Isla said.

Concern lined Martha's forehead. "But at any moment, you may be called back to your time."

"I realize that. And so does Simon. But it is just as likely that I will remain here."

"Do you wish to stay?" Martha asked.

"If I am given the option," Isla said, "I will choose to stay with Simon."

Martha gasped, the consternation on her face melting away. "That would make us all so happy."

"Can I say something now?" Simon asked.

"Not yet," his sister said, moving toward them.

Simon released Isla and stepped away so that Martha could embrace her.

"I suspected Simon was developing feelings for you," she said, "but I was so afraid that no matter your inclinations, he would be hurt again by your leaving."

"So, you do like me after all?" Simon said to his sister.

"Only on occasion. But my boys adore you, so I suppose I must offer you leniency on the day I catch you kissing your betrothed in my parlor."

With a chuckle, he leaned forward and brushed his sister's cheek with his lips. "Thank you, Martha."

"No more kissing," she warned.

"None," he promised. "At least, not in your presence."

Martha gave him a long-suffering look, but before she could lecture him further, the sound of the front door opening and closing reached them.

"I did not hear a knock," Martha said. "It may be Hugh returning."

Sure enough, moments later, Maidstone appeared at the parlor doorway, still wearing his cloak and hat.

"Do you have news?" Simon asked.

"I do." He removed his hat. "I spoke to Suffolk. He remains skeptical that the letter is anything more than a prank, but Cecil disagrees. By way of compromise, Cecil agreed to do nothing until he had spoken with the king. The king returned today, and upon reading Isla's missive, he insisted that a thorough search be made of the entire Palace of Westminster."

"Thank goodness," Isla breathed.

"Indeed," Maidstone said. "The news was a long time coming, but thankfully, it is what we wished to hear. Suffolk was asked to conduct the search. He will begin at daybreak tomorrow and will be accompanied by Monteagle. He has vowed to send word when they have completed the assignment and has agreed to inform me of what they find."

"Your connections to these gentlemen have been invaluable, Maidstone," Simon said.

"I am glad that I have been able to contribute to this essential effort in some small measure." He sighed. "We have but one day remaining until November 5, but God willing, we shall yet beat the conspirators at their game."

CHAPTER 19

Guy used the tip of his dagger to scrape more soil out of the narrow channel he'd dug in the dirt floor beneath the barrel of gunpowder and then leaned back to survey his work. The groove was little more than the width of his smallest finger, but that was all that was needed. Wide enough to hold the fuse in place, small enough to go unnoticed. With a satisfied smirk, he reached for the cord at his waist and tucked one end into the newly created space beneath the barrel. It fit perfectly. Threading the cord carefully through his fingers, he set the remainder in a straight line. There must be no slowing the hungry flame.

He had practiced lighting various lengths of cord at Percy's lodging. Countless times. To make a mistake with something so seemingly simple was pure foolishness. This fuse was precisely the right measurement. From the time he lit one end to the time it reached the other would be exactly fifteen minutes—just enough time for him to leave the undercroft, reclaim his horse from its hiding place behind the abbey, and gallop to the dock, where a ship was waiting to take him to Flanders.

The lantern he'd placed on the nearby wooden chair shed sufficient light to illuminate his handiwork, but the shadows cast by the barrels served to hide the newly set fuse. Guy rose to his feet, brushed the dirt off his knees, and walked to the door. From this position, one would have to know what to look for to notice the faint line cutting across the floor. How likely was it that anyone would visit the undercroft in the next twenty-four hours with so specific an assignment? He scowled. A fortnight ago, he would have put those chances at nil. Now, however, he could not be so sure.

Given the information Cecil had received, the king's adviser may suspect arson. And more often than not, arson involved fuses. Crossing to the opposite corner, Guy seized the rickety old table the previous tenant had left behind. It was not sturdy enough to hold anything of any substance, but it was bulky and would further darken the floor where the cord lay. He set it over the cord and moved back to survey the scene. A leaning table, two chairs, a single lantern, and a blanket sat before barrels of gunpowder that were indistinguishable from the barrels of wine and cider stacked around them. Wood, chopped and set in tidy piles atop the barrels further disguised the primary contents of the room, and in the far corner, hidden behind a broom, was a small bundle containing a flagon of ale and a loaf of bread. It was minimal nourishment, but as long as he kept the rats from it, the bread would be sufficient to keep him from going hungry during the long vigil ahead.

He opened the purse that hung from his belt and withdrew a smooth, round pocket watch. The metal glistened in the lantern light and sent a beam of light dancing across the shadowy barrels. Guy had never owned anything so elegant. Percy had given it to him as he'd prepared to leave. The nobleman had said the miniature clock was necessary so that Guy could mark the time correctly as he awaited the arrival of the king and his cabinet in the room above. In Guy's mind, it also served as a well-deserved token of appreciation. During the months he had spent living under the guise of Percy's manservant, Guy had played his part well. And with extraordinary tolerance. As far as Guy was concerned, Percy was an extremely fortunate fellow. Few men with so important a role in the course of history as Guy would deign take on the role of a retainer, no matter the noble lineage of his coconspirator.

He checked the time. Almost noon. By this time tomorrow, King James and his lords would be no more. The explosion would kill others, of course. There were always innocents affected when men resorted to violence. But countless blameless Catholics had died because of oppressive Protestant laws. It was time for Protestants to experience a similar loss. The flames of hate and justification burning in his soul grew stronger. Annihilation of the current regime was the only way to make a change. And if unsuspecting Catholics died in the explosion, they would die as martyrs.

Voices sounded outside. Guy froze. Then slowly, carefully, he slid the pocket watch back into his purse and crossed to the nearest chair. The sword at his side thumped against his thigh, and the spurs on his heels clinked. The light jingle was a good reminder to stand still if anyone approached. A servant taking inventory in his master's wine cellar might carry a sword to ward off undesirables, but he would have no need of spurs. An arsonist anticipating a swift escape on horseback, however, would desire both.

The voices were louder now, and they were accompanied by the steady thud of footsteps. Guy seized the logs lying on the closest barrel of wine and set them on the poor excuse for a table. Taking his knife, he pried the cork from the hole on the barrel's lid. Instantly, the sweet aroma of fermented grapes filled the room.

There was a scrape of a key in the lock. Guy tensed. Upon entering the undercroft, he had locked the door behind him, and the key was safely in his purse. Whoever was about to enter had access to another key. The door opened, and three men entered. One held a lantern. Guy recognized him immediately as the fellow who had rented this room to Percy. Frustration simmered beneath Guy's falsely placid expression. Percy should have insisted that every copy of the key to this door be handed over with the signing of the lease.

The two other intruders were unknown to him, but based on their finery, they were gentlemen of some means.

"Who are you?" the taller of the men demanded.

"John Johnson, m' lord," Guy said. "Manservant to Lord Percy."

"And what are you doing in here?" The taller man spoke again.

"His Lordship requested a tally of his best wine, m' lord. He is planning a dinner party after the opening of Parliament tomorrow."

The second nobleman stepped into the small circle of light coming from Guy's lantern and studied the stacked casks. "That would seem an inordinately large amount of firewood for a gentleman who spends much of his time away from London," he said.

"I daresay." Guy followed the direction of his gaze. "Though with his position in court, and the king returned, I believe he aims to be here most of the winter."

"Hmm." The skeptical nobleman turned to the other. "What do you make of this unusual supply, Suffolk?"

"I find it odd that a gentleman would keep his wood so far from his fireplace, but otherwise, I cannot fault the fellow for wishing to stay warm." The Earl of Suffolk sniffed the air.

"I would hazard a guess that Percy keeps a well-stocked wine cellar. He is known for his fondness for madeira."

"Well stocked indeed," the other man said, eyeing the nearest barrels.

Guy maintained his silence even as a drip of sweat trickled down his back. The tall nobleman was standing close enough to the end of the fuse that if he shifted his foot a fraction to the left, he would displace it from its shallow groove.

"Is this cellar let to Percy, Whynniard?" Suffolk asked the leaser.

"It is, m' lord. And this 'ere is 'is servant. Mr. Johnson was with 'Is Lordship when 'e signed the papers t' use th' place."

"I believe we can leave the man to his business, Monteagle," Suffolk said. "If Whynniard can vouch for him, we should move on to the next room."

The tall gentleman slowly walked the length of the stack of barrels, studying those in the shadows with particular attention. Guy remained completely still. Out of the corner of his eye, he saw the fuse twitch as the nobleman named Monteagle stepped on it, but as of yet, no one had noticed the sword and spurs Guy wore.

There was a whisper of movement in the corner. All three visitors swiveled in time to see the beady eyes of a rat gleaming in the lantern light. Monteagle muttered an oath, and the creature scuttled back behind the barrels.

"Percy can keep the vermin-infested place," Suffolk said. "Let us all pray that the creatures stay belowstairs."

Guy repressed a contemptuous snort. As far as he was concerned, the room above their heads housed the truly threatening vermin.

"We should go," Monteagle said. "Our search must be completed before evening."

Guy's chest tightened. So, it was a search. Under whose orders? If Cecil had requested it, why were he and his henchmen not conducting it themselves? He wanted to ask, but a servant would never be so forward.

Whynniard was already opening the door.

"Good day to you, m' lords," Guy said.

The noblemen ignored him. It was as he'd expected, but he inclined his head deferentially regardless. This would be the last time he did it. And the last time he would see any of them.

———— · ✸ · ————

Isla poked at the small piece of carrot on the plate before her. She'd managed to eat three bites of bread, one bite of roast goose, and two bites of carrot. It was a poor excuse for an evening meal, but it was all she could manage. And if the barely touched dishes on the rest of the table were any indication, Simon and the Maidstones were struggling with a similar lack of appetite.

"We should have heard by now." Simon set his knife down on his pewter plate, the clatter sounding especially loud in the unusually quiet dining room.

Lord Maidstone glanced at the darkened window. "Suffolk wished to have every room in the palace searched by nightfall."

"Perhaps he did, and the crisis is averted." Martha made a valiant attempt to infuse her words with hope. "Suffolk and Monteagle may have already captured Fawkes or Catsby or whoever else was lurking around where they should not be."

Isla said nothing. She had lain awake much of the night, attempting to remember the names of the men who were credited with arresting Guy Fawkes. She'd come close to capturing the names lodged somewhere in the deepest recesses of her memory, but up until now, they had eluded her. Unfortunately, she was quite certain neither of those soon-to-be heroes was named Suffolk or Monteagle.

"I shall go to Suffolk's residence," Simon said, coming to his feet. "If he has not yet sent a missive, he can deliver the news to me in person."

"Is that wise?" Lord Maidstone asked. "At a time filled with whispers of treason, I would not wish seemingly undue curiosity to cause suspicion to fall upon you or any member of this household."

"I am open to another suggestion, as long as it does not involve simply sitting here waiting."

A knock sounded on the front door. Simon pivoted. Lord Maidstone pushed away from the table and was on his feet when Grantham entered.

"A note was delivered for you, my lord," the servant said.

"Thank you, Grantham." Lord Maidstone accepted the sealed paper with practiced calm and waited until the servant closed the door behind him before resuming his seat.

"Open it," Martha begged.

Isla's throat tightened. Simon stepped up behind her. She knew he was as anxious as she was, yet the feel of his hand resting upon her shoulder brought an unexpected measure of comfort.

Lord Maidstone broke the seal and opened the paper. He cleared his throat, then read,

> *Maidstone,*
>
> *Monteagle and I conducted a thorough search of the palace buildings and found no sign of subversive activity. I have reported as much to the king. The writer of Monteagle's mysterious and anonymous letter*

undoubtedly wished to spread mischief rather than truth. The opening of Parliament is to go forth as previously scheduled.

Sincerely, Suffolk

"Nothing!" Martha cried. "How could they find nothing?"

Lord Maidstone met Isla's eyes. "You remain fully convinced that a threat exists?" He raised the paper in his hand. "Even after this report?"

"Yes." She leaned forward. "You must believe me. The noblemen did not find anything because Guy Fawkes has hidden the barrels of gunpowder amongst caskets of wine. If the king's guards went back to the undercroft beneath the House of Lords, they would discover it."

Simon's grip on her shoulder tightened. "I will go."

"No!" Isla reached for his hand. "It must be armed guards."

"I am armed." Simon patted the sword at his side.

"Without a key to the room or the presence of someone with the authority to enter, you will get nowhere," Lord Maidstone said.

"Very well. I shall find someone who fits one of those criteria," Simon said.

Isla pressed her palm to her forehead, willing her memory to return. What were the names of the men who had confronted Guy Fawkes?

"Try Knyvett," Lord Maidstone said. "His townhome is not far from here, and as a magistrate, he wields sufficient power to reopen the cellar."

"That's it!" Isla cried. "Knyvett! It is such an unusual name that I could not remember it. Knyvett must go to the undercroft, accompanied by a guard."

"And me," Simon said firmly. "I shall ensure Fawkes is taken into custody once and for all."

"I shall join you," Lord Maidstone said.

Simon shook his head. "There is too much at stake. We cannot have the entire success of this endeavor contingent upon me successfully persuading Knyvett to act. If our timing is off or Isla has forgotten an important but minute detail, all could be lost. There must be an alternate plan. Go to Cecil. He will give you audience without an appointment. Have him send men to the undercroft. God willing, Knyvett, a guard of his choosing, and I shall meet them there."

"Go with Hugh to Sir Cecil, Simon," Martha said. "Sir Cecil can send for Sir Knyvett and a troop of armed men. It is far too dangerous for you to approach the undercroft without an armed-guard escort."

Isla rose, grateful when Simon wrapped his arms around her. "Don't go," she begged. "Martha is right. There is still time for Sir Cecil to send word to Sir Knyvett."

"I must," he said. "We do not know where either gentleman is at present. If Cecil is with the king or has already retired for the night, it will take too long to alert the guards."

Isla placed her hands on his chest, desperate for Simon to understand the impending peril. "Guy Fawkes is a cunning and dangerous man. For years, he has lived as a mercenary. He has nothing but contempt for English law and the men who govern this land. This conspiracy has been his sole focus for months, and he will stop at nothing to see it through."

"I understand," Simon said.

Tears pricked her eyes. The words were easy to say, but she doubted Simon had ever faced anyone so fixated on a goal that all respect for the lives of others had fled.

"Martha," Simon said. "Turn away."

"Turn away?"

"Now," Simon warned. And then without waiting to see if she complied, he drew Isla closer and kissed her with a fervor that had her knees trembling and her heart aching. "I love you, Isla Crawford," he whispered. "I shall not do anything foolhardy. You have my word."

"I love you, too, Simon." Isla spoke through her tears. "Please be safe."

"We'd best be on our way, Bancroft." Lord Maidstone's voice came from the door. Perhaps he'd kissed his wife farewell while Simon had been kissing her. Isla didn't know, and now was not the time to look at Martha. She had a horrible feeling that her friend's face would reflect the fear and anxiety on her own.

Simon dropped one last soft kiss on Isla's forehead. Then he released her and walked out of the room.

CHAPTER 20

The Old Palace Yard was shrouded in blackness. Clouds covered the moon and stars, and an air of foreboding hung over the square. Sitting astride Blaze, Simon rolled his shoulders to release some of the tension building there. When he'd come here with Isla, he'd been struck by the portentous aura that had hung over the buildings he knew so well. He had not enjoyed the new sensation. He liked it even less now that it was even stronger.

Knyvett rode at his right. The gentleman had been eating his evening meal when Simon had arrived at his house. Thankfully, it seemed magistrates were better used to interruptions than most gentlemen, and when he heard that Simon had come on pressing business that involved the safety of the king, he had left his table to hear what Simon had to say. Choosing his words carefully, Simon had explained that as one who had personally heard the contents of the letter delivered to Monteagle, he was convinced that it contained a real threat. He'd also hinted that in Suffolk's desire to accomplish his assigned task quickly, the nobleman may have overlooked some highly suspicious barrels in the undercroft below the House of Lords. The promise of a second search being limited to one room had been enough to convince Knyvett to call for his horse.

Doubleday, the broad-shouldered guard who had delivered Knyvett's mount, had arrived with a lantern and a mount of his own. Both had been a welcome sight.

Doubleday had ridden ahead of them, keeping the lantern aloft, but now that they had reached the courtyard, he reined his horse to a stop to await further instructions.

"Over there, Knyvett," Simon said, pointing to a black rectangular object painted onto the lower portion of the building near the corner. "Do you see it? We may need to move closer to be sure, but the darkened portion looks to be a door."

"Agreed." Knyvett dismounted. "We do not know who or what we shall find inside, so I believe it would behoove us to approach quietly." He took his reins and tossed them around the lower branch of a nearby tree. Without a word, Simon and Doubleday did the same. "If you would light our way once more, Doubleday, we shall proceed to the undercroft."

From the direction of the Thames, a man shouted. Another shout and the creak of timber followed. It was an eerie sound. Simon pulled his cloak more closely around himself and surveyed the darkened space behind them. Not a soul in sight. Did Fawkes have any accomplices about? One gentleman against three was fair odds. Then again, one madman against three leveled the playing field.

"It's a door, Sir Knyvett." Leading the way, Doubleday had the best view of what lay ahead. "An' there's a few steps leadin' down to it."

"Have your weapon ready, Doubleday," Knyvett said. The zing of metal on metal filled the air as both Simon and the guard unsheathed their swords. For his part, Knyvett removed a large key ring from his belt. "As a member of the late queen's privy chamber and with my current position as a London magistrate, I enjoy greater access to the palace than most." He stepped into the circle of lantern light, the keys jangling as he sorted through them. He turned three over before claiming the next. "I shall knock. If there is no response, I shall unlock the door." He gave Doubleday a warning look. "Be prepared for a fight."

Doubleday's teeth glistened in the lantern's light. "Yes, m' lord."

The guard took a position at Knyvett's right and held the light above the keyhole. Simon stood at Knyvett's left. The magistrate knocked. Simon thought he heard the scrape of chair legs but then nothing.

Knyvett knocked again. The silence persisted. He slid the key into the lock. "On the count of three, gentlemen," he muttered.

He counted slowly, and then the bolt drew back with a solid thud. Knyvett pushed open the door, and Doubleday entered with Simon only one step behind.

The room was chilly and lit by a single lantern. A lone man stood before them, wearing a dark cloak and stovepipe hat. In his hand, he held a sword.

"What is the meaning of this?" His voice was low and filled with indignation.

"I could ask the same." Yet to raise his sword, Knyvett approached the man boldly. "As a London magistrate, I demand to know your name and reason for being within the walls of the House of Lords at this time of night."

The man's expression turned from outraged to calculating. "John Johnson," he said. "Manservant to Lord Percy, who leases this undercroft." He gestured to the caskets. "His are the wine caskets you see here."

Simon narrowed his eyes, scrutinizing the undercroft's contents. Percy was a known Catholic sympathizer, and Isla had mentioned his name as one who was involved with the conspiracy. "If this is truly Percy's wine cellar, the gentleman's collection rivals that of the most frequented inns in London." Simon turned his attention back to the man in black. "Of course, a gentleman with access to so vast a space may choose to store other things also."

The stranger's eyes flashed with menace. It was an unlikely reaction for a subservient manservant. However, it was exactly what Simon would expect from a mercenary and treasonous conspirator.

"Sir Knyvett," Simon said, keeping his eyes on the glowering man, "might I suggest that one of us checks the contents of these caskets? I fear Mr. Fawkes may not be telling the whole truth."

At Simon's use of his real name, Fawkes's shoulders stiffened, and he raised his sword a fraction.

Knyvett must have caught the subtle shift in Fawkes's stance because his hand moved to hover over the hilt of the weapon at his side. "Fawkes, is it?"

When Fawkes did not respond, Knyvett inclined his head toward the barrels. "Check them, Bancroft."

Much like a prize greyhound intent on his prey, Fawkes lunged forward. With barely enough time to unsheathe his blade, Knyvett would have fallen had Doubleday not leaped to parry Fawkes's sword with his own. The clash of steel rang through the cellar. Knyvett stepped back, allowing Doubleday room to maneuver into a better position while readying himself to enter the fight.

"Now, Bancroft," Knyvett yelled. "We have him."

Tightening his grip on his own weapon, Simon darted across the room. The lantern on the small table illuminated a long dagger beside an open bundle of food. He ignored the signs of Fawkes's simple meal and rounded the furniture. The faint scent of wine lingered over the nearest barrel. He ignored it. If the conspirators had placed casks of wine in the cellar to discourage curious visitors, those decoys were surely at the front of the stack.

Leaning over the first row of casks, he plunged his sword into the side of the nearest barrel in the next row. He twisted the blade and withdrew it. Instantly, a stream of dark liquid trickled down the wooden side. He swiveled, pulled back his arm, and pierced the next barrel. Grunts, heavy footsteps, and the ring of metal continued behind him. Trusting that Knyvett or Doubleday would shout a warning if needed, Simon twisted his blade. The wood cracked and splintered. He withdrew his sword, and this time, a stream of black powder followed.

"Gunpowder," he yelled. Isla had been right. About everything. Which meant he needed to search no longer. He knew what he would find. "Enough to blow up the entire Palace of Westminster and beyond."

"Yield, Fawkes," Knyvett shouted. "You are under arrest for treason."

"Never." The words dripped with loathing. "You and your inconsequential titles mean nothing." He lunged at Doubleday. The guard deflected, forcing Fawkes back two paces. "My purpose here is greater than you and greater than me."

Doubleday had him backing toward the furniture. Not wanting to distract the guard, Simon dropped to his knees and crawled beneath the table. His fingertips brushed against something long, thin, and smooth pressed into the dirt. He clawed it loose and pulled. The end of the cord appeared, grating across the base of the wooden barrel as he yanked it free. A fuse. Heaven help them. Were there more? And would Fawkes set them alight even now?

With a new level of urgency, Simon scrambled to his feet. Doubleday had set his lantern near the door, but Fawkes's was on the table, which meant a burning flame was within arm's reach of their opponent. Doubleday had Fawkes cornered. The man had to be desperate. But desperate enough to kill himself along with everyone else? Simon did not need to think on the answer. The unnerving determination on Fawkes's face spoke more clearly than words.

Fawkes's left arm swung wide across the table. Simon dove forward, pushing the lantern out of the conspirator's reach one heartbeat before Fawkes could have grasped it. Fawkes growled in anger. Simon shifted slightly and lunged again, this time reaching for the lantern's handle and lifting it off the table. Undaunted, Fawkes swung his arm wide and seized the dagger. Swiveling, he turned on Simon and let the weapon fly.

Simon had no time to react. The dagger had only the width of the table to travel before it entered his abdomen. He heard his cry as if from a distance, and then pain, sharp and intense, started on his left side and spread to encompass his entire torso. His sword clattered to the floor. The lantern in his other hand wavered. He could not drop it. Not while he was surrounded by gunpowder.

Vaguely aware that Knyvett was shouting and Doubleday had Fawkes on the floor, Simon looked down. The hilt of Fawkes's dagger was all that remained in view. Shock was instantly followed by a wave of nausea. Gritting his teeth, he set his hand around the dagger's handle and pulled it free. Blood covered the blade and dripped to the floor. He raised his eyes, not willing to view his doublet. Wetness coated his fingers and abdomen.

"Tie his arms." Knyvett was barking orders.

"There's a cord." The words came out in a groan. Simon could no longer remember where he'd tossed the fuse. Perhaps it did not matter. Doubleday was a guard. He surely had something on his person that he could use.

Pressing his hand to his wound, Simon attempted to move past the table toward the door. His legs trembled, and the lantern swayed.

"Bancroft!" Knyvett was at his side.

"Take the lantern," Simon gasped through waves of pain. "We will all be blown to the heavens if it falls."

Knyvett pried the metal ring from Simon's fingers. As soon as the weight of the lantern was gone, Simon dropped his head and arm. Breathing deeply, he took another faltering step. He staggered. An arm came around him.

"This way, m' lord." Doubleday half carried him to the door and slowly lowered him to the floor.

"Fawkes?" Simon managed.

"Trussed up with his own fuse," Doubleday said with satisfaction.

Knyvett stood above him, but Simon could not see beyond his shoes. Raising his head took too great an effort.

"We must take him to the king directly," Knyvett said. "Are you well enough to travel to the Palace of Whitehall if we assist you onto your mount?"

It was noble of Knyvett to not simply abandon him, but it was a ludicrous question.

"Go." Simon leaned his head against the wall. "Take Fawkes. Maidstone has gone for Cecil. They will arrive soon enough with extra men who can assist me."

Knyvett did not waste time arguing. He surely knew that attempting to move Simon would simply slow them down and be an exercise in futility. Every man in that dank room was fully aware that there was no recovery from a deep dagger wound to the abdomen.

"We shall leave a lantern and will return when we have handed Fawkes over to the king," Knyvett said.

Doubleday reached for the man sitting near the table with his hands tied behind his back. He hauled him to his feet and dragged him roughly toward the door. "The king first," Doubleday growled. "An' after that, the Tower."

Ignoring them both, Fawkes shot Simon a contemptuous look. "I daresay you shall see the other side before me, my lord. May you be suitably punished for your work here this night."

With all the strength Simon had remaining to him, he raised his head and kept it up until Doubleday had heaved Fawkes outside and Knyvett had closed the door behind them. He heard Knyvett's voice and the men's heavy footsteps. Then they were gone.

Breathing through the agony that encircled his core, Simon closed his eyes to the shadowy forms of the perilous barrels, closed his ears to the scratching of rats, and thought of Isla. Sorrow filled him, bringing the sting of tears to his eyes. The gunpowder plot was undone. The life of the king, members of Parliament, and countless innocent people had been saved, and yet Simon had failed. No matter his vow to the contrary, he would not return to her. The pain in his heart threatened to outweigh the pain at his side, but he pictured her beside him, their fingers intertwined.

"Forgive me, Isla," he whispered into the darkness. "I may not be with you, but I shall always love you."

———— · ✳ · ————

Something was wrong. Isla could feel it as surely as she could feel the heat from the fireplace and the draft from the window. She paced the distance between those two locations in Martha's parlor for the tenth or eleventh time. What she wouldn't give for mobile phone service right now! A brief call—or even a one-word text—from Simon was all it would take to put her mind at ease. Instead, she was consigned to this torturous waiting and fretting. Was there something she'd forgotten? Something about the capture of Guy Fawkes that she was missing?

"Surely one of the gentlemen shall return soon." Martha was sitting on the edge of the nearest chair, her hands clasped, her expression tense. She'd made the same statement twice already.

"I sincerely hope so." Isla paused her mindless march to anxiously run her hands down her cream-colored gown, realizing as she did so that it was the dress she'd been wearing when she'd first arrived at Copfield Hall. She had been afraid then too. But for very different reasons. The terrified young lady standing on the manor's doorstep that evening could never have anticipated how much she would come to love the Maidstones and Simon. She swallowed the lump in her throat. Especially Simon.

In the fireplace, a log shifted. Isla's thoughts did the same. There should be no reason to fear. Her history books had reported that the general search at the Palace of Westminster had come up empty and that it was Knyvett and a guard who had captured Guy Fawkes later that night. Simon had gone for Knyvett. Surely the magistrate and his associate must have been willing and had responded to the call. After all, the two men would be hailed as heroes and be well rewarded for their actions.

The two men. Isla's deliberations tumbled to a screeching halt. *The two men.* She reached for the back of the nearest chair to steady herself. If Simon had accompanied Knyvett and the guard to the undercroft, there were *three* men with Fawkes.

Simon would not simply walk away when Fawkes was taken into custody. He would want to ensure that the traitor was safely delivered to the king. But if that had happened, there would have been a record of it.

Isla's grip on the chairback tightened. Had there been any casualties during the capture of Guy Fawkes? With every man in the vicinity bearing a sword, it seemed almost impossible to believe that no one had been injured—or worse. The air left Isla's lungs. Was there no mention of Simon in the history books because he had not made it out of the undercroft alive?

She fought for composure. "Martha, I need a horse."

Her friend looked at her as though she had lost her mind. Perhaps she had. But with this new revelation, there was no way she could stay in the parlor another second.

"But it is full dark outside," Martha said.

"I know, but I must go to Westminster."

Fear entered Martha's eyes, and she rose to her feet. "What have you recalled?"

She should have known Martha would guess the reason for her request. But she could not tell her. Moving closer, she took her friend's hands in hers. "As much as I hate to leave you here alone, I really think Simon needs me more right now."

"You cannot go out alone. London is no place for a young lady—"

"I must, Martha," Isla interrupted. Nothing she was about to do fell under the prescribed codes of conduct for women in the seventeenth century, but at this point, she didn't care. "Can you find me a horse? I don't have any time to lose."

"You must have an escort."

"No. That is one more horse to locate and more time wasted." She squeezed Martha's hands. "Please. I wouldn't ask this of you if it weren't desperately important."

"Is Simon in danger?" she asked.

Isla released her hands and stepped back. "If you would send Grantham for a horse, I will run upstairs for my cloak." Not waiting for an answer, she lifted her skirts and ran out of the room.

CHAPTER 21

Isla clung to the reins for dear life. Her short canter on Stormy a few days before had been poor preparation for riding a much larger and unknown horse in the dark and on her own. But adrenaline was a powerful tool, particularly when it was combined with desperation.

Grateful that the moon had appeared from behind the clouds long enough for her to spot a few familiar landmarks, Isla released a sigh of relief when the entrance to the New Palace Yard materialized before her. She had no idea how long it had taken her to get here. Dispensing with her farthingale and donning her cloak had been fast and easy. Grantham had assisted her into the saddle after he'd arrived from the nearest stable, drawing a large, black horse behind him on the run. Mounting without Simon's strong arms around her had been challenging, but it had been nothing when compared to the terrifying sensation of tearing down the Strand toward Charing Cross, not knowing if she had the strength or skill necessary to remain in the saddle. And now, with her final destination ahead, she faced the daunting task of dismounting without breaking a bone.

Offering the most recent of many silent and fervent prayers, Isla reined in her racing mount. The horse shook its head disapprovingly, but with a compliant snort, it gradually slowed its gait, and by the time they entered the Old Palace Yard, the horse was walking sedately, and Isla was attempting to control her ragged breathing.

"Quietly, boy," she whispered. The horse snorted, and from somewhere nearby, there was an answering nicker. Isla tensed. Where had the sound come from? And was there a person waiting in the darkness with the other horse? Martha's stricken face as she'd watched her leave flooded Isla's mind. "This may be the worst idea I've ever had," she muttered, "but I'm here now, and I'm not leaving until I know that Simon is all right."

Up ahead, the specter-like outline of a tree took shape. Isla made for it. Another nicker told her the invisible horse was close. Her mount's ears twitched. Which was better: to remain on the horse in case she needed to flee or to get off while she still could? Shadowy outlines made it difficult to gauge her distance to the ground, but her memory of the courtyard was of a fairly even, hard-packed ground. In the dark, she would take that surface over cobblestones.

Reining her horse to a halt, she slipped one foot out of the stirrup and lifted her leg over the pommel. For a full five seconds, she sat completely still, willing herself to jump. Her horse stepped sideways, and Isla dropped. She hit the ground hard but miraculously remained upright. Swinging around, she bumped into her horse and fumbled for the leather straps.

"Come on," she said softly. "You're going to wait here."

Leading the horse behind her, she approached the tree. Two eyes glistened in the darkness. Isla's heart missed a beat. She froze. And then came the welcoming nicker.

"Blaze?" Scarcely daring to believe it was Simon's horse, she inched forward. "Blaze, is that you?"

Tossing her own reins over a branch and hoping it would be enough to keep the loaned horse close by, Isla extended a tentative hand toward the second horse. Almost immediately, a friendly nose brushed against it.

"Oh, Blaze!" Isla murmured. "Where is Simon?"

There were no other horses nearby. Did that mean Simon had come here alone? Or did it mean that he was the only one who hadn't left? Tamping down her mounting fear, Isla ran toward the building Simon had told her was the House of Lords. The main entrance was visible in the moonlight, but that was not what she wanted. Hurrying past it, she followed the front of the building, searching for another door. She had almost reached the corner when she spotted a few steps that led to a door set in the wall just below ground level. Lifting her skirts a couple of inches, she ran down the few stairs and stood at the door in a tortured state of indecision. What now? She had no way of knowing who—if anyone—was inside or how dangerous they might be. Leaning forward, she pressed her ear to the narrow crack between the door and the doorframe. Nothing. She closed her eyes, trying to block out the sounds of the slight breeze, the distant river, and a nightingale. And then she heard it. A faint, muffled moan. Without another thought, she opened the door.

A lantern sat on the floor not far from the door, casting a flickering light over a few pieces of furniture, barrels, and chopped wood. For two seconds, Isla stood staring into a rustic room seemingly devoid of people, and then she heard the moan again. She pivoted, her breath catching as she glimpsed a man lying on the floor a few feet to her right. Grabbing the lantern, she lifted it high.

"Simon!" Crossing the distance between them in three rapid strides, Isla fell to her knees beside him. A large red stain covered the left side of his jacket, and more blood marked the floor around him. His face was pale, but at her cry, his eyelids fluttered open.

"Isla?" His voice was barely above a whisper. "You are come."

"Yes." Vaguely aware that tears were rolling down her cheeks, she set the lantern down and took his hand. "Yes, I'm here."

"For . . . forgive me," he said. "It was Fawkes's knife. There was no time to defend myself."

A sob escaped her. "This is all my fault. I didn't think through the events well enough."

His smile was weak, but he raised his hand to touch her face. "You are not accountable for the actions of others, my beloved one. Only your own."

"But that's just it. I should have known . . . I should have prevented you from coming here . . ."

"I had to come. Fawkes needed to be stopped." He coughed and then grimaced with pain. "It is done, Isla. Knyvett and Doubleday will see him delivered to the king. My life may be over, but together we have saved innumerable others."

"No!" She turned her head to press her lips to his fingers. "We will get you away from here. Sir Cecil's men will come, and they can transport you to the Maidstones' house. Martha will know what to do."

Regret crossed his ashen face. "I fear that no matter my desires or yours, there is no recovering from an injury such as this."

"Yes, there is! There is!"

A flicker of understanding filled his pain-filled eyes. "But not here. Not now." He lowered his trembling hand from its position cupped around her face. "I love you, Isla."

There was no stemming her tears now. "I love you too."

He closed his eyes. She lowered her head, unaware that the door had opened wide until a gust of cold air swirled around her ankles.

"Ah, there you are, Isla!" A white-haired woman wearing a purple dress and purple shoes walked in carrying something made of pale-blue fabric over her arm. "I have found the Wendy dress at last."

Isla blinked and then blinked again. "Mrs. McQuivey?"

"Yes, dear. I'm sorry it took me so long."

"It took you until now to find a dress?" Isla looked at her incredulously. "I've been here for weeks!" Indignation heated her chest. "You left me here all alone! You never answered when I called for help. The changing room door was gone. And . . . and now Simon is seriously injured, and I don't know how to help him!"

"Oh my! I apologize if you've been waiting for me, but I'm here now, and I have what you need."

"I don't want the Wendy dress." Isla's voice broke. How could the woman talk about finding a costume with Simon lying beside her in a pool of blood? "Don't you see?" she cried, gesturing at Simon. "He's dying."

"Good heavens!" Mrs. McQuivey stepped closer and gazed down at Simon through her wire-rimmed glasses. "What ever happened to this poor young man?"

"He was stabbed with a dagger."

"Well, we must get him some medical attention right away."

"I . . . I told him that too," Isla said. "But he says there's nothing that can be done for him."

"Nonsense. The doctors at the Royal London Hospital will know exactly what to do."

Isla stilled. "Are you talking about the big hospital on White-chapel Road?"

"Of course I am."

Was that even possible? Mrs. McQuivey was referring to a twenty-first-century hospital with twenty-first-century doctors and modern medicine. "Can . . . can we take him there?"

"We must! I wouldn't want to attempt transporting him myself, you understand, not when he's lost so much blood. But we can call an ambulance. It shouldn't take them long to get to the shop."

Isla was not sure how she could go from utter despair to overjoyed in a matter of seconds, but it had happened. "Simon. Simon, can you hear me?"

His eyes fluttered open. "Forgive me, Isla . . ." He licked his lips. "It is difficult to . . ." His voice trailed off, and he stared at Mrs. McQuivey. "Who . . . I beg your pardon, but who are you?"

"This is Mrs. McQuivey," Isla answered for her. "From the costume shop."

Simon's eyes widened slightly. "The . . . the costume shop you visited?"

"Yes." Isla met his gaze, willing him to understand even in his weakened state. "She says you can come back with me."

"We'll call an ambulance right away, dear. The medics will help you."

"What is an ambulance?" Simon's voice was fading again.

"It's a big car with flashing lights that takes people with serious injuries to doctors who can heal them."

His answering smile was faint, but it was there. Isla's heart felt like it might burst. She leaned over and softly kissed his forehead. "Come with me," she whispered. "And when you are well again, I will teach you to drive a car."

"I would like that more than I can say," he murmured.

"You have only to walk through the door," she said.

He turned his head until he could see the exit. "That door?"

"Yes. Mrs. McQuivey and I will help you."

"To enter the future, never to return?"

She nodded. It was a prospect they'd never considered. And it was a lot to ask.

He managed a crooked smile. "Martha would miss me terribly."

An ache filled Isla's chest. Martha was probably going to lose him no matter what he decided. "She would."

"Almost . . ." He winced and pressed his hand to his wound. "Almost as much as I would miss her."

Isla battled a new rush of fear. "Simon?"

He moaned, but when he looked up, fresh determination filled his eyes. "Martha . . . she belongs with Maidstone and the boys, Isla. And no matter what century it may be, I belong with you." He reached for her. "I wish to go."

With tears blurring her vision, Isla took his hand. "Hurry, Mrs. McQuivey!"

The older lady set the Wendy dress on the table beside a small bundle of food, and then returned to Simon's side. Sliding one arm beneath his back, she took ahold of his left arm with her other hand. Isla mirrored her position on Simon's right.

"On the count of three," Isla said.

Mrs. McQuivey did her part with extraordinary ability. And though Simon groaned in agony and beads of sweat appeared along his forehead, he staggered to his feet.

"One moment," he gasped, struggling for balance.

Isla waited, her heart pounding. "Only a few more steps. Can you manage it?"

"Yes." He lowered his head, his breathing labored.

"Take your time, young man," Mrs. McQuivey said, her hazel eyes twinkling in the lantern light. "We all have as much of that as you need."

"I thank you." Simon exhaled, raising his head again.

Isla looked at him. Was he truly prepared for what lay ahead?

As if he could read her mind, he leaned forward and brushed her cheek with his lips. "I shall be with you, Isla. I will be okay."

"My kind of okay does not involve horses," she warned.

"So you have told me," he said, his pained expression filled with hope and love. "But I am ready to experience it."

EPILOGUE

Two Years Later

Isla slid a printed copy of Audrey Marshall's recent speech on housing reform into the filing cabinet and closed the drawer with a satisfied push. Her boss was not scheduled to make another public appearance for a week. It was a welcome reprieve after a fortnight of back-to-back commitments.

"Hey, Isla." Chloe popped her head around the office door. "Simon's on his way up."

Isla smiled, her heart lifting in anticipation of the evening she had planned with her husband. "Great," she said, locking the filing cabinet. "I'll be right there."

Taking a moment to switch off the light, Isla closed the door on Ms. Marshall's room and walked out into the main office just as Simon entered through the doors that led to the lifts. Dressed in well-fitting jeans, a navy T-shirt, and a black jacket, his dark, wavy hair cut short and his neatly trimmed beard replaced by a light scruff, he was, simply put, thoroughly modern and distractingly handsome.

"Hi, Simon," Chloe called from her desk. "How are all the king's horses and all the king's men today?"

Simon chuckled. His position as Riding Master at the Royal Mews inevitably invited this question from Chloe. "Well, I cannot speak for all of them, but this one is very well. How are you?"

"Oh, you know. Livin' the dream."

A slight crease appeared on Simon's forehead. It was an all-too-common occurrence when he spoke to Chloe. Modern idioms and seventeenth-century English were a tricky mix.

"And that is a good thing?" he guessed.

"Yeah," Chloe said with a smile. "I suppose it is."

Isla stepped up to rescue him. "Hi."

He swung around, his arms instantly circling her. "Hi to you too." He kissed her softly. "You know what one of my favorite things is about this era?" he whispered.

She raised her eyebrows expectantly. "What?"

"I can kiss you in public, and no one even gasps."

Isla laughed softly. "That's definitely a bonus, but nothing compares to the miracle of having you standing here, whole and healthy."

He didn't need to say anything for Isla to know that they were both thinking back to the day he'd staggered out of the McQuivey Costume Shop's changing room, weak from the loss of blood and pain. Mrs. McQuivey had called for the ambulance and had handed Isla a large bag.

"The clothes you were wearing when you first arrived," she'd said. "And a few things for your young man." She'd leaned a little closer and lowered her voice as though not wishing to offend Simon. "An American lumberjack costume is not exactly what the best-dressed men in London are wearing, but I thought jeans, boots, and a plaid shirt might be an improvement over his current ensemble."

Emotion had all but stolen Isla's voice, but she'd hugged the older lady tightly and had held on to the bag during the seemingly interminable wait for the ambulance, the ride to the hospital, and the surgery that had followed. The doctors had removed Simon's punctured spleen and given him high-powered antibiotics to counter the effects of Guy Fawkes's filthy dagger. But it was only when Isla had removed the clothing from the bag that she'd discovered Mrs. McQuivey's hidden gift. An official birth certificate for a Simon Hartworth Bancroft, born in Derbyshire in 1997, and a reference letter for the Lord Chamberlain's Office, recommending Simon for the position of Liveried Helper at the Royal Mews.

Working with horses as a member of the royal staff had been the perfect starting job for Simon, particularly while he had adjusted to living in a world so far removed from the one he'd always known, but his confidence and skill as a rider along with his experience with harnesses and carriages had quickly elevated him to the prestigious position of Riding Master. And not long afterward, they had ended their fake betrothal with a very real, private wedding.

Simon slid his fingers down her arm to claim her hand. "Are you ready to go?"

"Yes." She lifted her bag onto her shoulder. "Are you okay locking up tonight, Chloe?"

"No problem." Chloe eyed them curiously. "D'you two have big plans for Guy Fawkes Night?"

"We're headed to Surrey for the evening," Isla said.

"Isn't that where you met?"

"It is." Simon gave Isla's hand a gentle tug. "And if we are to leave ahead of the rush-hour traffic, we'd best depart right away."

Chloe sighed. She was used to Simon's occasional use of older English, but it always produced a dreamy look in her eyes. "I think I need to make a visit to Surrey to find a Simon of my own."

Isla bit back a smile. "Good idea. I'll let you know if I spot another one while we're there."

With a light laugh, Chloe slid a pile of papers onto the corner of her desk. "Have a good time. I'll see you tomorrow."

———— · ✳ · ————

Two hours later, Simon pulled their red Vauxhall Corsa into the small parking area at Copfield Park.

"It still feels odd to come here and not see the Maidstones' manor waiting for us," Isla said. "But I'm glad the county council turned the land into a public park."

"As am I." He turned off the ignition, marveling at how instinctive the action was now. Just as Isla had suggested when they'd ridden their horses here so long ago, he'd taken to driving immediately. It didn't matter if it was on the motorway or on the narrow, winding back roads in the country, the power of a car's engine both thrilled and fascinated him. "I believe Maidstone would be glad that his land is now available for all to enjoy." He got out and walked around the vehicle to open Isla's door. "Do you think we've arrived early enough to claim our bench?"

"I hope so." She took his hand.

His heart instantly responded, filling the spots that always felt a little empty when they returned to this place. He thought of Martha often and still missed being with Sam and Will.

"They continued to love you even after you left, you know," she said.

Simon gave Isla a startled look. He shouldn't be surprised. She always seemed to sense what was on his mind without him saying a word. They both hoped that Maidstone had found the Wendy costume Mrs. McQuivey had left behind in the undercroft. If so, he and Martha would have known exactly what had happened and would have understood. It would have been hard for them to explain it to their sons though.

"I hope the boys remembered me into their adulthood," he said.

"They did."

They started down the path that led to the lookout.

"How can you be so sure?"

She smiled. "You always remember the people you allow into your heart. And the twins had a special place in theirs for you."

"And that presumably explains why I shall never forget them," he said.

"Exactly." She squeezed his hand gently. "But the best part is, adding someone new does not diminish the fond memories of those already there."

He nodded, recognizing the truth of her words. Amid all the challenges and changes he'd experienced over the last two years, Isla had been his constant support. His anchor and his light. She always would be, but over the intervening months, he'd also added her parents, siblings, and nephews to those who were important to him.

"There it is." He pointed to a familiar spot up ahead. The old fallen oak was long gone, but where it had once been, a wooden bench now stood.

"And it's empty," Isla said.

They sat down together. In the valley below, the once tiny hamlet of Little Twinning was a mass of twinkling lights. A string of vehicle lights moved swiftly along the roads that now crisscrossed the formally rural area.

"I see the bonfire," Isla said, pointing to a flickering fire in a field just beyond the outskirts of the town. Like milling ants, the distant people moved around the flames, their shadowy forms barely visible through the smoke rising from the enormous pyre. "I imagine they'll start the fireworks soon."

Simon put his arm around Isla and pulled her close. Tonight, all around the country, there would be bonfires like this burning. People would drink hot apple cider or hot chocolate and eat donuts and toffee apples. Fireworks would fly heavenward to celebrate the saving of the English government and the capture of Guy Fawkes. It was a night of celebration, but for him and Isla, it was also a night of poignant reflection. In this special spot, the anniversary of that unparalleled event held deep meaning.

"*Remember, remember, the fifth of November. Gunpowder, treason, and plot*," Isla chanted softly.

"I think it is safe to say that neither you nor I shall ever forget," Simon said.

"No." She paused. "Have you ever wondered what we should tell our children? What you'd want them to know about what happened in 1605?"

"I've thought about it a little," he admitted. "Have you?"

"Yes. Especially in the last few weeks."

"Because this date was drawing near?"

"Partly." She turned so that her eyes were on his. "But mostly because this time next year, we'll be sharing the bench with someone else."

He stared at her, replaying her words in his mind. Was she saying what he thought she was saying? "Isla? You know how I struggle with modern English. I don't want to misinterpret or misunderstand what you—"

The look in her eyes softened. "We're having a baby, Simon."

His heart was pounding so hard, he could barely think. "You are sure?"

She laughed quietly. "I am sure. He or she will be here early next summer."

They were having a baby! He drew Isla into his arms, the wonder and joy of this moment threatening to overwhelm him. "Perhaps we shall have twins."

"Probably not." She smiled at him. "But I did think that if it's a boy, we could call him William or Samuel."

"And if it's a girl?"

She tilted her head back to see his face more clearly. "How do you feel about the name Martha?"

"Would she order me around like her namesake did?"

"If we have a little girl, I don't think it will matter what she is called; you will be at her beck and call from the day she is born."

She was right. There was no question in his mind. "My sister would be pleased."

"And you? Are you pleased with the news?"

"*Pleased* is not precisely the word I would use."

"It's not?" There was a hint of concern in her voice.

It was something he had to eliminate immediately. "No, my sweet Isla." He set a soft kiss atop the lines on her forehead. "*Ecstatic, overjoyed, elated,* and *overwhelmed* by my love for you. Those descriptions are far better."

"Oh." She relaxed against him, her arms circling his neck. "I like those words better too."

He smiled. "Well, okay, then."

Her soft laughter filled his heart to overflowing, and as the first fireworks exploded in the sky above, he lowered his head and pressed his lips to hers.

AUTHOR'S NOTE

On the evening of November 5, people all over the UK gather as families, friends, and communities to celebrate Guy Fawkes Night. For most, it is an evening of celebration, with bonfires, fireworks, and food. Occasionally, those who adhere to the old traditions will burn a scarecrow-like effigy of Guy Fawkes on the fire. It's a gruesome custom that harks back centuries and is a solemn reminder of a period of time that was brutally difficult for those who lived through it.

This book is a work of fiction, and I have made a few small changes to the historical account, including having Guy Fawkes rather than Wintour accompany Catsby to question Tresham in the Royal Forest of Epping Chase and shortening the amount of time between Monteagle's dinner and Fawkes's capture by three days. In almost all other respects, however, I have stayed true to the timeline of events surrounding the infamous Gunpowder Plot of 1605. The names and roles of the thirteen coconspirators along with Monteagle, Ward, Cecil, Knyvett, and Doubleday are real. So, too, are the references to the persecution of Catholics, the paranoia of Cecil, and the prevalence of the Black Death.

There are a great many historical details and anecdotes surrounding this unprecedented conspiracy that I was unable to share in a novel of this length, but I hope this story will encourage readers to discover those facts for themselves. There are also several still-unanswered questions. One of the most intriguing is the mystery surrounding who sent the warning note to Lord Monteagle. The original letter is held by the National Archives in London, and although it is a subject that divides historians, most believe that despite Catsby's belief in his cousin's innocence, it was most likely Tresham who penned it. They may be correct. Then again . . . none of those historians is aware of the presence of Miss Isla Crawford at Lord Monteagle's dinner.

Guy Fawkes was taken before the king at four o'clock in the morning on November 5. Afterward, Fawkes was incarcerated in the Tower of London. Within a week of Fawkes's arrest, all the original conspirators, except Robert Wintour, had been killed or arrested. Robert Wintour was taken into custody in January 1606, and at the end of that month, all the conspirators who remained alive, including Guy Fawkes, were executed.

ACKNOWLEDGMENTS

In the summer of 2023, Heidi Gordon, the production manager at Shadow Mountain Publishing, approached me about writing a time-slip series. Her invitation took me by surprise. I'd never considered writing in this subgenre before. In fact, the concept was sufficiently daunting that I might have turned it down had it not been for two things: first, the unqualified support and encouragement of my husband, Kent, and my editor, Sam; and second, the opportunity to launch a new series alongside my incredibly talented friend Sarah Eden.

Now, several months later, *A Time Traveler's Masquerade* is out in the world. The list of names of all the unsung heroes at Shadow Mountain who have played a pivotal role in the release of this book is too long for this short acknowledgment. But I do wish to express a special thank-you to Heidi Gordon for asking me to take on this project and for believing in my ability to do it; to Samantha Millburn for helping me polish this novel into what it is today; to Halle Ballingham for creating such a stunning cover; to Amy Parker and her marketing team for constantly thinking outside the box and always having my back; and to Sarah Eden for being such a beacon of light to readers and writers alike.

ACKNOWLEDGMENTS

Creating a fictional piece of work that closely follows a historical event involves significant research. I'm very grateful to Nick Holland, whose book, *The Real Guy Fawkes*, taught me a great deal about the notorious man whose name is known by many but whose life is shrouded in mystery. Thank you, Kent, for offering me sympathy and encouragement when the research and writing was hard. And thank you, Traci Abramson, for telling me to keep typing whenever I wanted to stop and bake cookies instead.

Finally, I'd like to thank my parents for my childhood memories of standing around a bonfire with a sparkler in my hand each November 5. I may not have understood exactly what we were celebrating, and I certainly had no idea that I would one day write a book about Guy Fawkes, but I am grateful for all those years of participating in a centuries' old tradition.

ABOUT THE AUTHOR

SIAN ANN BESSEY was born in Cambridge, England, and grew up on the island of Anglesey off the coast of North Wales. She left her homeland to attend university in the US, where she earned a bachelor's degree in communications, with a minor in English.

She began her writing career publishing several articles in magazines while still in college. Since then, she has published historical romance and romantic suspense novels, along with a variety of children's books. She is a *USA Today* best-selling author, a RONE Award runner-up, a Foreword Reviews Book of the Year finalist, and a Whitney Award finalist.

Sian and her husband, Kent, are the parents of five children and the grandparents of four beautiful girls and two handsome boys. They currently live in southeast Idaho, and although Sian doesn't have the opportunity to speak Welsh very often anymore, *Llanfairpwllgwyngyllgogerychwyrndrobwllllantysiliogogogoch* still rolls off her tongue.

Traveling, reading, cooking, and being with her grandchildren are some of Sian's favorite activities. She also loves hearing from her readers. If you would like to contact her, she can be reached through her website at www.sianannbessey.com. You can also follow her Facebook page, Sian Ann Bessey, or join her Facebook group, Author Sian Ann Bessey's Corner. Find her on Instagram, @sian_bessey.

COMING IN 2026

THE MAID OF
SHERWOOD
FOREST

A MCQUIVEY'S COSTUME SHOP ROMANCE